HIGHLAND WARRIOR

Books by Hannah Howell

ONLY FOR YOU

MY VALIANT KNIGHT

UNCONQUERED

WILD ROSES

A TASTE OF FIRE

HIGHLAND DESTINY

HIGHLAND HONOR

HIGHLAND PROMISE

A STOCKINGFUL OF JOY

HIGHLAND VOW

HIGHLAND KNIGHT

HIGHLAND HEARTS

HIGHLAND BRIDE

HIGHLAND ANGEL

HIGHLAND GROOM

HIGHLAND WARRIOR

Published by Zebra Books

HIGHLAND WARRIOR

Hannah Howell

ZEBRA BOOKS
KENSINGTON PUBLISHING CORP.

ZEBRA BOOKS are published by

Kensington Publishing Corp.
850 Third Avenue
New York, NY 10022

ISBN 0-7394-4272-4

Printed in the United States of America

Chapter 1

Scotland—1472

"Satan's big toe!"

Fiona cautiously stood up, steadied herself, and vainly tried to rub away the throbbing pain in her backside as she watched her horse disappear over the hill. Her brothers were going to kill her, slowly. Gillyanne, her sister by marriage, would probably not come to her aid this time. Fiona had the lowering feeling that she had sunk herself deep into trouble this time, had, in fact, been utterly witless. She was miles from home, had no supplies, and the sun was rapidly sinking below the horizon. Even worse, no one at Deilcladach knew where she had gone.

"Weel, ye certainly showed Connor who is in control, didnae ye," she muttered as she tried to discern exactly where that cursed horse had dropped her. "If only Connor had asked nicely instead of commanding me in that irritating way he has. Nay, nay, this isnae his fault. Tis yours and yours alone, Fiona MacEnroy. Tis ye who is to blame for this disaster."

She looked around and realized it was not only the people of Deilcladach who did not know where she was. She did not know, either. Her annoying mount had dropped her in a place she had never been before. The wild ride she had just survived left her uncertain of which direction she should turn in to head home; not that she was very good at finding her way around under the best of circumstances.

This was undoubtedly the most reckless thing she had ever done. There was only one good thing about it that she could think of. The madman who had precipitated her long confinement at Deilcladach could not possibly know where she was, either. The man may have succeeded in causing her to do something completely witless, but at least he would not benefit from it.

Fiona idly rubbed her finger over the scar marring her left cheek. *He* had given it to her the first time he had cornered her, along with a matching one on her right cheek. She could almost feel the others he had inflicted before her family had caged her behind the thick walls of Deilcladach until they could hunt the madman down and kill him. Just thinking about the man sent chills of fear throughout her body, yet she had briefly, foolishly, forgotten that danger. She had succumbed to a raging need to ride free after too many months of confinement.

A sound caught her attention and she tensed.

Horses were coming her way, fast. Even as she looked for a place to hide, the riders crested the small rise directly in front of her. Fiona drew her sword and dagger, then stood with her feet apart. She knew she had no chance of successfully defending herself against ten or more men, but decided it was better to die fighting than to allow that madman Menzies to keep slicing away at her.

Then she realized Menzies rarely had more than a few men with him. There were at least a dozen riders in front of her. One good look at the huge dark man at the fore of the troop told her this was not Menzies. Fiona held steady in her fighting stance, but had to fight back a wave of fear. Menzies might be insane, but he did not want her dead. She could not be sure these men would have that much restraint.

"Jesu, look there, Ewan!"

Ewan MacFingal just grunted in response to his brother Gregor's cry. He was looking, but he was not sure he was seeing too clearly. Surely there could not be a small female facing them with a sword in one hand and a dagger in the other? Could she not count? There were twelve of them and only one of her, a very small, delicate one.

Signaling his men to halt, Ewan slowly rode toward the woman. She was dressed as a lad in a jerkin, breeches, and boots, but there was no doubt that she was a woman. It was not just the long, thick honey gold braid hanging down to her slim hips which gave her away, either. The lad's clothing could not fully disguise her lithe feminine shape.

Her face was definitely that of a woman, as well. A very beautiful woman.

When he was close enough to see her eyes, he felt his breath catch in his throat. They were big eyes, the long thick lashes surrounding them several shades darker than her hair, as were her finely arched brows. They were also the color of violets. He did not think he had ever seen eyes that color, or eyes so stunningly beautiful.

The rest of her heart-shaped face was equally captivating. She had delicate bones, from the soft curve of her high cheekbones to the line of her faintly stubborn jaw. Her nose was small and straight, her skin clear and fine with a hint of gold to it as if she had been gently gilded by the sun, and her lips were full and tempting. He idly wondered where she had gotten the scars, one on each cheek. They were neat, a rather gentle mark beneath each of her lovely cheekbones.

He silently cursed as he dismounted and drew his sword. If he was thinking that even her scars were beautiful, she was more dangerous than she looked. Ewan knew how intimidating he looked so was rather surprised when she only blinked once, slowly, looked him over, and then tensed in the way a warrior does when braced for an attack.

"Ye cannae be thinking to fight with me, lass," he said, scowling at her.

"And why shouldnae I?" Fiona asked.

"Because I am a mon, bigger than ye in height and breadth."

"I did notice that."

It was impossible not to notice that, Fiona mused. He had to be a foot or more taller than her own meager five feet three inches, if she stood very straight. She suspected he might even be taller than her brothers. He was broad of shoulder, lean of hip, and had long, well-formed legs. His loosely fitted jerkin and breeches did little to hide the strength in his body. His sword looked rather impressive as well.

Fiona knew she ought to be shaking in her boots, but she was not. It puzzled her, for there was no softness to be found in his harsh features. There was a predatory look to the man. His bone structure was good, from the high cheekbones to the strong jaw, but there was a hardness to the face that stole away the elegant handsomeness it should have had. His nose had probably once been long and straight, but a break or two had left a bump at the bridge of it, giving it a hawkish look. Despite his dark scowl, she could see that his mouth was well shaped, a hint of fullness to his lips. His eyes were an intriguing bluish gray, like a clear summer sky when the clouds of approaching night started to seep into it. And he was lucky to still have both of them, she mused, as she glanced at the scar that ran from just above his right eyebrow, down his right cheek to his jaw, passing within a hair's breadth of the corner of his eye. There was a hint of softness to be found in those eyes, however, in the long, thick lashes and neat brows that held the touch of an arch. His long, thick, pitch-black hair, hanging several inches past his broad shoulders, was braided on either side of his face and only added to his look of a fierce, dark warrior.

And he was very dark, indeed, she thought. Even his skin was dark, and something told her it

was not from the sun. There was the inky shadow
of an emerging beard, which only made his face
even darker. Fiona wondered why she, a woman
who had spent her life surrounded by fair, handsome men, should find this dark man so attractive.

"Then ye will nay be fighting with me," Ewan
said, subduing the urge to back away from her intense study.

"They do say that the bigger a mon is, the harder
he will fall," she murmured.

"Then old Ewan ought to fair shake the ground,"
said the young man holding the reins of the dark
man's horse, and the other men chuckled.

"I willnae fight with a wee lass," Ewan said.

"Ah, that is a relief as I had no real urge to get
all asweat and weary. So, I accept your surrender."

"I didnae surrender."

That deep, rough voice produced an impressive
growl, Fiona decided. "If ye arenae going to fight
and ye arenae going to surrender, then what *are* ye
planning to do? Stand there all day blocking out
the sun?"

If Ewan had not suspected it would be a serious
error in judgment to turn his back on this woman,
he would have scowled at his snickering men. "Now
that ye have had your wee jest, I suggest *ye* surrender."

Fiona knew she had little choice, which made
her feel distinctly contrary. She still felt no real fear,
either. The man had made no attempt to attack or
disarm her. The amusement of his men did not carry
the taint of anger or cruelty. There was also a look
upon the dark warrior's face that she found oddly
comforting. It was the same look her brothers gave

her when they found her to be excessively irritating and were heartily wishing she was not a female so that they could punch her in the nose. Fiona knew instinctively that this man would not strike her any more than her brothers would.

"I wasnae jesting," she said and smiled sweetly. "I am ready to accept your surrender now. Ye can just pile your weapons up neatly by my feet."

"And just what do ye plan to do with a dozen prisoners?"

"Ransom ye."

"I see. And we are all supposed to just sit quiet like good, wee lads, and let ye rob our clan."

"Oh, I dinnae wish to rob your clan. All I want is a horse and a few supplies."

"Ah, lost yours, have ye?"

"Mayhap I ne'er had one."

"Ye are miles from anywhere. Do ye expect me to believe ye just popped up out of the heather, ye daft wench?"

"Wench? Did ye just call me a wench?"

Ewan did not think he had ever seen a woman's humor change so rapidly. He had just begun to understand her game. In an almost playful way, she had been testing him, trying to see if he could be spurred to violence against a woman. She had begun to relax. Now it appeared that, with one ill-chosen word, he had set her back up and set the progress of their odd negotiations back several steps. Before he could say anything to mend matters, his brother Gregor spoke up and made the situation even worse.

"Actually, he called ye a daft wench," said Gregor.

"I hate being called a wench," Fiona said.

She sheathed her dagger, grasped her sword with both hands, and attacked so swiftly and gracefully, Ewan was struck with admiration. So struck that he came very close to getting wounded. As he met her attack, however, he realized it would have been little more than a scratch, that she had not been aiming for anything vital. He also realized that she had been well trained. She might lack the strength and stamina to outlast a man in a long, hard battle, but she definitely had the skill and agility to give herself a fighting chance. A touch of good fortune or an error on the man's part and she could win a fight. The silence of his men told Ewan they also recognized her skill. What he did not understand was why she had attacked him. He was sure it was not because he had called her a name she did not like. Ewan wondered if this was another test of some sort, one to judge his skill or to see just how hard he would try not to hurt her.

Fiona knew within minutes that this man did not want to harm her. He was fighting her defensively and she was certain that was not his way. Even as she wondered how she could now extract herself from this confrontation, it was ended. He blocked the swing of her sword and somehow ended up within inches of her. The next thing Fiona knew, her sword was gone from her hand, her feet were pulled out from beneath her, and she landed flat on her back, hard enough to knock the breath out of her. As she struggled to catch her breath, she braced for the blow of his body landing on top of her. It not only surprised her, but impressed her, when he somehow managed to completely pin her to the ground with his body yet rested very little of his weight upon her.

"Now, are we all done with this troublesome nonsense?" Ewan demanded, fighting to ignore the feel of her beneath him and pushing away the tempting images it tried to set in his mind.

"Aye," Fiona replied, panting a little as she regained her ability to breathe. "I will accept your surrender now." The man truly could growl impressively, she mused, and wondered why that rough noise should send small, pleasurable shivers down her back.

"Enough," he snapped. "Ye are now my prisoner. Do ye have any other weapons?" he asked as he took the knife sheathed at her waist and tossed it aside, his brother Gregor quickly appearing to collect it along with her sword.

"Nay," she answered and could tell by the way his eyes narrowed that he knew she lied.

"Surrender your weapons, woman."

"I told ye, I dinnae have any more." Fiona wondered if the fact that the knife sheathed at the back of her waist was digging painfully into her back was the reason her ability to lie was so hampered.

That thought had barely finished forming when she found herself caught up in a fierce wrestling match with the man as he tried to search her for weapons. She got some pleasure out of his curses and grunts, which revealed she was at least discomforting him. Unfortunately, it did not deter him. He quickly began to find all of her knives. His curses increased as he took the two strapped to her wrists just inside the sleeves of her jerkin, the two tucked inside her boots, and the one sheathed at her back. He even found the subtle slits in her breeches that allowed her to reach the knife strapped to each of her thighs and took those. All her struggling halted abruptly when he ran his big, long-fingered hands over her breasts and found the knife sheathed between them. As he tossed that to the man collecting her weapons, he yanked her to her feet, and she wondered why she could still feel the warmth of his touch.

Ewan stared at the collection of weapons a widely grinning Gregor had piled up. He suddenly realized that, at any point during their confrontation, she could have pulled out one of those well-hidden knives and thrown it at him, or slipped it between his ribs. There was no doubt in his mind that she could have done so with speed, stealth, and deadly accuracy. He had obviously not failed any of those tests she had been putting him through. When he looked at her and she smiled sweetly, he immediately grew suspicious.

"Any more?" he asked.

"Of course not." She met his narrow-eyed stare for a full minute before she sighed. "Just one."

"Hand it to me."

His eyes widened as she reached behind her head and pulled a knife from out of the thick coils of her braid. When she slapped it into his out-stretched hand, he ignored the hilarity of his men and studied the weapon. It was long with a narrow blade, sheathed in thick, soft leather, and the hilt had been made in such a way it looked like no more than an ornate hair ornament, yet was still perfectly usable.

"Why are ye so heavily armed?"

"Weel, it wouldnae be wise to ride about alone without a few weapons," Fiona replied as she undid her sword belt and tossed it down with the other weapons, then began to remove the sheaths for her knives that she could reach discreetly.

"Tis nay wise to ride about alone nay matter how weel armed ye are."

She scowled at him and he tried to fix his attention on her ill humor, but it was not easy. His gaze kept falling to where her hand had slipped inside the clever slits in her breeches to remove the knife sheaths strapped around each slender thigh. Ewan could all too clearly recall the feel of that soft skin. It had taken a lot of willpower to resist the urge to linger there, to stroke that soft skin, and to recall that he was disarming her beneath the amused gazes of his men.

Even worse, his palms still itched with the need to feel those firm, plump breasts again. He had all too briefly felt how perfectly they had nestled into his hands as he had searched her for more weapons. Despite her clothes and the fact that she had been bristling with weapons, he could not ignore the fact that she was a woman, a soft, temptingly shaped woman. Worse still, he seemed incapable of ignoring the fact that he desired her.

"What is your name?" he asked her as Gregor put all of her weapons in a sack.

"Fiona," she replied and met his hard stare, one that demanded more information, with a smile.

"Fiona what? What clan? What place?"

"Do ye expect me to sweetly reply and give ye all that is needed to rob me and mine?"

Cleverness in a female could be extremely irritating, Ewan decided. "Where were ye headed?"

"Nowhere in particular. I was just riding about enjoying the rare sunny day."

"Then how did ye end up here?"

"Ah, weel, my mount is a contrary beast. He bolted. I think I must have hit my head on the saddle pommel or the like, for after a rough ride, I became quite dazed. When I finally came to my senses, the wretched beast was moving at a calmer pace, but as soon as I tried to grab the reins, which had slipped from my hands, the horse bolted again. After yet another long, rough ride, he tossed me to the ground and left me here."

"Is that the beast over there?"

Fiona looked to where he pointed and softly cursed. The big, gray gelding stood only a few yards away, idly feasting on soft grass. If she had known he was so close, she would have tried to catch him, might even have escaped the trouble she now found herself in. Then, she sighed, accepting her fate. Since she had truly needed a horse, it was certain that aggravating beast would never have allowed himself to be caught.

"Aye, that is him," she replied.

"What is the name it answers to?"

"Several, actually, but if he is feeling particularly contrary, the best one to use is Wretched."

"Wretched? Ye call your mount Wretched?"

"'Tis short for Wretched Pain in the Arse. He is also called Curse to All Mankind, Limb of Satan . . ." She stopped when he held up his hand.

"Mayhap he wouldnae be so contrary if ye gave him a proper name," Ewan said.

"He has one. Tis Stormcloud. He doesnae often answer to it, however. And he has weel earned the others."

"If he is so much trouble, why do ye ride him?"

"He is big, strong, fast, and can go for miles without a rest. Of course, that isnae such a fine thing at the moment," she muttered and glared at her horse, who looked at her, neighed, and tossed his fine head as if he were enjoying a fine laugh at her expense.

"Stay here," Ewan commanded. "Watch her, Gregor." He started toward the horse.

Fiona crossd her arms over her chest and watched him approach Stormcloud. To her utter surprise and a flash of extreme irritation, the man easily caught Stormcloud. The horse did not even try to elude him, seemed positively enraptured. She cursed as he led the horse back to her. When the animal looked at her and gave her a horsey snicker, she stuck her tongue out at him. Her captors found that worthy of a hearty laugh. Even the big man holding Stormcloud's reins grinned.

"Mayhap, if ye spoke sweetly to the beast," Ewan suggested, "he would feel more kindly toward ye."

"I *have* spoken sweetly to him, in the beginning, when I thought he was a reasonable beast," Fiona replied. "I spoke so sweetly honey fair dripped from every word. It ne'er worked. Watch." She stepped closer to the horse and began to flatter him. "Such a fine gentlemon, ye are, Stormcloud. Big, strong, fair to look upon." She concentrated on keeping her voice low and coaxing, struggling to think of every compliment she could as she wooed him.

Ewan quickly lost interest in the game she played with her horse. He was caught firm in the magic of

her voice. It was low, slightly husky, and dangerously seductive. The flattery she filled the horse's
ears with could all too easily flatter a man as well.
He glanced at his men and realized they were being
as seduced as he was, or nearly so. Ewan hoped
their bodies were not growing as taut with need as
his was or there could be trouble.

Just as he was about to end the game, to try to
break the spell she wove, she reached for the reins.
The horse lowered his head and shoved her away
forcefully enough to cause her to sprawl on her
back on the ground. Stormcloud then produced
that sound which all too closely resembled a human
snickering. Ewan tried his best not to laugh, but
the loud hilarity of his men broke his control.

Fiona cursed softly as she got to her feet and
brushed herself off, then glared at the laughing
men. "I dinnae suppose ye would have let me ride
on him anyway."

"Nay, I wouldnae," Ewan said. "Ye are our hostage."

"Might I learn just who plots to drag me off to
his lair and try to use me to pick clean the purses
of my kinsmen?"

"We are the MacFingals. I am Sir Ewan, the laird
of Scarglas, and the mon weighted down with your
vast array of weaponry is my brother Gregor. Ye
can learn the names of the rest when we camp for
the night."

"Just how far away are ye taking me?" she asked
as he searched her saddle and packs, handing
Gregor her second sword and three more knives.

"Ye didnae think ten knives and one sword were
enough?"

"I might have lost one or two weapons in a battle. What are ye doing?" she asked when he mounted Stormcloud.

Ewan grabbed her by the hand, relieved when she nimbly swung up behind him and offered no argument. "I am riding this horse. He has had more rest than my own. I am taking ye to Scarglas, a little o'er a day's ride from here. When we get there, ye will tell me who ye are and where ye are from. Or ye can save us all a lot of trouble and do it ere we get there."

Before she could tell him exactly how small his chances were of her granting that wish, he kicked Stormcloud into a gallop and left her with no choice but to hang on. He might have a lot of questions for her when they camped for the night, and she might even give him a few answers. She had a few questions of her own, however, such as who in the world were the MacFingals of Scarglas?

Chapter 2

"She is muttering," said Gregor as he leaned against the tree next to Ewan and joined him in watching Fiona.

Ewan almost smiled. The moment they had camped, he had ordered Fiona to prepare a meal. She had obeyed him, but made no secret of her annoyance. The fact that only Simon, the youngest of his men at sixteen and his half-brother, was helping her seemed to have added to her irritation. She was, indeed, muttering, when she was not sweetly telling an obviously infatuated Simon what to do. Ewan had caught only a few words of her disgruntled litany, and had decided it would be best to distance himself.

"I suppose that, because she believes she is a mon, she finds the chore demeaning," continued Gregor.

"Oh, I dinnae think she believes she is a mon," murmured Ewan.

"But her skill with weapons—"

"She has been purposefully trained. I have nay doubt of that. And she has been trained weel."

"Why would someone train a lass to fight?"

"I can think of many reasons. Mayhap a dangerous shortage of fighting men, mayhap she comes from a place where battles are frequent, danger all round, or mayhap she was reared mostly by men who didnae ken how else to deal with her. I favor the latter. She moves about in the lad's clothing as if she is accustomed to such attire."

Gregor watched Fiona closely for a moment and nodded. "Aye, she does. She e'en moves more as a lad does than a lass."

"She also shows little fear about being amongst us, a lone woman amongst a dozen men."

"Oh. Mayhap she is no maid, is accustomed to men in all ways."

"Nay."

"Ye sound so certain of that."

"As certain as I can be. I make my judgment based upon how she acts." And, he reluctantly admitted to himself, because he felt a strange, but fierce, loathing of the possibility that Fiona had been touched by any man, let alone many. "She has faced us with weapons, burned our ears with insults, and tries to thwart our plan to ransom her by simply refusing to tell us her full name or where she comes from. There has been nay one small attempt to flirt with any of us, to use any feminine wiles. And look ye at how besotted our Simon is, yet she makes no use of that weak spot in our ranks. There isnae e'en the hint of seduction in her actions."

"Ah, aye. She appears to treat him as a younger

brother or the like." Gregor smiled faintly. "Tis fair certain that is why Simon is so enthralled. Shy and virginal is our Simon. A few maids at Scarglas have sought to catch his eye, but he is proving verra skittish. I was thinking I should take him to a whore soon who will teach the lad a thing or two."

Ewan thought of the time his father had thrust him into a woman's bed, insisting it was time he became a man. He had been fifteen, tall and bone thin, and painfully shy. He had also already begun to be appalled by his father's apparent attempt to breed his own clan, keeping his current wife and far too many other women pregnant year after year. Ewan shuddered at the memory of the night he had lost his virginity. It had been a night full of failures, embarrassments, and awkwardness, all performed in the arms of a hard-eyed woman who outweighed him by at least five stone and badly needed a bath.

"Nay," he said sharply and pretended not to see Gregor's look of surprise. "Leave the lad be. He will take that step when he is ready and 'tis best done that way."

Gregor shrugged. "As ye wish. It just seemed to me that he was a wee bit slow to get the itch."

"I am sure he gets the itch, but 'tis best if we let him choose his own time to scratch it." He studied Simon, who reminded him a great deal of himself at that age. "He probably just needs to get beyond seeing himself as naught but sharp bones and a pair of too big feet."

"Is that how ye felt?" Gregor just smiled when Ewan scowled at him.

"Nay all of us are blessed with your confidence and bonnie face."

"Thank ye for nay saying vanity."

"Ye are welcome. Of course, ye might consider resting your parts now and again ere ye wear them out." He almost smiled when Gregor cast a startled glance at his groin, then glared at him.

"We cannae all be the monk ye are," Gregor grumbled.

"I am nay a monk," Ewan snapped.

Gregor rolled his eyes. "Bedding a woman once a year is monkish. I dinnae ken how ye can do it."

"Tis called restraint. Tis better than breeding a bushel of bastards."

"I only have two. We have all tried to do as ye have asked. A mon has needs, however, and we dinnae all have your strength. Some of us cannae help but wonder if that restraint is why ye are so dark of humor."

Ewan sighed and shook his head. It was an old argument. It was difficult to teach restraint when the patriarch of the clan showed none. The fact that Scarglas had far too many women within its walls who were free with their favors did not help, either. He had had some success since wresting the laird's seat from his father five years ago, but not as much as he would have liked. Ewan looked at Fiona and could not stop himself from wondering what she would think of Scarglas and its people.

"Mayhap that lass will give the lad confidence," murmured Gregor. "If Simon can learn to be at ease with a lass as fair as that one, he may gain some ease with others. Weel, if that lass will be staying with us for a while."

"Oh, I think she will be our guest for a long while, unless ye can think of a way to get her to tell us exactly who she is."

"Ye could always try to seduce the truth out of her. Where are ye going?" Gregor asked when, after one furious glare, Ewan started to stride off into the woods.

"Hunting," Ewan replied. "Better I try to kill some beastie and put meat on our table than run my sword through ye. I might just start to regret that in a year or two."

It did not surprise Ewan when he soon heard Gregor trailing him. The dangers surrounding him and his family meant that he was never allowed to go off on his own. He also knew he would do no hunting, would only catch something if it was unfortunate enough to stumble across his path. It annoyed him to admit it, even if only to himself, but he was trying to escape the temptation of Gregor's suggestion.

Seduce a woman as beautiful as Fiona? It was laughable, or would be if it did not stir up so many thoughts and feelings he was trying so hard to bury deep within himself. He was a big man, dark of looks and nature. Fiona was all sunlight, beautiful, spirited, and so very alive. She was so far above his touch, it was almost dizzying to look at her. Only hours in her company and he was already fighting a craving for what he knew he could never have. Somehow he was going to have to find out who she was, ransom her, and get her out of his life before he succumbed to his desires, tried to reach for her, and made an utter fool of himself.

*   *   *

"Where did a weelborn lass learn to cook so weel?" asked Simon, taking a deep, appreciative sniff of the rabbit stew Fiona was making.

"Now, why would ye think me weelborn?" Fiona asked as she stirred the stew, wondering if it would be enough for so many people. She had two full pots bubbling over the two fires Simon had made, but twelve men could probably devour it in minutes.

"Ye may nay be dressed as a lady or act much like one, but I ken ye are one. Your clothes and weapons, e'en your mount, are those of a weelborn lass or lad. Ye e'en speak verra weel. And"—Simon blushed—"ye are clean and smell verra nice."

"Ah, weel, aye, I am weelborn, but the first years of my life were spent living like the poorest crofter." She tossed the wild onions one of the men had gathered into the stew, and smiled at Simon, who obviously expected a tale now. "For too many years our clan and two others tore each other apart. Finally, there came a time when there was naught left but rubble, burned fields, slaughtered livestock, widows, and orphans. We who survived the last battle which killed the lairds and too many of the grown men rose up from the destruction and swore that it would end on that day. No more feuding, killing, raiding, and all of that. And so it was. Howbeit, for many years, survival and rebuilding took all our few resources. All of us, from the poorest to the laird himself, turned a hand to whate'er work needed doing."

"Is that why ye were taught to fight?"

"Aye, although, praise God, the peace held and there was little of that. Howbeit, we were so weakened, we would have been easy prey for anyone. It was a hard life, verra hard, yet I can see that some good came of it. We all have gained a wide array of skills, and I believe we are, weel, closer than others. We no longer have to fight each day just to survive, but we ken we can do so if we must, and we ken that every mon, woman, and child in the clan can do the same, willingly and skillfully. Tis a good thing."

"Aye," agreed Simon. "Yet, ye must have a laird, aye? One who stands above the others?"

"One who *leads* the others, aye. But because of what we suffered, everyone is certain our laird will, if necessary, work side by side with his people, whether tilling a field or thatching a roof. They also ken that he will ne'er fill his belly whilst they hunger or sit warm in his great hall whilst they shiver in the cold. There is also the rather comforting knowledge that their laird willnae thrust them into war at the slightest hint of insult, that he willnae allow pride to stop him from trying to reach some compromise or less bloody solution. That, too, is most comforting."

"Twould be nice. Our old laird fights with everyone, or did. Five years ago Ewan took o'er as laird, and he works mightily to make alliances. Tisnae going weel. Our father made some hard enemies."

"Oh, ye are Sir Ewan's brother, too?"

"Half-brother. Bastard born. There are a lot of us. Near three dozen at last counting."

And what could one say to that? mused Fiona. Since her brother Diarmot had five bastard chil-

dren, it would seem somewhat hypocritical to con-
demn such a thing. Yet, the old laird seemed to
have gone a bit too far. Such rampant profligacy
was probably one reason Sir Ewan was now the laird.
That and the hint Simon gave that the old laird
had a true skill at offending people, thus leaving
his clan surrounded by enemies. Fiona wondered
just what sort of place she was being taken to.

For a brief moment, she considered telling Sir
Ewan exactly who she was so that she could be
quickly ransomed and returned to Deilcladach.
Then she inwardly shook her head. Her clan was
not so rich it could afford its coffers being emptied because she had been fool enough to get lost
and captured. Her family would worry about her,
but there was no way she could let them know she
was all right without exposing them to what could
be some rather exhorbitant ransom demands. There
was, actually, one small advantage to the difficulty
she now found herself in, although she felt a little
guilty for even considering it. Menzies would not
find her, could not possibly know where she was.
For a little while, she decided, she would be selfish
and enjoy that fact.

Declaring the meal ready, Fiona took her share
and forced Simon to take his as well. Sir Ewan and
Gregor were just walking back into the camp when
she told the men they could eat. She quickly moved
out of the way, sitting with her back against a tree.
She smiled her thanks to Simon when he slipped
up next to her and gave her a chunk of bread.

"Your laird travels weel supplied," she murmured.

"Ah, weel, this bread was given us by two sisters
who were quite taken with our Gregor," said Simon.

"The lasses do like our Gregor." Simon shook his head. "He has two bastards, ye ken. Tis a mon's way, but it troubles me. It marks a lad. Tis a mark ye can ne'er be rid of. It marks the lass who bears the bairns, as weel."

Fiona nodded. "It does, true enough. I have a brother who has five bastards, although he may nay be the father of them all. The women said he was when they left the bairns at his door and he accepted them. He is a verra fortunate mon for his new wife has also accepted them."

"Och, that is fine. My mother found herself a husband, but he didnae want me about, so Ewan took me in. I was just a wee bairn, only three years, and wasnae any use to the mon. Just another mouth to feed, ye ken. Twas for the best. If he had kept me, I would be struggling to make a crop grow in poor land or trying to keep a few beasties alive to sell for a pittance. Instead, I am being trained as a warrior."

It was not easy, but Fiona murmured an agreement. Fiona would never allow him to see the strong surge of pity she felt for him. It was born of the thought of a small fatherless boy tossed aside by his own mother. Simon was right to say he had a better life than he might have had otherwise. She also suspected he had found acceptance, perhaps even a rough affection, amongst his half-brothers and the others. There had to be some scars upon the boy's soul, but his sweet, shy nature made her believe that they were not deep ones. Simon had survived and was thriving. That was, in the end, the most important thing.

She was distracted from her thoughts on Simon's

sad beginnings by the other men. One by one, they dropped their emptied plates in front of her. Fiona supposed those grunts they made as they did so were intended as thanks or compliments. It was clear that they expected her to clean up after them. That was irritating, but not unexpected. The look of amusement upon Sir Ewan's face, however, acted upon her temper as stinging nettles did upon her skin. Only Simon's quick offer to help saved the man from having his ears vigorously clouted. Grumbling under her breath, she worked with Simon to clean up after the meal she had been ordered to cook.

"What are ye about?" Ewan asked Gregor when his brother carefully studied his back as they walked away from Fiona and Simon.

"Looking for the daggers," Gregor drawled, and grinned.

Ewan briefly smiled. "Tis indeed fortunate I found all her knives. I suspect I owe Simon a boon for speaking up so quickly and saving me from a sound thrashing." He chuckled and felt almost as surprised as Gregor looked.

"Ye find her looking as if she wants to gut ye amusing?"

"Aye. Tis a clean, clear anger. Much like a mon's or a lad's. I can see it and, I suspicion, soon I will be able to tell what will stir it. That could prove helpful."

Gregor nodded. "Ye might be able to get her to spill out a few truths if ye get her into a rage."

"That I might. Tis a far better plan than the one ye had," he added in a soft growl.

"Seduction is a proven way to pull secrets from a woman," said Gregor. "If ye havenae the urge to try it, I could—"

"Nay." Ewan inwardly grimaced over how quickly and vehemently he had spoken. "We dinnae need any more enemies, and I think we will gain some if she is used ere she is ransomed." Ewan decided that sounded very reasonable and stoutly ignored his brother's look of amusement.

"So be it. Shall I secure her for the night? Nay sure how to do so, but 'tis needed, I believe. I suspicion that lass could cause us a great deal of trouble if she put her mind to it."

Ewan cursed softly as he turned to look at Fiona. Gregor was right. She needed to be secured in some way. It would not be that difficult to alter the guard schedule he had arranged, ensuring that she was watched closely throughout the night. To his dismay, he could not bring himself to enact that very sensible plan. He did not like the thought of any man remaining so close to Fiona as she slept, or having the opportunity to gain her interest.

Utter madness, he thought crossly. And a weakness that could easily bring him a great deal of grief. If he were back at Scarglas, there would be places he could go, work he could do, in an attempt to put her out of sight and mind. There was no place to hide here.

He sighed, accepting his own contrariness. He did not want another man too close to her for too long, so he would have to be the one to guard her during the night. It could answer a few questions, such as just how great a weakness he suffered and how difficult it would be to fight the attraction he felt for her. It could also prove to be a very long, sleepless night.

"I will guard her," he said. "The night guard has already been arranged. Tis easier to just leave it as it stands. I just need a wee bit of rope."

"Rope?" Gregor asked as he followed Ewan to where their supplies were. "Ye plan to tie her up?"

"That would be the better plan, but nay. If naught else, I wouldnae wish to try and explain to the men why a mon of my size feels the need to tie up such a wee lass just so that he can sleep. I will just leash her to me so that she cannae slip away in the night."

Without another word to Gregor, Ewan walked toward Fiona, who was just finishing the chore of cleaning up after the meal. Her lovely eyes widened at the sight of the rope he held, then narrowed. Before she could retreat, however, he caught both her slender wrists in the grip of one hand. He saw her leg tense as she slowly drew it back.

"I willnae be pleased if ye kick me, lass," he drawled as he dragged her toward the spot where Gregor hastened to spread out a blanket for them to sleep upon.

"Weel, that would certainly keep me weeping for most of the night," Fiona said, giving up her futile attempts to free her wrists. The man's grasp was not really painful, but it was unbreakable. "Just what do ye plan to do with that rope?"

Ewan did not reply. He secured one end of the rope around her wrists and the other end to one of his own wrists. After checking that the bonds were secure, he met her gaze. She looked as if she wanted to wrap the rope around his neck and strangle him—slowly. He wondered why he found that amusing and decided that lust was disordering his wits.

Fiona silently called him every foul name she could think of as he gently, but firmly, pushed her down onto the blanket. He sprawled at her side, then spread another blanket over the top of them. When he crossed one arm beneath his head and draped the one she was bound to over his stomach, she found herself forced onto her side, facing him.

"I dinnae suppose ye would accept my vow to nay try to escape?" she asked as she shifted around a little in a vain attempt to find a comfortable position.

"Nay. I dinnae ken who ye are and ye dinnae plan to tell me, do ye, Fiona-of-the-ten-knives?"

She almost smiled over the name he gave her, then grimaced. Fiona-of-the-eleven-knives would be better, for that would mean that she still had one hidden away and could cut herself free. There were worse things he could have done to make sure she gave him no trouble during the night, but this would make sleep difficult.

So would this enforced closeness, she realized as she suddenly became aware of a few disconcerting facts. She was far too aware of the big, strong body so close to hers. He was enticingly warm and smelled nice, clean and with his own personal scent that she found dangerously attractive. Fiona abruptly recalled their wrestling together as he had relieved her of her weapons. A blush singed her cheeks as she realized she wanted to feel those big hands on her again; only this time they would linger and caress. It was madness, but she instinctively knew it would be very difficult to cure herself of it.

Closing her eyes, she tried to revive the fear of strangers, of men, that Menzies's perverted pursuit had bred in her, but it would not come. For reasons of its own, her heart would not allow her to fear this big, dark man. Feelings she had never experienced before, for any man, were stirring to life within her. A part of her wanted to let those feelings grow and soar. A saner part of her wanted to bury them. Not only was this a very bad time to discover she could be attracted to a man, could even feel passion for one, but it could prove to be a very unwise choice. After silently cursing long and hard, Fiona fought to clear her mind of all troubling thoughts. Perhaps after some sleep, she could find the strength to stand back and see everything more clearly.

Ewan chanced a look at the woman he was leashed to. His gaze lingered when he realized she was asleep. The softness sleep brought to her face and the moonlight made her only more beautiful. He silently cursed as he was forced to admit that he could look at that small heart-shaped face for a very long time and never tire of doing so. Ewan knew that a lot of men would find her flawed because of the scars upon her face, but in his eyes, they did nothing to lessen her beauty.

He clenched his hands into tight fists as he fought the urge to touch Fiona. The memory of the silken warmth of her skin beneath his hands as he had searched her for weapons was a hard one to banish. Nay, it was impossible, he admitted. He ached to feel that warmth again, to linger over it, from the soles of her small feet to her smooth brow.

Simply thinking of touching her soon had him aroused to the point where it was painful. Ewan wanted to feel those firm, plump breasts nestling into his palms. He wanted those long, strong legs of hers to be wrapped around his waist. He desperately wanted to hear her cry out his name whilst caught fast in the throes of the passion he would stir within her.

It was madness. The dreams of a fool. He was big, dark in looks and in humor, and badly scarred. Women did not flock to him as they did to Gregor. Once a year he spent a night with a whore, who took his coin and never begged him to return soon. If a woman ever cried out his name, it was in fear.

Ewan closed his eyes and swore he would kill this attraction. For many reasons, he had decided to remain a man alone. If he was not careful, did not guard his feelings, he feared his lovely hostage could easily change his mind, could make him try to reach for what he could never have.

Chapter 3

Fiona dreamed of her horse tossing her to the ground and running away, leaving her to her fate. She scowled, wondering why she felt as if the contrary beast had thrown her, then fallen on top of her. Still more asleep than awake, she opened her eyes, but she saw neither grass nor rocky ground, only a blanket. That made no sense. People did not leave blankets spread about ready to catch someone thrown from their horse.

Forcing the lingering clouds of sleep from her mind, Fiona raised a hand to rub her eyes, only to gape. Her wrists were tied together. A heartbeat later, her memory returned and her mind cleared. It was no horse on top of her, squeezing all the breath from her lungs, but her captor.

She tried to wriggle out from beneath him, but he had her firmly pinned to the blanket. All she accomplished was to rouse him enough to make him shift his position a little. Fiona nearly gasped aloud when she became aware of exactly what was now nudging against her backside. She not only had a very big man crushing her; she had a very big *aroused* man crushing her. Although she told herself the way her heart raced was due to fear, she knew she was lying. There was a faint touch of alarm within her, for the man felt to be impressively well endowed. What truly upset her, however, was the sudden urge to move her hips and nudge him back. Obviously, a night's sleep had not restored her senses at all.

When she felt him nuzzle the side of her neck, a strange warmth flooded her body. Even as she savored that feeling, she could hear her brother's wife laughingly say that a man often rises with the sun. Her blood cooled. Sir Ewan was probably not even fully awake. He had simply *risen* with the sun, felt a warm female body at his side, and was planning to make use of it. Well, if he was going to nuzzle and nudge, she thought crossly, he could at least know whom he was doing it to.

"Get off me, ye great ox," she muttered, moving whatever part of her body she could in a vain attempt to push him away. "I cannae breathe."

Ewan opened his eyes and stared down at the woman he was sprawled on top of. He was tired, having gotten little sleep, but he woke up quickly when he realized the position he was in. God's teeth, he had been nuzzling her neck and he was as hard as a rock. Even worse, he had obviously been rubbing that hardness against her lovely backside. The position they were in was so deliciously suggestive, he trembled faintly from the sheer strength of his desire. Silently cursing, he moved off her so abruptly, he sharply yanked on her bound wrists.

"Pardon," he mumbled and, hearing his men begin to stir, reached over to untie her.

Fiona slowly sat up and took several deep breaths to calm herself. She had the unsettling feeling it was going to be a long while before she could forget the feel of his big, strong, and highly aroused body pressed so close to hers. That both frightened and annoyed her. Not only did she know nothing about this man, but it was a very poor time for her to be suffering such an attraction, or infatuation, or whatever it was that was plaguing her. She already had one too many men in her life, she thought angrily as she stood up, brushed herself off, and started toward the trees.

"Where do ye think ye are going?" he demanded as he leapt to his feet and began to follow her.

"Tis morning. What do most people have to do in the morning when they first awake, ye fool?" When she heard him continue to follow her, she whirled around to confront him, and was pleased when he hastily backed up a step. "I dinnae need any assistance."

"But ye *do* need guarding." He swiftly looped one end of the rope he still held around her wrist and retied the other end around his own. "Weel? Go on." He almost backed up another step when she glared at him.

For one brief moment, Fiona considered not going. It would be humiliating to relieve herself with him standing so close by. Unfortunately, her

full bladder was making it all too clear that she
would regret that decision, would humiliate herself even more if she did not hurry on her way.
Muttering curses against all men, she started on
her way again, glaring hard at his broad back when
he took the lead.

As she found herself on one side of a tangled
clump of shrubs with him on the other a few minutes later, Fiona did wonder why she was so disturbed
by it all. She had been raised by her five brothers,
and there had been very little refinement or deli-
cacy at Deilcladach for the first thirteen years of
her life. When Gillyanne had arrived, some gen-
tling of their rough ways had followed, but she
doubted anyone would consider the MacEnroys
refined. Performing a basic, necessary function within the hearing of another should not be troubling
her as much as it was. It troubled her so much that,
despite her desperate need, she was unable to relieve
herself until he began. When had she become such
a delicate flower of womanhood? Fiona prayed that
her sudden sensitivity was not because she had some
mad wish to appeal to the man.

"I need to wash," she said when he began to drag
her back to the campsite.

Ewan looked at her, idly wondering why he
should think she looked so tempting when she was
scowling at him. "Ye do understand that ye are a
hostage, dinnae ye, and nay a guest?"

Fiona looked pointedly at the rope leashing her
to his side, then looked back at him. "I believe my
poor, wee woman's mind has begun to grasp that
fact. I still want to wash."

"I think ye were raised with too light a hand upon

the reins," he grumbled as he led her to a small
brook several yards away.

"I think I was raised perfectly."

She ignored his grunt and tried to ignore the
rope on her wrist as they both knelt by the brook
to wash their faces and hands. Taking from her
pocket a small square of embroidered linen Gilly
insisted she carry at all times, Fiona dampened it
in the cold waters. She was rubbing her teeth clean
when an abrupt sense of approaching danger
made her tense. A heartbeat later, as she searched
the wood for some sign of what had stirred her
alarm, she felt Ewan tense.

"Enemies?" she asked in a near whisper even as
she stood up with him. "So close to your lands?"

"On every side and round every corner," he
muttered. "How fast can ye run?"

"If we werenae tied together, I could beat ye
back to the camp."

"Just keeping pace with me will do for now." He
caught the glint of sunlight hitting metal in the
thick wood on the other side of the brook. "Now."

They had not run far when Fiona pulled a little
ahead and Ewan realized she had not been giving
him some idle boast. She was not only swift, but
agile, nimbly dodging or leaping over every obstacle in their path. The moment they reached the
camp, he untied the rope around their wrist as he
curtly told his men to prepare for an attack. He
shoved Fiona toward Simon and commanded the
youth to guard and protect her.

Fiona bit back a protest as Simon dragged her
to a spot near the horses and to the rear of Ewan
and his men. Now was not a good time to argue over

her right and ability to defend herself. She did wish she had her sword, however. It felt wrong to stand there completely unarmed, a youth of but sixteen summers her only shield against any enemy who might reach them.

That enemy reached the camp but a moment later. They swarmed out of the wood from two different directions so swiftly and silently, Fiona was astonished that the MacFingals were not startled into a dangerous moment of hesitation. Instead, they met the attack with a speed and ferocity that was awe inspiring. Although Simon was doing an admirable job of watching for any man approaching them, Fiona did the same. She kept an especially keen watch upon the horses. This might not be a raid, but that would not stop anyone from trying to steal whatever they could get their hands on.

The MacFingals were efficiently decimating their enemy even though the odds against them were nearly three to one, and Fiona began to relax. She hated fighting and bloodshed, but was pleased that her captor and his men were so skilled. These men had not come to make peace, but to kill. What did trouble her was what the great skill of the MacFingals implied. It seemed they were far too accustomed to people trying to kill them. Staying with the MacFingals might provide her with a haven Menzies could not find, but it appeared it would not be a particularly safe haven.

Just as the enemy began to retreat, Simon cursed and shoved her more firmly behind him. A huge, filthy, hirsute man ran toward them, stopping just out of the reach of Simon's sword. The man grinned, revealing rotting teeth through his greasy beard. Fiona tensed when she realized none of the other MacFingals had noticed that one of the enemy had slipped past them. Instinct told her that Simon was skilled with his sword despite his youth, but he was facing a man nearly a foot taller and several stone heavier.

"Give up, laddie. Ye cannae win against me," growled the man.

"Beating ye willnae e'en raise a sweat," drawled Simon.

Fiona had to admit that, for such a sweet lad, Simon could produce an impressively chilling smile.

"Boastful wee maggot, arenae ye. I mean to gut ye, wean, and then I will plow the lass o'er your bleeding carcass."

Something in the way Simon shifted his weight on his feet told Fiona the fight was about to begin. Cursing her helplessness, she moved away from Simon, not wishing to impede him in any way. The first clash of their swords made her wince despite the other sounds of battle assaulting her ears. Simon quickly revealed his greater skill, but she knew it might not be enough. If his bigger and stronger opponent could hold on long enough, he could wear Simon down. There was also the simple fact that Simon was only sixteen and could not have gained the battle experience his opponent had.

She began to look for some way to help. Her weapons were with the horses, but she resisted the urge to go after them. Not only would she be putting herself at risk by traversing such open ground, un-armed, in the midst of a battle, but if Simon sensed her leaving, it could fatally distract him.

A cry from Simon drew her full attention back to him. He was bleeding from what appeared to be a serious wound on his arm. Although it was not his sword arm, the loss of blood would quickly weaken him. She prayed fervently as she again searched for something to use as a weapon, only to hear a groan and a thud to her right. One of the enemy had staggered away wounded from the battle and had collapsed from a loss of blood just a few feet away. It was a rather gruesome answer to her prayer, but she was not about to disdain it. Fiona did not hesitate to relieve the fallen man of his sword and dagger.

Even as she turned back to Simon, she saw him falter. The youth had not leaped clear of his foe's sword quickly enough and now had a wound on his belly. Simon fell to his knees and his opponent smiled. The way the man prepared to swing his sword told Fiona he had every intention of severing Simon's head from his shoulders. Fiona did not hesitate. She thrust her sword into the big man's side. When he screamed and turned to look at her, she plunged her dagger into his heart. The man staggered back a step then slowly fell down, his gaze never wavering from her face.

Fiona shuddered, appalled by what she had done despite the necessity of it. She watched the man's eyes empty of life and fought the urge to empty her belly. This was sure to haunt her dreams for a very long time.

Slowly, she became aware that the battle had ended and wondered how long she had been staring at the grim results of her actions. Fiona forced herself to turn her attention to Simon, who still knelt upon the ground. As she knelt by his side, Ewan and Gregor ran up to them. She supposed that, once she had recovered from the horror of killing a man, she would appreciate the looks of astonishment and respect the two men were giving her.

"Get Simon on a blanket and bare his wounds," she said as she stumbled to her feet. "I will need that small leather bag from my saddle. It carries what I shall need to tend his injuries. I will return in a moment." She raced to the wood, knowing that she could no longer control the urge to be sick.

"Shouldnae ye follow her?" asked Gregor as he picked Simon up in his arms.

"Nay, she will return," replied Ewan as he moved toward the horses to get what was needed for Simon's care. "She will be back to tend Simon." Ewan was a little surprised at how certain he felt about that.

"Weel, if she means to tend him, why did she run off at all?"

"I suspicion she has gone to empty her belly into the bushes."

"Ah, I used to do the same when I was a lad."

By the time he and Gregor had gotten Simon settled on a blanket, his shirt removed, the boy appeared to revive a little. "She moved like lightning, Ewan," he rasped as Ewan bathed away the blood from his torso.

"Aye, she was quick," agreed Ewan, pleased to see that the wounds were shallow ones.

"I failed ye. If she hadnae found those weapons, she would have died once the mon finished me off."

"Ye didnae fail me. The mon was bigger, stronger, battle-hardened, and had a longer reach than ye. Ye have the skill to win in an even match or a fair fight. Ye just have to learn the skills to win in the uneven and unfair ones. As soon as ye heal, we will begin those lessons."

Ewan saw Fiona returning. Her stride was steady, but she looked wan, and when she drew closer, he could see that she had wept. He was glad to see that the body of the man she had killed had been taken away. She needed to be steady of hand and clear of mind to tend Simon.

"Ye saved my life," Simon began when Fiona knelt beside him, only to be hushed when she gently pressed her fingers against his lips.

"Ye put yourself between a sword and my heart. Twas my duty to see that ye didnae die for it. Now, let us see to these wee cuts."

"Do ye ken much about tending such wounds?" Ewan asked.

"Aye, I was taught a great deal about healing from our Gilly and her kin," she replied as she gently bathed Simon's wounds, checking carefully for any dirt or bits of cloth that might have become trapped within. "These are nay verra dire wounds and have bled freely, cleaning themselves weel. Some salve, some stitches, and some rest until they close and all should be weel."

"Can he be moved once ye stitch him?"

"How far do ye have to go and is it rough ground?" Fiona knew it would be best if Simon rested for a few days before he was moved, but understood that their safety required them to leave this place.

"Near half a day, but nay too hard a ride. A pallet wouldnae be too rough on him."

"And 'tis verra necessary to leave here right now? Hold him steady, please. I fear this will burn some, Simon." As soon as Gregor and Ewan pinned Simon to the blanket, Fiona washed his wounds with uisque-beatha. "Ah, good, that sent him into a swoon."

"Why did ye pour that onto his wounds?"

"It has proven to be a help. The wounds dinnae seem to get infected when ye bathe them in the drink. Now, if ye would be so kind as to keep holding him still, I will stitch him up."

Ewan watched the skillful way she worked, her stitches done quickly, but neatly. Simon would be left with scars, but her small, tidy stitches ensured those scars would not be like the ugly, ragged ones marring his flesh. The swift efficiency with which she worked assured him that she had not lied or boasted when she had claimed knowledge of healing. Then Ewan recalled her question about the necessity of moving Simon.

"The men who attacked us were Grays," he said as she completed her stitching and began to cover Simon's wounds with a salve. "Some fled. They could gather more men and return within but a few hours. Now that they ken we are here, I think that it exactly what they will do."

"So, this wasnae a planned attack?" She tied off the bandage she had wrapped around the wound on Simon's arm and, with Gregor's help, began to wrap a bandage around the youth's stomach.

"Nay, I think they just stumbled upon us. I am certain they will be eager to try again, however."

"Then we move on. Can Simon be taken upon a pallet without costing us too much time?"

"Aye, I planned to do that. Tis why I feel we will need half a day to reach Scarglas."

Fiona nodded as she stood up. "Make the bed of it as soft as ye can with blankets and tie him to it. Twill lessen the roughness of the journey." She picked up her bag. "I will see if there are any other injuries that need tending."

"A few wee ones. We were lucky. We lost no one. We had warning enough to be ready for them."

Ewan watched her move toward his men even as he ordered two men to make a pallet for Simon. She was suffering over what she had done. He could see it in her eyes, hear it in her voice. Although someone had trained her how to fight, and trained her well, Ewan felt sure she had never had to kill a man before.

He sighed, feeling both regret and anger. She now had blood on her hands because of his family. His father had ensured that they were surrounded by enemies, too many of whom would like to rid the world of anyone who claimed Scarglas as his home. Ewan could not recall when, if ever, he had been able to spend a day, even an hour, without watching for an attack. It was wrong to drag her into the midst of all that trouble, yet he had no choice. He could not leave her wandering about such a dangerous land on her own, nor could he deny his clan the chance to gain some much-needed ransom for her. The best he could do was work hard to make certain her stay in this benighted land was not a long one.

Which was not going to be easy if she continued

to refuse to tell them who she was and where she
was from, he thought as he helped prepare the pallet for Simon. Ewan considered threatening her,
frightening her into telling him what he needed to
know, then quickly shrugged aside that idea. Not
only did he doubt he would do so effectively since
he could not actually carry out any of his threats,
but he doubted it would work. Instinct told him
that threats and intimidation would either be dis-
believed by Fiona or would simply make her even
more determined to tell him nothing.

Once prepared to leave, Ewan found himself with
yet another problem. It should have been a simple
one to solve, but his own contadictory emotions
made it difficult. Fiona had to ride with someone,
but he found he was reluctant to have her share a
saddle with any of his men. Inwardly cursing, he
set her on his saddle and mounted behind her.
Having her so close was undoubtedly going to make
the ride to Scarglas a long and uncomfortable one.
Unfortunately, he suspected watching her ride along
in another man's arms would be even worse.

After only an hour of feeling her slender body
so close to his, catching her sweet scent each time
he breathed, Ewan knew he needed to distance or
distract himself. "Is today the first time ye have
been in a battle?"

"Aye," Fiona replied, fighting the urge to nestle
back against him. "I have been in a few wee fights,
e'en wounded a mon or two, but I have ne'er killed
a mon." She shivered as the image of the man's
empty, staring eyes filled her mind.

"He was about to take Simon's head from his
shoulders."

"I ken it." Feeling chilled and her back aching from the struggle to keep a distance between them, Fiona cautiously began to relax against him. "There wasnae any other choice. E'en if I could have borne letting Simon die, I still had to do it. Once Simon fell, the mon was coming for me." She sighed and relaxed against Ewan's broad chest a little more. "I always feared I would hesitate when it came to actually killing a mon."

"But ye didnae."

"Nay, God save my soul, I didnae. My brother was right. When confronted with someone who wants to kill me or kill someone I preferred to keep alive, I was able to find the stomach to do what I needed to. I just wish he had been wrong about how I would feel after I was safe again."

"Twill pass. Your brother sounds a wise laird."

She laughed softly as she felt her weariness begin to weight her limbs. "Nay always wise, but he kens how to keep us safe." Fiona had the unsettling feeling she had just given Ewan some small hint about who she was, but was too tired to worry about it. A small hint would not help him much, and she would simply be more cautious in watching out for a trap. Too many carelessly dropped small hints could quickly add up to enough of a whole to end her game. After she had rested, she would try to recall all she may have let slip already, and be more wary in her answers and her conversation with everyone. As she closed her eyes, she prayed exhaustion would keep the dark dreams away for a little while.

Ewan grimaced as his body responded immediately to the soft woman resting against him, but then he smiled. Fiona was not so very skilled at deception. She could not hold all the truth inside. He would not need threats to gain the truth, just time. When at ease, Fiona spoke freely, unable to guard her tongue as closely as she needed to. He would warn everyone to listen carefully to all she said. It would take time, but he was certain that, piece by tiny piece, Fiona would reveal who she was, whom she belonged to, and where she was from. When he slipped his arm around her small waist to hold her steady, he told himself he was pleased. He sternly told himself he would be glad to see her leave and ignored the sneering inner voice that called him a liar.

Chapter 4

Intimidating was the first word that came to mind when Fiona got her first look at Scarglas. Dark, eerie, and lonely were her next impressions. The way it loomed up ahead, cold and somewhat threatening, tickled at a memory in Fiona's mind. It made her think of sorcery and murder, but she could not think why. If she had ever heard of Scarglas or the MacFingals, the memory was proving obstinately elusive at the moment.

Scarglas Keep sat on a small rise in the midst of a brutally cleared area. Its outer walls were thick and high. A wide moat encircled those walls, and she knew it was probably dangerously deep. Several yards outside the moat was an encircling berm as tall as a man, yet another barrier an enemy must cross before reaching those trecherously high walls. Off in the distance, in a direct line with the four corners of the keep, she could see the tops of four wooden watchtowers. Everything about Scarglas bespoke a keep under constant siege.

The passage through the high berm was barely wide enough for a wagon. Fiona was not surprised to find that the bridge over the moat was the same. No enemy could approach the tall, iron-studded gates of Scarglas in any great number. The somewhat narrow strip of land between the edge of the moat and the base of the walls was cluttered with small stone cottages. Another obstacle, Fiona realized. Even if the thatched roofs were fired, that would impede the attackers far more than the defenders, and she doubted such fires would do any damage to those walls.

She wondered how long the MacFingals had held Scarglas. To build such a place would take many years and a lot of coin, something few Scots had. If the clan had been upon these lands for a long time, then why had she never heard of them? Fiona knew her knowledge of the various clans was not very extensive, but any clan so contentious it was surrounded by enemies would surely have been talked about. Yet, she had never heard one word about them, or could not recall one.

A brief glimpse of a village to the north of the keep, and an intriguing circle of standing stone to the south, softened the stark look of the place, but not by much. Fiona repressed the urge to shiver as they rode through the gates. Scarglas was certainly strong enough to protect her from Menzies if he was ever able to track her to it. Unfortunately, it seemed that hiding from one man was putting her in the path of many another eager to raze this place to the ground. It might be time to rethink her plan.

Ewan was just setting her on the ground when a tall man burst out of the keep. He flung open the heavy doors so ominously decorated with iron spikes as if they weighed nothing. Although his hair was white, the resemblance to Ewan was unmistakable. Fiona prepared herself to meet the man who apparently bred children and enemies with equal abandon. She was annoyed when he completely ignored her.

"Been in a fight, have ye, lad?" the man asked, glancing only briefly at Simon. "Lost the boy, did ye?"

"Nay, Simon is but wounded," replied Ewan. "Twas the Grays."

"Set a trap for ye?"

"Nay. I believe they but stumbled upon us and thought they had enough men to beat us."

"Hah! The Grays were always fools. So, got yourself a prisoner, eh?" The man frowned at Fiona. "She doesnae look much like a Gray."

"We didnae take her from the Grays," Ewan began.

"Ah, so ye have finally found yourself a bride. That pleases me, laddie. I was beginning to get concerned."

Fiona noticed the heat of a blush darken Ewan's cheeks. "Concerned about what?" she asked, but both men ignored her.

"She isnae my bride. We found her, lost and on foot. Decided to hold fast to her until she tells us who her clan is. Then we can ransom her back to them." Noting the telltale licentious glint entering his father's eyes as he studied Fiona, Ewan held her by the arm and tugged her a little closer to his side. "Father, this is Fiona. Fiona, my father, Sir Fingal MacFingal."

"Fiona what? Of where?" demanded Sir Fingal, scowling at Fiona.

Fiona scowled right back. "Just Fiona. Tis all I am willing to say."

"Tis for the best she isnae your bride, I be thinking, Ewan," said Sir Fingal, looking Fiona over in a way that made her want to strike him. "Too small, dresses like a wee lad, and she is scarred."

It was not easy, but Fiona resisted the urge to cover her scarred cheeks with her hands. The man was insulting, arrogant, and rude, but that was not the reason she was beginning to heartily dislike him. It was the way the man acted concerning Simon that had her aching to kick him. Sir Fingal had appeared completely unmoved by the possibility that the boy, his own son, was dead. He had barely glanced at the boy and, when told that Simon was only wounded, had not even asked where or how badly.

"We need to get Simon into a bed," Fiona said, looking up at Ewan. "I need to look at his wounds."

"Mab will see to the lad," Sir Fingal said and he looked toward the keep.

Following his gaze, Fiona saw a small, plump woman hurrying toward them. Her graying light brown hair was a wild tangle around her round face, and her clothes looked equally disordered. She stopped every few steps to pick up something she had dropped and put it back into the overfilled basket that swung wildly on her arm. If her healing supplies were in that basket, they were now well sprinkled with the dirt from the ground of the inner bailey.

Just as Fiona was about to curtly order the woman to stay away, she got a good look at the woman's face. There was a kindness in the woman, a sweetness that Fiona suspected ran bone deep. Mab frowned in confusion as she noticed all the various bandages on the men. Fiona caught a glimpse of disappointment as well as fear upon her face and inwardly grimaced. Mab was undoubtedly the healer of Scarglas and Fiona had just trespassed upon her territory. The fact that Mab looked uneasy instead of furious told Fiona the woman did not feel secure in the position she had probably claimed for herself. Mab would not fight if Fiona turned her away, but Fiona knew she would feel like an ogre if she did that.

"I tended the wounds, Mistress Mab," Fiona said, noting that Mab's big brown eyes held only curiosity when the woman looked at her. "There was a battle which left a few men bleeding and I thought they would make the rest of the journey here in more comfort if those wee holes in them were corked."

"Ye have some healing skills?" Mab asked.

"Some. I had some training, was taught by several weel-respected healers."

"Who? Mayhap I will ken the name."

Fiona thought out her answer carefully before replying, "I spent some time with Lady Maldie Murray when I was younger." She felt that made the association sound appropriately vague, thus useless to Ewan.

Mab gasped and clutched her small, plump hands against her generous bosom, causing several things to tumble out of her basket to the ground. "Oh, how verra fortunate ye are. Lady Maldie is a lauded healer. How I wish I could have met her ere I came to Scarglas."

Not sure why Mab's coming to Scarglas would mean the woman would never have the chance to meet Lady Maldie, Fiona picked up Mab's things and put them back in her basket. Somehow she was going to have to keep this woman from using any of those now filthy items on the wounded men. She could not shame this woman or push her from her place in the clan, not in Mab's eyes or those of the MacFingals, but Fiona was going to have to teach Mab a few things before she left Scarglas.

"Mayhap ye should find a basket with a top or use a bag as I do, mistress," Fiona said. "Twould save ye the extra work of having to clean the things which fall upon the ground." Fiona could tell by the look upon Mab's face that the woman had not intended to clean the things nor knew why she should.

"Oh, of course," Mab said. "I was in such a rush to see to the lads, ye ken, and just threw all my things into the first thing I could find."

Inwardly, Fiona breathed a hearty sigh of relief. She had found the path to take. It would not be easy to make every lesson sound as if she was simply stating a fact Mab already knew, but she would try. Instinct told her that Mab would not take offense at more direct speech, but Fiona would do that only when they were alone or Mab asked a question. Somehow she knew that Mab desperately needed her place as the clan's healer and Fiona could never be so cruel as to take it away, especially since she was not staying at Scarglas for very long.

"I need to get Simon to a bed, mistress, so that we may look at his wounds," Fiona said. "The ride here may have opened them."

"Of course, of course." Mab looked at the two men who had unhitched Simon's pallet from the back of Gregor's horse. "If ye two could bring the lad along with us, please?" Mab grasped Fiona by the arm and started to lead her toward the keep. "Twill be wondrous to speak to someone who trained with Lady Maldie Murray. Just wondrous. I am always trying to find cures, ye ken. Tis my duty to keep the lads hale. I have recently mixed a cream that will make scars fade. I shall have to give ye some."

A glance over her shoulder brought Fiona's gaze in line with Ewan's and Gregor's. Both men quickly shook their heads and she understood. Mab's tender feelings were obviously protected by a lot of people. Mab's cures, however, were obviously meant to be avoided. Somehow she was going to have to convince Mab that she was happy with her scars. Since that was a lie, it would not be easy. Fiona shook the concern aside and followed Mab into the keep, forcing her thoughts to the more important matter of caring for Simon.

"I thought ye said she was a hostage," grumbled Sir Fingal, scowling after Mab and Fiona.

"She is," replied Ewan as he started toward the keep, Gregor and their father falling into step on either side of him.

"She doesnae act like one. Nay sure 'tis wise to let a hostage treat our men's wounds."

"Fiona has a true skill. She willnae be using it against the men, either."

"How can ye be so certain of that? Ye dinnae e'en ken who the lass is. She could have been sent here by one of our enemies, could be here to kill me or ye, or to spy on us."

Ewan considered that possibility as they entered the great hall, but could not rouse more than the faintest glimmer of suspicion. That was unusual, for he had learned long ago not to put much trust in women. He did not like to think he was letting lust and a pair of beautiful violet eyes steal his wits.

As he, Gregor, and their father took their seats at the head table, two maids swiftly setting ale, bread, and cheese before them, Ewan felt his briefly wavering conviction return. He could trust Fiona to care for Simon, for any of the people of Scarglas. The way she had tended the wounds of Simon and his men revealed that she was a healer to the very marrow of her bones. She would never use those skills to cause harm.

In every other thing concerning her, he would be wise to use caution, to carefully weigh her every word and deed. Despite that warning to himself, he still could not fully believe she had been sent to spy on them. Their meeting could not possibly have been planned. That still left the chance that she had been journeying to Scarglas to spy upon them and had simply stumbled into their path. Women, especially young, beautiful women, made excellent weapons and spies. It was a fact he would have to keep reminding himself of.

"How did ye get a hold on the lass?" Fingal asked.

Gregor answered and Ewan only half listened as

he drank some ale and took the edge off his hunger
with some bread and cheese. He did think Gregor
found far too much amusement in the confrontation. Later, when he wrestled the unwise attraction
he felt for Fiona into submission, Ewan knew he
would also find it humorous. At the moment, however, he could only view Fiona's advent into his life
as a curse. He did not think it a good sign that his
father saw little humor in the tale, however. His father saw enemies around every corner, and although
the man did have far too many, he often carried caution to excessive lengths.

"Tis all verra suspicious," muttered Fingal. "I
think we ought to toss the lass out."

"Nay," said Ewan. "Ye cannae send a wee lass like
that out alone. There is too much danger out there."

"Ye may have brought danger right into our keep.
I say she could be a spy, sent here to sniff out our
weaknesses, mayhap e'en to find a way to let some
of our enemies into the verra heart of Scarglas."

"Then we watch her closely until we can find out
who she belongs to and ransom her back to them."

"And just why havenae ye found out who she is?"

"She willnae tell me. Says she willnae help me
pick clean the pockets of her kinsmen."

Fingal cursed softly. "So we make her tell us. I
ken many ways to make someone spill the truth."

There was a chilling implication behind his father's words that Ewan did not want to think on
too long. When Fingal felt threatened, he could
act callously, even cruelly. The man saw threats
and insults everywhere and often reacted without
thought, which was one reason they found themselves ringed by enemies. About the only things

that kept his father diverted from thinking vast hordes of people were striving to steal all he had, betray him, or kill him were money and women. Since Ewan found the thought of his father turning his lecherous gaze upon Fiona extremely distasteful, he would have to make the man believe that she could greatly enrich them.

"There isnae any need to exert ourselves," Ewan said. "We must simply take careful note of all she says. The truth will slip out. It may come in bits and pieces, but it will come."

"How can ye be sure?"

"'Tis already happening. I ken her brother is a laird, there is a close female relation named Gilly, and she has the sort of connections that would allow her to train with Lady Maldie Murray, a legendary healer. Once I can speak with Simon, I suspect I will discover e'en more, for she talked with him a great deal last eve."

"Weel, that might work. No lass can hold tight to a secret. But are ye sure she will e'en be worth a ransoming? She isnae dressed as a fine lady and she had no escort as a fine lady should."

"Her clothing is of a verra fine quality as are her weapons. Her mount is also one only a weelborn lass could afford. Despite her odd attire and skill with weapons, all else bespeaks a lass of good blood. Aye, someone will pay to have her returned, and 'tis best if she is returned to them unharmed and with no tales of cruelty to tell."

Ewan breathed a silent sigh of relief when his father nodded, his attention distracted by Bonnie, a plump maid who was the current object of his father's lust. Fingal had abandoned his role of coldhearted warrior to become the warm-blooded lecher all too well known to the people of Scarglas. It was his father's constantly changing moods, his inability to keep his attention and energy set on any single path for long, as well as his inability to control his emotions, that had allowed Ewan to take the man's place as laird. The fact that Fingal had not cared about the change in leadership made it all too clear that he did not really want the burden of leading and caring for his clan.

It was such erratic behavior which had made the people of Scarglas accept Ewan's place as laird. It was also such behavior which made Ewan, and far too many others, uncertain about the health of Fingal's mind. Ewan would watch his father act with no restraint or shift from one mood or thought to another within a heartbeat and fear that madness lurked there. It was that fear which made Ewan strive for control and restraint in all things. At times he could feel fierce emotions and desires stir to life within him and would fight hard to banish them, chilled by the fear that he might be just like his father. Fiona stirred such emotions within him, which was why he intended to do his best to ignore and avoid her.

There was a beast within him, a creature of strong emotion and fierce desires. That beast was nudged awake every time he looked at Fiona. He had thought he had tamed it, but he now knew he had only caged it. For the sake of his own sanity and the welfare of the people of Scarglas, he had to keep it caged. That meant that he had to keep his distance from Fiona even as he rooted out the truth of who she was. The days ahead looked to be long and troublesome, he thought, and then tried to turn his father's attention back to matters of importance and away from the sway of Bonnie's ample hips.

"Do ye truly believe such cleanliness is necessary?" asked Mab as she frowned down at a sleeping Simon.

"Aye," replied Fiona, slouching in a chair on the other side of Simon's bed. "I cannae say why it is, but wounds kept clean heal faster and better. They dinnae go putrid, risking the life of the wounded one. There is less chance of a dangerous fever as weel. Since infection and fever can cause e'en the smallest injury to become mortal, I am willing to do anything to fend them off, e'en if I dinnae ken the why of it."

Mab nodded. "I confess that I have but a meager skill. When I came here, there wasnae anyone who truly wished to be a healer, so I took that place for myself. Twill be verra helpful to learn from ye as I can see that ye have a true skill and much knowledge." She smiled at Fiona. "I am verra good at making potions and salves, however. I am certain I shall soon hit upon a grand cure for something."

Before Mab could yet again suggest Fiona try her cure for scars, Fiona asked, "Ye say ye came here? Ye arenae from Scarglas? Ye arenae a MacFingal?"

"Nay. I came here, oh, ten years ago, I think it was. I am a Drummond. Weel, I was a Drummond. They made it verra clear they didnae want me anymore." Mab sighed. "I still dinnae understand where

I went wrong. My salve should have worked. And I am verra certain I mixed that potion right. They must have all had verra delicate stomachs for it to work so swifty and fiercely. And I did offer to clean up the mess, foul though it was. I tried to explain to the laird that the potion wasnae a poison, that 'tis good to purge the body now and then. But he wouldnae listen. Wouldnae listen to my assurances that my salve would grow his hair back on that odd bald spot and that the strange green shade to his hair would assuredly grow out in time. He would-nae heed a word, just tossed me and my belongings out."

Fiona tried to picture the results of Mab's potion and salve, then quickly ceased. It was not a pleasant picture. "So ye came here? Ye had heard of the MacFingals?"

"Och, nay. I had ne'er heard of them. The old laird found me hurrying away from a village." Mab grimaced. "I was just trying to be helpful and I did rid that vile woman's hair of lice. And it was a rather nice color in her hair, much akin to bluebells. But I must nay brood o'er such things. As I left, I met the old laird, and, weel"—Mab blushed—"he was so charming, so ardent. I was quite swept away. Twas a wee bit disconcerting to arrive here and discover that he had a wife, but I needed a home, didnae I? So, I stayed and took my place as the healer. My laddie is nine now and is seeking his place within the clan. This week he works with the armorer to see if he would like to learn that skill."

"Ye bore the laird a son?"

"Aye, my wee Ned. A lovely laddie and the joy of my life. I was afeared that I would be sent away by the laird's wife, but she was dead ere anyone noticed I was carrying. Killed by lightning whilst trysting with a Gray."

"Oh, and that is what began the feud, is it?"

"Nay. The old laird had already made enemies of near everyone by then." Mab idly smoothed the blanket over Simon. "The Grays have been our enemies from the verra beginning. They wanted Scarglas and werenae happy when Fingal got his hands on it. They claim it was promised to them, but the mon who held it gave it to the old laird, who was his cousin. Fingal was blood after all. Twas only right."

Before Fiona could ask anything else, a plump, dark-haired woman entered the room, set a large tray of food and wine on a table near the fireplace, and left. She said not one word. The only notice she gave of the other occupants of the room was a brief, fierce glare aimed at Mab. Fiona moved to sit in a chair near the table and waved Mab into the other seat. For a moment, she sipped her wine and nibbled on a thick piece of bread.

"Who was that woman?" asked Fiona as she cut herself a piece of mutton.

"Clare," replied Mab. "She doesnae like anyone. Used to be a MacKenzie, but fled her clan. She is thrice a widow, and when her third husband died, many thought she was killing them. She doesnae care for the women who bed the old laird, especially the ones who did so when he had a wife. I suspicion she lowered herself to bring this food to us because she was curious about ye. She has been here, oh, near to a dozen years. She married Angus the stablemaster near ten years past and he still lives, so I think her other husbands were just an ill-favored lot."

"So, she is now a MacFingal, too. Just who *are* the MacFingals? I have ne'er heard of them yet they must have held this land for many years as it was a kinsmon who gave it to the old laird."

"He wasnae a MacFingal. The MacFingals are a new clan." Mab chuckled. "Verra new. Tis the truth, the old laird started it. He had a falling-out with his kinsmen and turned his back on them. Decided to start his own clan, named it after himself. Fingal came here a few months before his cousin died, a verra distant cousin, and obviously wooed the mon into naming him his heir. Fingal married the mon's daughter to secure it all, e'en though she was promised to another. She gave Fingal one son ere she died."

"Then what is the name of his kinsmen's clan?" Fiona was astonished when Mab suddenly looked fearful, even going a little pale.

"We cannae say the name. Tis forbidden."

"I dinnae think anyone will hear ye, Mab."

Mab shook her head. "Tis forbidden. If the old laird kens anyone has said it, he goes into a rage which can last for hours. Nay, 'tis best if ye just see us all as MacFingals."

Fiona began to think she had landed in a keep full of lunatics, the old laird being the worst. Lunatics, broken men, and castoffs. The banished and the bedeviled. Her curiosity was roused, however. Before she left Scarglas, she was determined to find out exactly who Fingal MacFingal was and why he had turned his back on his kinsmen. A small inner voice sneered that her interest was stirred more because of a tall, dark warrior named Ewan than by some angry old man, but she ignored it.

Chapter 5

The sound of the door being unbarred brought Fiona to her feet. She had been both annoyed and relieved when she had been secured inside the room with Simon. A soft pallet had been made for her by the fire and even her demand for a bath had been fulfilled, a painted wooden screen set up in the corner of the room to give her privacy. Fresh clothing had been brought to her and Fiona thought she looked rather nice in the soft woolen gown, the deep blue complementing her eyes. Mab had left to be with her son, Simon had passed a peaceful night, and she had slept well, too. There was no reason for her to feel irritated, for her treatment as a hostage had, thus far, been exemplary. She knew, to her disgust, that the lack of any word or sight of her captor was the cause of her annoyance. That implied that she had missed him and she cursed her own weakness.

Gregor entered the room, followed by Mab, and he smiled at Fiona. "Ye clean up weel, lass."

Fiona inwardly cursed the blush she felt sting her cheeks. "Thank ye."

"How fares the lad?" he asked as he moved to the side of the bed to look at Simon.

"No hint of fever," said Mab who, after setting a tray holding a bowl of broth and some water on the small table by the bed, felt Simon's forehead and cheeks.

"He passed a quiet night." Fiona stood at the foot of the bed and smiled at Simon, who blushed when Mab yanked down the covers to look at his bandaged wounds. "The wounds looked clean when I changed the bandages this morning and put a wee bit of salve on them. Do they look clean to ye, Mab?"

Gently easing aside the bandages enough to peek at the wounds, Mab nodded. "Verra clean. Ye must tell what your salve is, for 'tis clear that it works wonders." She tugged the blankets back up and, with Gregor's assistance, eased Simon into a partially seated position against the pillows. "I have broth, water, and some cider for ye, laddie. And dinnae make that face. Ye ken ye must nay eat too heartily for a wee while." She looked at Fiona. "A day or two, aye?"

"Aye. Broth today, I think, and if there is still no sign of fever or infection, something a wee bit heartier on the morrow. They werenae verra deep wounds."

"Mere scratches," said Simon. "I will be out of this bed soon."

"Nay until Mab and I say ye can or we will be

lashing ye to that bed. The wound upon your belly could be set to bleeding verra easily. Ye will be in bed until it closes and then ye will be verra, verra careful for a while after that. It wasnae deep enough to gut ye, but 'tis more than a scratch. I will see it closed tight ere I let ye prance about."

"I ne'er prance," grumbled Simon, and sighed when everyone just grinned at him.

"I brought a potion to give him to ease the pain," Mab said, glancing nervously at Fiona.

Fiona almost laughed at the looks of alarm that swiftly passed over Simon and Gregor's faces. "Weel, he slept easily all night without a potion, Mab. True, that could have been because he was too exhausted to be troubled by any pain. Best we leave it to Simon to decide." She had to grin at the identical looks of relief the brothers quickly hid from Mab.

"Do ye need something for the pain, lad?" Mab asked Simon.

"Nay, Mab," Simon replied. "I willnae say it doesnae hurt, but 'tis nay bad enough to drink a potion. Those things make my head ache and my stomach churn when I wake up again."

"Come then, Fiona-of-the-ten-knives," Gregor said, grinning as he took her by the arm and led her toward the door. "Time to break your fast."

"Why did he call her that verra odd name?" Mab asked Simon.

Fiona sighed as she and Gregor stepped into the hall and he shut the door on Simon's reply. She supposed it had been too much to hope for that all the details of her capture would not be told. There had been twelve heartily amused men

there, after all. The people of Scarglas were going
to think she was very odd, she mused, then almost
laughed. Recalling all Mab had told her, odd was
almost a rite of passage at Scarglas.

"Simon *will* heal, will he not?" asked Gregor as
they entered the great hall. "He looked weel
enough. Better than I had expected."

"I believe he will be just fine," replied Fiona. "Another day or two without a sign of fever or infection and then all one needs to worry about is
keeping him still enough to let his wounds close
tight." She hid her surprise when Gregor led her
to the laird's table.

"Would ye really lash him to the bed?"

"In a heartbeat," she replied, ignoring his soft
laughter. "If 'twas just the wound upon his arm, he
wouldnae have to be too confined, but the wound
upon his belly requires that he be verra still if it is
to close weel. Every time he moves his body, he
tugs at those stitches. In truth, 'twill be a week or
more ere I will e'en allow him to don the loosest of
clothing. So, if he tries to get up, he will have to do
so naked."

Gregor laughed again as he urged her into a
seat next to Ewan. "I believe he will stay abed."

Fiona simply nodded, too unsettled by being near
Ewan to think of a coherent reply. A part of her
found the way she reacted to Ewan fascinating,
even encouraging, for she had begun to think she
would never feel such interest in any man. She
never had before Menzies had begun tormenting
her, and she had feared that Menzies's actions had
killed all chance that she ever would. What irritated and alarmed her was that her body, perhaps

even her heart, would choose to be drawn to a man who had every intention of selling her back to her family.

"How is Simon?" asked Ewan after glaring at Gregor, who sat down on his right.

As Fiona replied, he studied her. Dressed as a lad, she had been beautiful, too beautiful for his peace of mind. Dressed as a woman, she took his breath away. She was temptation on two pretty feet. Just the sound of her slightly husky voice had him taut with need. A glance at his father revealed that the man found Fiona attractive, and Ewan scowled. The man could not possibly be thinking of trying his charms on a lass over thirty years younger than him, could he? Ewan not only found that distasteful, but realized a small part of him was afraid that his father might succeed. That tasted of jealousy and Ewan inwardly grimaced. He was in a lot more danger than he had realized.

"Why are ye still tending the lad?" demanded Sir Fingal.

"I was there when he was wounded," replied Fiona. "I believe in finishing whate'er I have begun."

"Mab can do it."

"Ah, but if we both tend the lad, we can both have time to rest, aye?"

"Where did ye get those scars?"

"Da," Ewan protested, but his father ignored him.

Fiona calmly finished the piece of honey-coated bread she had been eating and met Sir Fingal's gaze directly. "A mon felt my face needed some improvement."

"What do ye mean by that, ye daft wench?"

"I wouldnae call her a wench if I was ye, Da," murmured Gregor.

Ewan grabbed Fiona's hand when she reached for the knife used to cut the cheese. The feel of her small hand in his sent the heat of desire straight to his loins, but Ewan struggled to ignore the feeling. He was interested in her answer to his father's question.

"Explain," Ewan said and almost smiled at the way her violet eyes nearly sparked with annoyance.

"A mon sought my hand in marriage," she replied, fighting to ignore how strangely bereft she felt when he released her hand. "I refused him. Although I did so most kindly, he took offense. He hunts me, and each time he has caught me, he marks me. These were the first." She lightly touched the scar on her right cheek. "He has caught me three other times. He says he intends to make me unmarriagable, to force me to accept him if only because none other will have me."

"Who?"

"That can be of no interest to ye."

Ewan decided not to argue that just yet. "Then why were ye out riding alone?"

"Constant confinement, e'en if 'tis for one's own safety, can make a person act foolishly."

He nodded, understanding exactly what she meant. The fact that he could never go anywhere alone because they were surrounded by enemies often made him feel the same. One did not need high walls to feel confined. Ewan also wondered if one reason she was being such a complacent hostage was because she had come to her senses and realized the danger she had put herself in. She was now safely behind high walls again and well guarded.

"I think ye must tell me who this enemy is," he said, watching her closely. "He could follow ye here."

"Since I dinnae ken where *here* is, I dinnae think he will be able to find me."

"He trails ye, hunts ye. It isnae impossible for him to trail ye to our gates."

Fiona calmly finished her porridge as she thought over the matter. Only her family knew about her troubles with Menzies. Even if Ewan could find a kinsman of Menzies to speak to, she doubted many of Ranald's clan would know what he was doing to her or would admit it if they did. Since Menzies had caught her at times when she had thought herself safe, it was indeed possible that he could find her at Scarglas. The MacFingals did not need another trouble kicking at their gates. It would also be to her advantage to tell Ewan, for he would guard her against that threat. She just wished he would not be doing so only to protect her value as a hostage, but hastily shook aside the odd pang that knowledge caused her.

"His name is Sir Ranald Menzies," she finally said. "He rides with six men." She almost smiled when Ewan grunted in reply, for he reminded her very strongly of her brothers for a moment.

"So, this fool thinks to make ye worthless as a bride for any other," said Fingal, then scowled at her. "Has he bedded ye then?"

"Da!" Ewan and Gregor protested together.

"What!? Tis a reasonable question. Tis a sure way

to make her unweddable to another. Mon wants his wife untouched. Ye should have a virgin for a bride, Ewan."

"She isnae my bride," Ewan nearly shouted, "but a hostage for ransom."

It was foolish to be hurt by his adamant refusal of her as a bride, Fiona thought. He was simply telling the truth. She had not come to Scarglas as a bride, but as a hostage. Even so, she mused, he did not have to be so angered, even appalled, by the suggestion.

She only half listened as Ewan and his father argued. As she finished her porridge and reached for an apple, she looked around the great hall. Many of the men in it bore a strong resemblance to Sir Fingal, and those who did were Ewan's age or younger. The old fool was clearly trying to breed his own army. Fiona suspected the older men were all ones who had found their way to Scarglas and stayed, or remained after the previous laird died.

It was an impressive great hall with a massive fireplace at each end. Tapestries and weapons decorated the walls. The laird's table had carved oak chairs, while the other men sat on sturdy benches. The hall was also surprisingly clean, she realized. Whoever ran the household did so with an iron hand. Women and boys moved quietly amongst the tables, refilling jugs and taking away empty plates. Either Sir Fingal had money or the previous laird had. Deilcladach had only recently begun to enjoy some of the refinements she saw here. It would not be a bad place to live if it was not so besieged by enemies, she decided, and then her thoughts were abruptly pulled back to the argument between the MacFingals.

"Weel, if ye dinnae want the lass," snapped Sir Fingal, "Gregor can wed her. Time he wed and started a family."

"I have two sons," said Gregor, "and I will choose my own wife."

"And I will choose my own husband," said Fiona, glaring at Sir Fingal.

"Dinnae be daft," said Sir Fingal. "'Tis a mon's place to choose a mate for the lasses in his family."

"Nay in mine, it isnae. And *ye* arenae my kinsmon so 'tisnae your concern."

"Ye are under my rule now, lass."

Fiona snorted. "I dinnae think so. Now"—she stood up—"if ye will excuse me, I believe I will return to see how Simon is faring."

Ewan signaled to his brother Nathan, who quickly fell into step beside Fiona as she left the hall. He glanced at Gregor and was pleased to see that his brother was as amused as he was. Their father looked stunned. Ewan suspected it was the first time any woman had faced him squarely and denied him. Even his last wife had been cowed and submissive right up until the night she had run off. Despite all the trouble it was going to cause him to have Fiona around, Ewan knew he would enjoy watching a female stand up to his father. He would just make sure she did not pay too dearly for that.

"That lass was raised with too light a hand on the reins," Sir Fingal said.

It made Ewan wince to hear his father say something he himself had said. He was dismayed to think he had unknowingly accepted some of his father's attititudes into his heart and mind. Although he found some consolation in the fact that he did not fault Fiona for her strengths, Ewan swore to himself that he would try much harder to turn aside the lessons his father tried to teach him.

"She is right," Ewan said. "Ye arenae her kinsmon and have no right to pick a husband for her. She isnae here for that. She is here to be ransomed and fill our empty coffers."

"She might have a fine dower. That could do as weel as a ransom."

"Nay. She is to be ransomed."

"Dinnae ken why ye are being so obstinate. Ye need a wife and show no sign of getting one. With your face, it willnae be easy to woo a lass, either. Why not take one who fell into your grasp?"

"Da, leave it be," said Gregor. "Marrying her off to one of us could anger her clan and we dinnae need any more enemies."

Sir Fingal snorted. "And ye dinnae think holding the lass for ransom will irritate her clan?"

"Tis an accepted practice. I suspicion they now ken that she rode off alone and willnae blame us for taking advantage of how she fell into our grasp."

"Humph. Tis a sad waste of a young lass. She is bonnie enough despite the scars, and I think ye are right to say she is weelborn. Dinnae get many of that sort about this place."

"Leave it be, Da," Ewan said wearily, echoing Gregor's words. "Leave her be. Tis clear she isnae going to willingly fall in with your plans. None of us wants an unwilling bride."

His father glared and muttered, but said no more.

Ewan had the strong feeling the man had not changed his mind, however. Now, along with everything else he had to watch out for, he was going to have to guard against his father's plots to marry him off to Fiona. Or worse, marry her off to one of his brothers. Watching Fiona given to another, knowing that man shared her bed, would surely rouse the beast within him. It stirred to life at the mere thought of such a circumstance.

"I will warn the others of Father's plots," said Gregor as soon as their father had left the hall.

"Good." Ewan sighed and dragged his hand through his hair. "A woman as strong as Fiona is must come from a strong clan. As ye said, we dinnae need any more enemies."

"Have ye e'er heard of this Sir Ranald Menzies?"

"Nay, but there are Menzies nay too far from here."

"Do ye mean to seek out some word on the mon?"

"If I can think of a way to send one of our men safely about to ask a few questions, aye. I am nay sure he would learn much so I hesitate to risk a mon. This Sir Ranald sounds mad and I suspicion his kinsmen willnae be wanting to admit he is one of theirs. I will think on it." He finished off his ale and stood up. "Now, since Simon isnae suffering too badly, I believe I will have a wee talk with the lad. The sooner I discover who that lass belongs to, the sooner I can send her on her way."

Ignoring young Nathan, who stood guard in the doorway of the herb shed, Fiona listened to Mab tell her all about what she had at hand, how it was gathered, and how it was prepared. When she was not trying to find some clever cure, Mab was probably no danger to anyone. The woman knew something about herbs and was well versed in simple medicines. Fiona wondered if there was any gentle way to get the woman to cease being inventive.

It was difficult to keep her mind set on what Mab was saying, for Fiona kept wondering what Ewan wanted to speak to Simon about in private. Try as she would, she could not recall everything she had said to the youth. She prayed Simon could not, either. If Ewan searched for clues as to who she was, she did not want him to gather too many too quickly. It might be foolish, but she was attracted to the man. Fiona wanted to stay at Scarglas long enough to see what that might mean or if, by some miracle, it might be returned. A deep hurt might lie ahead, but she was beginning to think it would be foolish to flee in fear of that when staying might show her that her doubts and fears were unjustified.

Mab started to speak about a potion she was mixing, drawing Fiona's full attention. Before Mab could tell her what herbs she was stirring together, however, the woman's attention was diverted by a small, fair-haired boy. Fiona smiled when introduced to Mab's son, then shooed the pair out of the shed, assuring Mab that she would be fine on her own. After agreeing to meet Mab back in Simon's room, Fiona turned her attention to the potion Mab was creating. She was not sure she was skilled enough, but she would at least try to guess at what Mab was brewing up now.

Fiona was close to solving the puzzle when she

felt a presence directly behind her. Even before she looked behind her, she knew it was Ewan. The fact that, after so short an acquaintance, she could recognize his scent made her feel a little sad. She was obviously becoming more enthralled with the man with each passing hour, yet he showed no sign of suffering a similar affliction. Slowly, she turned around to face him.

"What are ye doing in here?" Ewan asked, clasping his hands behind his back in an attempt to kill the urge to touch her.

"Afraid I am mixing up a barrel of poison for the lot of you?" She shook her head when he just quirked one dark brow at her. "Dinnae be an idiot. I am just trying to guess what Mab has put into this potion she is mixing. She left ere she could tell me."

Ewan moved closer, leaning forward to sniff at the small bowl holding Mab's potion. His whole body tensed when he realized how close Fiona was now. When she took a deep, unsteady breath, her breasts brushed fleetingly against his chest. He nearly groaned and was not surprised to see that he had brought his hands forward to grasp the table on either side of her. He lifted his head just enough to bring his face even with hers. When she nervously licked her lips, he felt his belly clench with the strength of his desire.

"Do ye think 'tis her potion for scars?" he asked softly.

"Nay." Fiona fisted her hands tightly at her sides, fighting the nearly overwhelming urge to wrap her arms around him.

"They arenae so verra bad."

When he brushed his lips over one of the scars

on her cheeks, Fiona trembled. She turned her head slightly, intending to speak, only to find her lips brushing over his. He made an odd, strangled noise, and suddenly she found herself held firmly in his arms. She did not hesitate to wrap her arms around his neck. The heat of his soft lips against hers went rushing through her whole body. The feelings assailing her made her weak in the knees and she clung to him more tightly.

The first nudge of his tongue against her lips was all the persuasion she needed to open her mouth. He growled softly as he invaded her mouth with his tongue. With each stroke of his tongue, Fiona felt her need for him grow.

Then, abruptly, she was released. Fiona gripped the edge of the table tightly to keep her trembling body from sagging to the ground. The heat of desire was clear to see in Ewan's stormy gray eyes, but he looked utterly dismayed.

"I shouldnae have done that," he said, his deep voice hoarse and a little unsteady. "It willnae happen again," he added in a stronger voice before striding away.

Fiona took several deep breaths to steady herself as she stared in the direction he had gone. She now had the proof that he was as attracted to her as she was to him. It was also clear that he did not want to be, was determined to fight it. A slow smile curved her still kiss-warmed lips as she brushed down her skirts. Every instinct she had told her that Ewan MacFingal was her match, her soul mate. If the man thought he could escape that fate, she was ready and able to show him otherwise.

Chapter 6

"Where is Sir Ewan?"

Fiona ignored the faint smile on Gregor's hand-some face. For three days she had done her best to keep herself as close to Ewan as possible. With each day he had grown more elusive. She was be-ginning to fear she was wrong, that the kiss they had shared had not moved him as strongly as it had her. Worse, he might have simply uttered empty flattery when he had told her the scars upon her cheeks were not so dreadful. Men might boast of their own scars, but they did not like to see such marks upon a woman.

"He rode out an hour ago," replied Gregor. "Took six men with him. Intended to look for signs of the Grays."

She scowled at the gates Ewan had escaped through. "The question is, is he fleeing from me or his father?" she muttered.

"Both," Gregor replied and laughed when she blushed.

"Ewan isnae one for the lasses, ye ken," said Nathan, his blue eyes alight with laughter. "If ye mean to catch him, ye will have to run verra fast."

For one brief moment, Fiona considered soundly denying Nathan's implication, then sighed. He would never believe her. It was embarrassing that Ewan's brothers had guessed her game, but they could also prove useful. They certainly revealed no dislike of her plans and she found some comfort in that.

"What do ye mean when ye say that Ewan isnae one for the lasses?" she asked Nathan. "He doesnae like women?"

"Och, he likes them weel enough. His fierce looks tend to make the lasses turn away and he has no skill at wooing."

"'Tis the scar, is it?" When both Gregor and Nathan nodded, she shook her head in disgust. "My brother is scarred and that didnae stop our Gilly from thinking him verra fine indeed. And our Gilly came from a clan reknowned for its verra handsome men. Some of them are so bonnie they fair take a lass's breath away. I am surprised his being the laird hasnae changed their ways."

"Weel, I suspicion he could get a lass in his bed if he but asked," said Nathan. "The women here ken their place."

Gregor laughed at the outraged look upon Fiona's face. "Wheesht, lad, ye are risking life and limb talking like that."

"Are ye saying the women at Scarglas arenae allowed to say nay to a mon?" demanded Fiona, placing her fists upon her hips as she glared up at the young Nathan.

Nathan took a small step backward. "Weel, some do. But Da says—"

She held up her hand to silence him. "Dinnae repeat any of that mon's nonsense. I am weel aware of what he thinks a woman's place is. I did-nae realize the women here had accepted that non-sense as a great truth. Tis past time someone taught them how to say nay. Tis past time someone told them the real truth. Now, where is Mab?"

"Oh, um, in the herb hut."

Fiona almost smiled when her young guard blushed deeply. "Why does mention of Mab cause ye to blush?"

"I am nay blushing," said Nathan, shoving Gregor when he laughed.

"If ye arenae blushing, then I must believe that high color on your cheeks bespeaks a fever. That would mean that I had best send ye to bed after a good purging." She had to bite the inside of her cheek to stop herself from laughing at the young man's look of horror.

"Mab is in the herb hut making me a potion."

"Och, ye are a brave lad," Fiona murmured. "A potion for what?"

"Weel, 'tis a salve for my skin." He blushed again. "To clear up the spots."

Fiona studied Nathan's handsome face very closely. It was a little spotty, but she had seen far worse. "It doesnae look bad, Nathan. How old are ye?"

"Nineteen next month."

"Weel, the best cure for spots is to get older.

Also, keep your face verra clean. Scrub it weel at least once a day with soap and hot water, then rinse it verra clean. If the spots are particularly bad, after ye scrub your face, wipe the worst of the spots with a wee bit of uisque-beatha."

"Uisque-beatha? How will putting uisque-beatha on my face help?"

Fiona shrugged. "I dinnae ken. Mayhap it dries them out. I *do* ken that it helps."

"Mab says her potion will help."

"Mab is a dear, sweet woman who has a verra fine understanding of the more common cures, potions, and salves. I would strongly advise ye, however, to avoid any of her own special creations. I thought ye were all wary of them already." Gregor nodded vigorously, but Nathan frowned uncertainly. "Her special cures tend to go awry. Green hair, blue hair, swift and violent purging," she began.

"And frightening rashes," added Gregor.

"The last thing I need is more spots," said Nathan.

"I will go to her. If I can discover what she is mixing together, I can tell ye if ye can accept her aid and nay hurt her feelings or if ye had best start running."

Nathan kept his gaze fixed on Fiona as she strode toward the herb shed, but asked Gregor, "Did ye ken that Mab's cures arenae always safe?"

"Aye," replied Gregor. "Didnae ye ne'er wonder why so many of us are wary of whatever salve, powder, or drink she offers?"

"I thought ye were reluctant because it usually tastes or smells foul."

"That it does, but there were a few alarming results from her *cures* in the first few years she was here. Ye can trust her to tend a wound, set a bone, or soothe a fever, but ye had best avoid all else."

"I will remember that." Nathan smiled faintly. "I will thank Mab most kindly for her help, but do as Fiona says. Tis my hope that game can be played weel. Twould hurt Mab's feelings if I have to refuse her help."

"Dinnae worry. Fiona will see it right. She has been steering our Mab right since she first set foot in Scarglas, and hasnae hurt the woman's feelings yet. Mab dearly wants to be a good healer, and since Fiona was taught by this Lady Murray that Mab esteems so highly, Mab heeds all she says. And Fiona leads Mab in the right direction with a gentle, kind hand."

"Do ye think that is how Fiona intends to lead our brother?" Nathan asked, grinning broadly.

Gregor laughed and shook his head. "I fear she will need a whip and a stout rope."

"Why wouldnae he want such a bonnie lass?"

"Oh, he wants her, right enough. He just doesnae think he is worthy of her."

"She obviously thinks he is."

"Aye, but I think she frets too much o'er her scars as weel. It doesnae help that our father is meddling. That makes Ewan run and makes Fiona fret o'er any small attention Ewan does pay to her. Twill be a tangled, confusing courtship which I fear will cause a few bruises to both hearts."

"Mayhap we should do something, although I cannae think what. Talk to Ewan, mayhaps."

"Nay, we will do naught for now. Weel, aside from letting Ewan ken when he is acting a complete fool. In such matters, 'tis best if the pair thrash it out themselves. Now, if he discovers who she is and still sets himself to ransoming her, then we will step in. Ewan wants her, she wants him, and she will make a verra fine lady of Scarglas. I willnae allow fears and doubts, his or hers, to ruin what I see as a perfect match."

"I will be ready to lend a hand."

"So will every one of our brothers."

"Everyone sees what is happening?"

"Of course. Didnae ye think it odd that a wee, bonnie lass has been roaming the halls of Scarglas for days and yet nary one MacFingal lad has started sniffing about her skirts?" When Nathan started to laugh, Gregor swiftly joined him.

Change was not accepted gracefully at Scarglas, Fiona decided as she stared down the much larger Clare. Once assured that what Mab was mixing for Nathan was harmless, Fiona had hurried to where the women were doing the laundry, eager to offer them her soap, only to come up against a stone wall named Clare. It did not seem to matter to the woman that no criticism was offered, that the change was but a small, insignificant one. Clare obviously saw any suggestion as a gross trespass upon her territory. Fiona wished she had Gilly's skill at sensing people's feelings, seeing into the heart of them. She would find it extremely helpful at the moment to know how much of Clare's refusal was born of a fear of losing her place and how much of simply obstinancy.

"This will make the linens softer," Fiona said,

carefully setting the blocks of washing soap she had prepared on a stool. "Twill also cause less wear upon them and the clothes ye wash. It cleans just as weel as what ye use now." Fiona hoped the maids had not ceased scrubbing the laundry to watch her and Clare because they expected a battle to break out. "Twill also be much kinder to your hands."

"Ye arenae the mistress here," snapped Clare, her dark eyes hard. "Ye are naught but a hostage."

"True, but I dinnae see what that has to do with whether I ken a better soap to use or nay."

"Ye have no say in what is done at Scarglas. Go back to following that mad witch Mab about."

"Mab isnae mad and she isnae a witch."

Clare snorted with contempt. "She certainly isnae the healer she calls herself. Dinnae ken why the laird doesnae just toss the old whore and her bastard out of Scarglas ere she kills someone. Now, get ye gone, wench."

The shove Clare gave her caused Fiona to stumble back several steps, but she quickly steadied herself. Out of the corner of her eye she saw a scowling Nathan start toward them, and she heard all the maids gasp in shock, but neither of those things caused Fiona to hesitate. She leapt toward Clare, who had turned her back. One well-placed kick caused the woman to fall to her knees. Fiona grabbed the woman's right arm, twisting it tightly behind her back, even as she wrapped her other arm around the woman's throat. Bending down a little, she was able to speak into the woman's ear, but she made no effort to speak softly.

"Now, I might have been able to ignore the fact

that ye called me a wench and laid hands upon me," Fiona said, "but I cannae ignore what ye said about Mab."

"She—" began Clare.

Fiona tightened her arm around the woman's neck just a little in silent warning. "Mab is a sweet woman with a big heart who took on a chore no one else seemed to want. She isnae a whore, either. She but fell victim to a lecherous mon's sweet words, a mon who neglected to tell her he was wed. So, aim your scorn at the one who deserves it. And if ye dinnae wish your sharp tongue split, I strongly suggest ye dinnae whet it on her son." She shoved Clare away and stepped back. "So then, if ye are too pigheaded to try e'en the smallest change, so be it. I will wash my own clothes and linen."

As she stumbled to her feet, Clare sneered at Fiona even as she was careful to stay out of the smaller woman's reach. "And what would a wee fine lady like ye ken about honest work?"

"Judging without knowledge again? Ye are obviously a slow learner. I ken how to scrub clothes, thatch a roof, plant a field, mend a harness, and much more. I also ken how to silence a vicious tongue." Fiona snatched up the knife used to cut the cakes of washing soap, and threw it, neatly pinning the sleeve of Clare's dress to the post she stood in front of. "And ere ye think it, rest assured that blade is resting exactly where I intended it to." She picked up a cake of her soap and started to walk away. "Do as ye will with the soap. Tis my opinion that ye might try washing out your sour mouth with some of it."

As soon as Fiona had left, Nathan stepped up to Clare and pulled the knife free before meeting her wide-eyed stare. "She doesnae like to be called a wench."

"Who *is* she?" Clare asked in an unsteady voice.

"Weel, the laird calls her Fiona-of-the-ten-knives." He smiled grimly when Clare grew even paler. "Twas the number he found on her when he captured her." He leaned a little closer, his voice hard and cold as he said, "Most of us are fond of Mab, and her son is my brother. A wise woman might take a moment to recall just how many bastards there are at Scarglas ere she spits out her contempt of them. A wise woman might also keep her ears open enough to realize that that wee lass could verra weel be the next lady of Scarglas, the laird's wife." He turned away from a trembling Clare and started after Fiona. "In fact, I and near all of my brothers are determined to see it happen."

Nathan found Fiona standing in the midst of the bailey. She had her hands on her slim hips and was staring up at the sky. As he reached her side, he realized she was taking deep breaths and letting them out slowly.

"I lost my temper," Fiona said, keeping her gaze fixed upon the dark clouds that promised rain.

"Och, aye, ye did," said Nathan. "Ye had Clare fair to wetting herself."

Fiona sternly told herself that she should find no pleasure in that. "A lady shouldnae lose her temper. Our Gilly says that, when a lady does get angry, she certainly shouldnae be wrestling people to their knees or throwing knives at them."

"What should a lady do then?"

"Our Gilly says a lady politely makes her discontent understood, speaking firmly, but quietly."

"Weel, ye didnae shout."

She exchanged a brief grin with him, then sighed. "I wish I had our Gilly's gift. She can tell what a person feels, ye ken. Tis as if she can see into the verra heart of a person."

"It sounds a verra useful gift."

Fiona nodded. "It is. If I had it, I might be able to understand why Clare is so angry and bitter."

"Bile for blood?" He smiled when she chuckled, then fell into step at her side as she started back toward the keep.

"Tis true that some people are born with ill tempers and sour minds. Most are made that way as they grow. If one kens the why of it, one can often turn them up sweet again, or at least deal with them without wanting to cut out their tongues. Did Clare e'er bed down with your father?"

"Nay. Her husband says she doesnae bed down with him much, either." Nathan blushed. "Pardon. I shouldnae speak so to ye."

"Dinnae fret. I was raised by my five brothers until I was thirteen. Then our Gilly arrived and made a few changes, easing the rough way we all lived. We are still a wee bit rough, though. I doubt ye could say much to shock me, or that I havenae heard before." She frowned. "Why would Clare call Mab a witch?" She wondered why her question should make Nathan look so uncomfortable.

"Ah, weel, if ye stay here long enough, ye will hear that word cast our way a lot. I think the Grays

feed the rumors. It doesnae help that we are all so
dark and Scarglas is a wee bit forbidding. My father has had five wives and four of them died. That
causes a lot of rumors to start as weel. Tis said he
bewitches women." He relaxed a little when Fiona
snorted with contempt. "It doesnae help that he is
fond of cursing everyone."

Fiona suddenly stopped short and gaped at
Nathan. "Now I ken who ye are. I have heard the
tales, but ne'er paid much heed to the name. If 'tis
the Grays spreading those black rumors, they are
doing a verra good job of it if e'en I have heard a
few." She shook her head and started toward the
keep again. "I dinnae ken where my wits have
gone. I should have at least recognized this keep
for 'tis clearly described when the tales about ye
are told. When I first saw it, I felt a memory or two
stir to life, but couldnae quite grasp them. Thought
it was just the look of the place that made me think
of things such as sorcery and murder."

"Ye arenae afraid now?"

"Nay. I dinnae see it. Ye do seem to have collected an odd lot of people here, like old Iain, who
dances in the moonlight within that circle of stones.
Oh, and Peter, who is so afeared of water he must
be carrying ten years of filth upon his person."

"More like twenty."

"Aye, but I dinnae see witchcraft in any of it. A
harmless moon-madness, mayhap, but no sorcery.
And although I am nay too fond of your father, I
dinnae think he would kill a wife. Most like he
kept them constantly breeding and that shortened
their lives or caused them to flee. As for bewitch-

ing women, weel, he obviously has a true skill for wooing lasses into his bed and I suspicion he chooses ones foolish enough to believe his lies."

"Aye, he does. He also uses his position here to get the lasses into his bed. He and Ewan often argue about that." He stopped and looked toward the gates. "And speaking of Ewan, here he comes."

Fiona tried not to look too pleased by Ewan's return. She did not want to display her infatuation with the man too openly. The way he almost awkwardly dismounted, wincing and slumping a little when he reached the ground, shattered her pose of calm, friendly welcome. She rushed to his side, stung by the way he took a wary step back, but fighting to ignore it.

"Ye have been hurt," she said, looking him over carefully.

"Tis naught," he said, deeply moved by her concern and cursing that weakness in himself.

Seeing the blood soaking the breeches he wore, she gave him a disgusted look. "Ye are bleeding like a stuck pig. Best we get it cleaned and stitched as soon as possible."

Before Ewan could think of a way to refuse her help, he found himself being helped to his bedchamber by Nathan. Seeing the small trail of blood he left behind him, he decided there was no sensible argument he could give anyway. He could only hope that pain and loss of blood left him weak enough that he would not suffer any twinges of desire while she tended to his wound.

He decided he had grown dangerously weak when he made no more than a softly muttered protest when Nathan stripped him of his clothes. Ewan groaned as he nearly fell into his bed. As Nathan carefully arranged his bedcovers over him so that only his wounded leg and bare chest were exposed to view, Ewan struggled to conquer an attack of light-headedness.

"What happened?" asked Nathan as Fiona began to wash the blood off Ewan's leg.

"We caught some Grays stealing cattle," Ewan replied. "Unfortunately, there were half a dozen others close by, but out of sight. We were taken by surprise as we were busy routing the thieves. A few of the other men suffered some minor wounds."

"Oh, dear, I am nay sure where Mab is," said Fiona. "She may nay ken that she is needed."

"I will fetch her," Nathan said and hurried out of the room.

Ewan bit back the urge to tell Nathan to stay. He told himself he was a grown man, a man of strength and resolve. He should be able to be alone with Fiona and not give in to his base urges. She was touching his leg only to tend his wound, an innocent touch that could be ignored.

That resolve began to fade away with each touch of her fingers against his thigh. He almost welcomed the pain of having his wound bathed with uisque-beatha and stitched, for it quickly cooled his blood. That reprieve did not last long, however. He felt his ardor stir to life again as she bandaged his leg, her soft fingers brushing perilously close to his groin as she worked. A quick look revealed that the bedcovers were bunched up enough to hide his reaction to her touch, and he breathed a silent sigh of relief.

"Ye have blood upon your face," Fiona said as

she straightened up from tying off the bandage on his thigh.

"Tis naught," he said. "Tis just a wee scratch."

"It should still be cleaned."

When she leaned over him to bathe the cut above his ear, Ewan inhaled so sharply he nearly choked. Her breasts were within inches of his mouth. He found himself staring directly at the soft swells of her breasts above the neck of her gown. Her skin was a clear, soft honey shade. No matter how hard he tried, he could not dispel the urge to see if her skin would taste as sweet and warm as it looked.

Just as she started to move away, he wrapped his arm around her waist to hold her still. He kissed the top of each breast, inhaling deeply of her clean scent. She trembled and he heard her breath catch in her throat. Although he ached to linger there, to feast upon that soft skin, he kissed his way up her elegant throat to her lips. Her eyes were wide and held a look he was sure was one of a growing desire. Her full lips were slightly parted and he took quick advantage, kissing her deeply and with a fierce need he could not hold back.

With each stroke of his tongue, Fiona felt her desire grow. He moved his hand over her back and it felt as if fire trailed in its wake. A soft moan escaped her when he slid his other hand up her side and ever so gently squeezed her breast. None of the fear Menzies had bred in her was roused by Ewan's touch, only a greed to feel more.

She was just about to crawl up onto the bed with him, when he suddenly pushed her away. Hurt and confused, she struggled to steady herself as she looked at him. There was a slight flush upon his cheeks and his breathing was ragged, both signs of what she felt sure was desire. Then she heard Mab call her name and the sting of his abrupt rejection eased a little.

Ewan covered his eyes with an unsteady hand. "Go. Mab needs you."

Fiona hesitated only a moment before hurrying out of the room, meeting Mab just outside the door. She was frustrated by the abrupt end to their lovemaking, but knew it was for the best. Ewan was wounded and in no condition to consummate the passion they felt for each other. He was also still fighting that attraction. Now was not a good time to try to make him see that he did not have to resist. Ruthlessly suppressing all remnants of desire, she turned her full attention to helping Mab tend to the other wounded men. Ewan would not be able to run away or avoid her for several days, until his wound had begun to heal. There would be plenty of time to conquer his resistance.

Chapter 7

"I strongly suggest ye lie back down," Fiona said as she stepped into Ewan's room and caught him struggling to sit up on the edge of his bed. "Ye have only had those stitches in for two days. That wound cannae possibly be closing up so soon."

For a moment Ewan contemplated bluntly refusing to obey her, then told himself not to be a fool. He was dizzy and sweating and he had not even finished sitting up. Muttering curses over his weakness, he collapsed back against the pillows Mab had recently piled at his back. He scowled at the tray Fiona set down on the table by the bed.

"That better nay be gruel or broth," he grumbled.

"Tis neither. Tis mutton stew," she replied.

When she sat on the edge of the bed, holding the bowl and spoon in her hands, he snapped, "I can feed myself."

Fiona said nothing, just handed him the spoon,

but she kept a firm grip on the bowl. She watched along with him as he moved the spoon toward the bowl and she knew he was trying with all his might to still the trembling in his hand. Finally, he dropped it into the bowl, and slumped against the pillows.

"I am as weak as a bairn," he complained. "Tis because ye have been giving me naught but broth for two days."

She rolled her eyes as she shoved a spoonful of stew into his mouth. "Tis because ye bled so badly ere ye got the wound tended to. Tis also because ye just used what strength ye had regained by resting in trying to get out of bed too soon. I suspicion the knock on your head doesnae help, either."

"It only put me to sleep for a few minutes," he said quickly before she shoved another spoonful of stew into his mouth.

"Which means it was a good hard knock e'en if it didnae crack the bone."

He said nothing else, simply sat there feeling a little ridiculous as she spoon-fed him his stew. It would be far better for his peace of mind if only Mab tended to him, but he could not bring himself to demand such a thing. Ewan knew that such a refusal of Fiona's aid would hurt and insult her, especially when he could offer no good reason for doing so. One did not tell a lady that he wanted her gone because the mere sight of her made him hard as a rock. Whenever she was near him, the pain of his wounds seemed but minor twinges compared to the aching need she stirred within him.

If he took care, he would be healed by his birthday, he mused. Then he could go to the village, take one of the willing maids at the tavern to bed, and rut away this fever in his blood. The plan had barely formed in his mind when he had to admit to himself that it would be a waste of his time and money. Since he had not had a woman for a year, he suspected he would have no real difficulty performing, but he knew it would not satisfy him, would not dim his desire for Fiona by even the smallest degree.

It had been eight years since he had felt such a blind need for a woman, and he did not like the fact that he was tumbling into that snare again. Such a fierce desire and, he feared, such fierce emotions made a man weak and foolish. Ewan briefly touched the scar upon his face. Helena had taught him that, using his passion and love for her to betray him to his enemies. He could not allow himself to be so weak again.

A small voice told him that Fiona was no Helena, but he struggled to ignore it. It was true that Fiona seemed to be honest and caring, but she also refused to tell him exactly who she was. There were good reasons for such a refusal, but he could not ignore the fact that there could also be sinister reasons for it.

Just as he was about to tell her he had had enough stew, the door to his room was opened so forcefully it slammed against the wall. Ewan tensed when he saw his father standing there. The way his father was glaring at Fiona told him the man was in one of his furies. One could never be certain what Sir Fingal might do when he was in a rage. Ewan did not want to believe that his father would actually hurt Fiona, but did not feel as confident of that as he would like to be.

"Ye are meddling in things that are none of your business, woman," Sir Fingal yelled, pointing at Fiona.

"And what things would that be?" Fiona was pleased with how calm she sounded, for the enraged Sir Fingal made her a little nervous.

"Ye have been talking to the women."

"I hadnae realized that was forbidden."

"Dinnae be insolent. Ye ken exactly what I am talking about. I just told Bonnie to come to my bed and she said nay. Nay! To me!"

Ewan stared at his father as he chewed on a mouthful of mutton stew he had not really wanted. His father sounded an odd mixture of furious, outraged, and stunned. Out of the corner of his eye he saw a faint smile fleetingly grace Fiona's face. It appeared that she had purposefully done something she knew would infuriate the man and that astonished Ewan. What astonished him even more was that she appeared to be completely unaffected by Sir Fingal's fury.

"That is her right, isnae it?" Fiona asked, her expression one of gentle confusion and utter innocence.

"That is what she said *ye* told her. She said ye told her there was no law that she had to share my bed just because I had an itch to scratch."

"I dinnae believe I was wrong in that. I am sure there isnae a law that says she cannae refuse ye."

"There is *my* law! Tis *my* keep and I liked everything just as it was. Ye will cease putting foolish ideas into the heads of the women here or ye will be verra sorry." He turned to leave, stopped, sniffed the shirt he wore, and cursed. "And I ken ye are the reason all my linens and clothes smell like thrice-cursed lavender so ye can stop that, too." He slammed the door behind him as he left.

Ewan shook his head when she started to give him another spoonful of stew. He watched her set the bowl aside and pick up a tankard. She was looking very guilty. She would not look him in the eye and there was the hint of a blush upon her cheeks. He grasped the handle of the tankard, but she kept her hands curled around it to steady it as he took a drink. His gaze never wavered from her face, but he had nearly finished the drink before she sighed and reluctantly met his gaze.

"I ne'er thought to talk to the women," he said.

Fiona inwardly breathed a sigh of relief for he showed no hint of anger. "Weel, I dinnae mean to sound disrespectful, but I felt trying to talk your father into a little restraint might prove much akin to banging my head against a rock."

"Tis exactly what it would be like." He exchanged a brief smile with her, then grimaced in self-disgust. "I confess, it ne'er occurred to me that the women might not want to share his bed. My father has a true skill at wooing the lasses, ye ken. I fear I just assumed all the women were saying aye because they wanted to, because he had charmed them or the like."

"I suspect some do want to. I didnae lecture them about sin and all. I simply told them that, if they really didnae wish to be used by the old laird or any of the other men here, they had the right to say nay. After all, the church praises and preaches virtue and such, and surely they are a higher power than the old laird."

"Are ye telling me that such a thing worked where ye came from? Tis a common practice for the men of a keep to make use of the maids within its walls. Some are e'en offered to the guests."

"Just because 'tis common practice doesnae make it right. Where I come from, the women are treated with respect and can say aye or nay as they choose. A mon shouldnae use his position of power to get women into his bed. The women, or most of them, dinnae dare refuse a laird, or his father, or his brother, or any mon who rules o'er them. Whores gather where'er there is coin to be had. Let the men use one of them."

"Or woo a lass, as my father does?" Ewan found he was curious about her opinion of his father.

"Ah, weel, mayhap." Seeing that he had finished his drink, Fiona set the tankard down, then turned slightly so that she was seated more comfortably on the edge of the bed as she faced him. "There is a part of me that thinks a woman who allows her virtue to be stolen by nay more than pretty words and a bonnie smile deserves whatever trouble befalls her. Yet, another part of me thinks any mon who steals a lass's virtue with lies and walks away, leaving her to suffer whate'er consequences there may be, ought to be punished." She shrugged. "Contrary of me, I ken it. Yet, too often, that rogue has just robbed that lass of the only thing of value she might have. Tis the lying to get what one wants that angers me, I am thinking."

"Women lie to get what they want, too."

"Aye, and that isnae any better." She clasped her hands together in her lap and readied herself to ask a question she could no longer hold back. "Why was your father painted blue?"

It took Ewan a moment to grasp the abrupt change of subject, then he inwardly grimaced. When Fiona had made no mention of how his father had looked, Ewan had hoped she intended to simply ignore it. He had the feeling she had tried, but how could anyone really ignore a man who had blue markings over every bit of skin one could see? Fiona was clever enough to guess that those markings were also undoubtedly all over the skin one could not see.

"The moon is full tonight," he replied, then cursed softly when she just stared at him, her expression making it clear that she wanted a better explanation than that. "My father and several other men paint their bodies that way at every full moon and go out to dance about in the circle of stones. Naked."

"What does your priest have to say about such heathenish acts?"

"That old fool is right out there dancing with them."

Fiona told herself it would be unkind to laugh. Poor Ewan was clearly humiliated by his father's behavior. "Old Iain has already been out there."

"Aye, he just likes to leap about out there. He willnae put on the blue paint until the moon is full."

"I see." She was not surprised to hear the strain in her voice as the need to laugh was swiftly breaking all restraints she had put on it. "Why?"

"My father heard a tale that claimed the ancients

used to do it to ask the gods to make them stronger and fiercer in battle, and . . ." He hesitated, deeply reluctant to finish.

"And what?"

"More virile."

Fiona clapped a hand over her mouth and stared down at the bedclothes. She could feel the laughter shaking her body and clapped her other hand over her mouth as well. It was rude, perhaps even a little cruel to laugh, but how could one not laugh? The image of a group of aging men, painted blue and cavorting naked beneath a full moon, was, quite simply, hilarious. She choked a little as she struggled valiantly, but finally collapsed against the bedcovers in a fit of laughter.

At least she isnae horrified or afraid, Ewan mused. He briefly wondered if he ought to take offense, if only out of respect for his father, then shrugged the thought aside. What the man planned to do tonight was ridiculous. He would find it funny, too, if it did not cause so much trouble by feeding the rumors of witchcraft. After a moment, he started to smile, finding her laughter infectious.

As her laughter eased, Fiona sat up only to discover that she had edged closer to Ewan. Their faces were but inches apart. He was smiling and she wondered if he had any idea of how handsome he was. When his smile began to fade, she tensed, wondering which way he would turn this time. Would he pull her close or push her away? She wished the man would make up his mind about what he wanted from her. The way he was warm one minute and cold the next was proving a little hard to endure.

Ewan gently grasped her by the chin and, with

his other hand, wiped away a tear of laughter that glistened upon her flushed cheek. He fixed his gaze upon her mouth. When she licked her lips, he softly cursed his own weakness even as he slid his hand to the back of her slender neck and tugged her closer.

Just one kiss, he told himself. Surely he had the strength of will to steal one kiss without losing all control. The moment his lips touched hers, however, he began to doubt his own resolve. The sweet warmth of her mouth seemed to rush through his blood straight to his groin. When she parted her lips beneath his, he wrapped his arms around her and held her close as he greedily accepted that silent invitation.

Fiona felt as if she was melting from the heat of her own desire. She eagerly returned his kiss, making no attempt to control or hide the passion he stirred within her. When he ended the kiss, she tried yet failed to catch her breath as he kissed her throat, her cheeks, and the hollow behind her ear. She trembled and gasped when he stroked her breast.

As he began to kiss her again, he shifted their position until they were both on their sides. Fiona took quick advantage of the change, stroking his back and thrilling to the feel of his smooth, warm skin. Slowly, she slid her hand beneath the bedcovers to caress his taut buttocks and swallowed the groan that escaped him. A heartbeat later she found herself pushed away and Ewan turned onto his back.

Shaken and chilled by the abrupt ending of the embrace, she sat up and looked at Ewan. He had one arm draped across his eyes so it was difficult to read his expression. There was a slight flush upon his cheeks and he was breathing as raggedly as she was, however. Those had to be signs of a passion as strong as her own. Or signs of pain, she suddenly thought with a horrified glance at his wounded leg.

"Ewan," she began, appalled that she could have so completely forgotten that he was injured.

"Go away."

Fiona felt all her concern for him disappear in an instant, to be replaced by a pain so sharp she nearly cried out. He was not suffering from passion or pain, but regret, perhaps even shame. It was not passion or pain putting a flush upon his cheeks and making his breathing unsteady, but disgust. Whether it was with her or himself did not really matter.

"I think it would be best if Mab tended me from now on," he said.

"As ye wish."

Picking up the tray she had brought in, she left him. She wanted to run, to find somewhere to hide, but pride kept her from doing so. It did not please her to meet with Gregor only a few steps away from Ewan's door. The way his eyes narrowed as he looked at her told her that she was not hiding her tattered emotions as well as she had thought. She smiled her gratitude as a passing Bonnie relieved her of the tray, then clasped her hands behind her back.

"I left Simon sleeping," Gregor said, still watching her closely.

"Ah, good," Fiona replied. "Getting a lot of rest is the best medicine there is."

Gregor nodded. "Is something wrong? Ye are looking a wee bit pale and wan."

"I am just weary, 'tis all. I believe I will seek my bed and have a wee rest myself." Fiona started to walk around him. "If ye would excuse me?"

After watching her hurry away, Gregor scowled at the door to Ewan's bedchamber. He had not intended to visit Ewan, but was now determined to do so. If he judged the look upon Fiona's face correctly, his brother and laird had just delivered that lass a sound blow. It appeared he might be forced to knock some sense into Ewan's thick skull a lot sooner than he had anticipated.

The moment he stepped into Ewan's bedchamber and shut the door behind him, Gregor demanded, "What did ye do to the lass, ye fool?" He marched up to the bed and glared at Ewan, who did not look any happier than Fiona had.

Ewan sighed and rubbed his hands over his face. "Why would ye think I did anything to Fiona?"

"Mayhap because she looked as if ye had returned one of her daggers the hard way, by burying it in her heart?"

That implied that he had somehow hurt Fiona's feelings, and Ewan refused to believe that. "Ye mistake the matter."

Gregor crossed his arms over his broad chest. "Nay, I dinnae think so. I met her just outside your door and she didnae smile. Fiona always smiles. She didnae pause to have a wee talk, either. Nay, she looked pale as death and fled to her bedchamber. So, I ask again, what did ye say or do to her?"

It was not a subject Ewan wished to discuss with

Gregor, but he knew his brother would not leave it alone. Or worse, he would come to some conclusion of his own. Ewan sighed and decided he was also too tired and too heartsick to argue or lie.

"I told her to go away and that 'twould be best if Mab tended me from now on," Ewan replied and nearly flinched beneath the hard, overly sharp gaze Gregor fixed upon him.

"Why? The lass has tended ye faithfully and verra weel."

"Because I cannae be alone with her," Ewan snapped and dragged a hand through his hair. "I cannae keep my cursed hands off her."

"And ye see that as a bad thing?"

"Of course it is a bad thing. She is a hostage. And although she still hasnae admitted to it, she is a weelborn lass. Undoubtedly a virgin, too. She doesnae need some overgrown fool mauling her every time she chances to draw too near to him."

"Since ye arenae bruised or bleeding, I would think she isnae protesting the mauling too heartily," drawled Gregor.

The truth of that struck Ewan like a hard right to the jaw. Fiona did not resist his kisses. If he dared trust his own judgment, she melted in his arms, returned his passion in full measure. Perhaps it was foolish to keep pushing her away. What he ached for was, apparently, there for the taking. Any other man offered such a boon would take it, swiftly and greedily, so why not he?

Then he scowled, suspicion flaring to life within his mind and heart. Just why would a woman as lovely as Fiona feel any passion for him? Passion could be feigned, be no more than some base deceit used to weaken his guard and loosen his tongue. Although he had decried such a possibility to his father, and did not seem able to wholeheartedly believe it himself, he could not blindly discard it, either.

What he had told Gregor was also the truth, and one he needed to keep firmly fixed in his mind. If Fiona was not a spy and a threat, then she was a hostage. Many a man would think that gave him the right to use her, but he was not one of them. Fiona would be returned to her own people untouched. His honor demanded it. So did common sense. The very last thing he needed was to add another enemy to the lists of those arrayed against him and the people of Scarglas.

"She is a maid," said Ewan. "An innocent. Tisnae so difficult to overwhelm an innocent." He stoutly ignored Gregor's look of disgust. "And if she isnae an innocent, a hostage we can ransom, then she is one of the enemy set in the midst of us to cause trouble and 'twould be folly to let lust cloud my thinking. I fell into that trap once and have enough wit to recall a lesson weel learned."

"Fiona isnae like Helena."

"Nay? Helena seemed all that was sweet and innocent, then led me like a lamb to the slaughter."

"Sweet, mayhap, but I suspicion ye discovered she wasnae so verra innocent."

"I may be wrong about Fiona's innocence, too. There is only one way to be sure and that is to take her to my bed. If she *is* a virgin, then I will rob her of her chastity. That might lessen her worth when we ransom her, and 'twould surely leave her kinsmen thinking of vengeance. It could also set both of us before a priest, dragged there by our father or her kinsmen, and I want no wife. Whoever she turns out to be—innocent hostage or clever foe— the wisest thing for me to do is to leave her alone."

Gregor shook his head. "Ye think too much, Ewan. Ye chew o'er every riddle and thought as if 'tis a piece of tough meat. Sometimes things are exactly what they appear to be."

"Too often they are not. Now, tell me how matters stand," he ordered. "I will be stuck abed for several more days, I fear, and ye shall have to be my eyes and ears."

Ewan was pleased when Gregor accepted the change of subject even though it was clear he would have liked to say more concerning Fiona. To his relief, everything seemed to be peaceful for the moment. He soon grew too weary to continue the discussion, however. After Gregor left, Ewan slumped heavily against the pillows. He realized Fiona was right, that he had used up what little strength he had regained in his attempt to get out of bed too soon, and that annoyed him.

He sighed as he closed his eyes and fought to ignore the pain in his leg and the lingering ache in his head. Slowly, he ran his tongue over his lips. He could still taste the sweet warmth of Fiona's mouth. The clean womanly scent of her, touched with a hint of lavender, still lingered in the air. The heat of her small, soft hand was a potent memory against his skin. She was a heady brew, a fever in his blood that he feared was incurable.

So, why not feed that fever? he asked himself. Why not heedlessly reach out and take what she seemed so willing to give him, much to his amazement? He had the wit and strength to avoid any consequences. As laird, he ought to be able to hold firm against his father's ploys to marry him to Fiona. Most would consider his bedding a female hostage no great crime, even a right, just a part of the ransom. If her kinsmen cried out for revenge, well, what was one more enemy added to the vast hordes his father had already made? Maybe Gregor was right to think him a fool to keep pushing Fiona away.

Cursing softly, he struggled to clear his mind of all thought of Fiona, passion, and need. He was not his father, Ewan sternly told himself. He had restraint, could fight the natural urge to take what he wanted when he wanted it. All the reasons he had given Gregor for keeping a distance from Fiona were sound ones. The soundest one of all was the one he had not told his brother. Ewan knew, deep in his heart, that if he took Fiona into his bed, he would soon take her into his heart. That utterly terrified him.

Chapter 8

Fiona stared blindly out at the men cavorting in the moonlight within the circle of stones. The window in the solar, a room obviously intended for the lady of Scarglas to use, looked out over that strange configuration of stones. It was a place shrouded in age and mystery. If the spirits of the ancients still lingered there, she had to wonder what they thought of the dozen or so naked fools leaping and twirling about in the moonlight, pausing in their strange dance only to get themselves more to drink. She had come up here to watch them, thinking that such a sight would surely amuse her enough to pierce the shroud of gloom she was wrapped in. Instead, she was fighting the urge to weep, loudly and without restraint.

Had it been only a few hours since Ewan had so coldly pushed her aside? She had fled to her bedchamber to lick her wounds and try to regain her composure, something she still found elusive. She had wept, but it had not really eased the pain of his rejection or the humiliation she felt. In truth, all crying had done was make her head ache and her eyes grow swollen and red. She refused to indulge in such a useless weakness again. Since her eyes ached from the weight of the tears she held back, she feared her resolve was crumbling fast.

When Mab entered the room, several gowns draped over her arms, Fiona tried to smile at the woman. The quick, sharp look the woman gave her told Fiona it had obviously been a pathetic effort. Mab quite often seemed to be skipping along in her own little, happy world, easily distracted and caught up in grand plans to mix up some miraculous cure, but Fiona knew there was a sharp mind there. She just wished the woman had not chosen to fix those keen wits on her for the moment.

"Which of the old laird's wives did these gowns belong to?" she asked as Mab draped the gowns over a large oak chest banded with leather and iron.

"His second wife," Mab replied as she walked over to the window Fiona sat in front of. "She bore him Gregor, Adam, Brian, Ross, and Nathan. Annie lasted the longest of the old fool's wives. Nine years. Died shortly after bearing Nathan. I think old Fingal might actually have been fond of her in his way. Nay faithful or loving, but fond. Some blame his persistent unfaithfulness for her death. Tis said she looked out her bedchamber window, saw Fingal plowing a buxom maid, and when she tried to throw something verra heavy out the window at him, fell out. Died at his feet."

"Tis a shame she didnae land on him and take him with her," Fiona snapped and shook her head.

"The mon is like a spoiled child. Someone should beat some restraint and responsibility into the old fool. Ewan had a different mother?"

"Aye. Fingal's first wife, Mary, the daughter of the previous laird. She died birthing Ewan. Fingal liked to tell the lad he was such a big, strapping bairn no mere woman could bear more than one of him."

"Jesu. Does the mon ne'er think ere he speaks?" Despite her hurt and anger, Fiona felt a brief surge of pity for the boy Ewan had been, a child made to think he had caused his mother's death. "I suppose it shouldnae surprise me. Tis clear he doesnae think before he acts, either."

Scowling out the window at the moonlit figures prancing about in the circle of stones, Mab said, "True enough. Just look at the fool and his foolish friends. Skipping about naked in the moonlight, drinking until they fall on their faces, and painted blue like heathens. Dinnae ken how they can think such nonsense will enhance their virility. In this cold, 'tis certain their privates are looking as small as any bairn's by now." She smiled when Fiona laughed, then grew somber again. "Why am I now ordered to be the only one to tend to the laird?"

Startled by the abrupt question, Fiona answered truthfully. "Because he ordered it. He obviously cannae abide me near him." She cursed as she felt the warm sting of tears upon her cheeks.

Mab handed her a delicately embroidered square of linen. "Now, ye cannae truly believe that."

"Aye, I can. He was verra clear in his dismissal of me. I am such a fool," she whispered.

"Now why would ye think that?" Mab asked as she sat on the window bench next to Fiona.

Fiona stared at the now twisted and damp linen in her hands. For a moment, she considered changing the subject, or telling some lie. Then, she inwardly shrugged. Mab would not believe a lie and it might help to talk to someone about Ewan, about what she felt and how he was acting. She was failing miserably in trying to sort out the matter on her own.

"The mon pulls me close, then pushes me away," Fiona replied. "He kisses me senseless, then ignores me. This afternoon he kissed me, then coldly sent me away, and 'tis clear he wants me to stay away." She took a deep breath to steady herself and wiped the tears from her cheeks. "I thought 'twas just that he wanted me, but his sense of honor kept making him retreat. But today, weel, he was disgusted with me, disgusted that he could e'en think to sate his lusts upon me. I am certain of it."

"Are ye? Weel, ye may indeed be a fool if ye are thinking such things." She ignored Fiona's scowl. "How did he look? What told ye he was disgusted with ye?"

Trying not to let foolish hopes stir in her heart, Fiona told Mab exactly how Ewan had looked after he had abruptly ended their embrace. "I thought his wounds pained him, but when I said his name, he coldly told me to go away. Then he said he thought it would be best if ye tended to him from now on."

"I see no disgust there, Fiona. Of course, he would think it best for me to tend him as 'tis clear he cannae keep his hands off ye."

"Aye, because his monly lusts stir when a woman is near. Then he realizes which woman he holds and turns away. I suppose I should be glad he doesnae just take what he needs ere he opens his eyes."

"Fiona, Ewan ne'er just takes what he needs. He ne'er just reaches for a lass because of, er, monly lusts. I think he fears becoming too much like his father. Ewan isnae e'en like his brothers, who are lusty lads but show far more restraint than their father, a restraint taught them by Ewan. I have heard some of the lads call him Brother Ewan and tease him about his monkish ways."

"Ewan monkish?" Fiona found it difficult to believe the man who kissed her with such fierce passion could ever be monkish in his habits.

"Aye. He beds a woman but once a year. On his birthday, he goes to the village and spends a night with a whore. From what little I have learned, it sounds a wee bit, weel, cold-blooded. He favors none above the others, just chooses one who looks clean and takes her to bed. He leaves at dawn and doesnae return. Tis almost as if he takes some physic for his health, rather like an occasional bleeding to relieve one's body of any ill humors."

Fiona laughed briefly, unable to resist the humor of Mab's words, but quickly grew serious again. "Once a year? Are ye certain, Mab?" Hope was again stirring in her heart and that frightened Fiona.

"Verra certain. There was one time, near eight years past, that he broke with that habit. A lass named Helena came to Scarglas. Ewan was besotted, I fear. There was talk of marriage."

The thought of Ewan being besotted with some woman, even eight years ago, was painful. Fiona told herself not to be such an idiot. The man was nearly nine-and-twenty. It would be strange indeed if he had not suffered some infatuation at least.

"What happened? He didnae marry her, did he?"

"Nay. She was sent here by one of Scarglas's enemies. That lass led poor Ewan into a trap that nearly cost him his life. Tis where he got that scar upon his face." Mab sighed. "Ewan was always a serious lad, but what lightness of spirit he did have faded on that day. Ewan returned to his habit of indulging his monly lusts but once a year."

"Mayhap he but nears the end of his year of celibacy."

"Idiot. I told ye all of that so that ye would see and understand that Ewan is a mon of great resolve and restraint. Do ye think none of the lasses about here have tried to pull him into their beds? He may nay be the bonniest of the brothers, or e'en verra skilled at wooing a lass, but he *is* the laird. And before that, he was the laird's chosen heir. A mon like that doesnae just grab a lass because he has an itch. Nay, not unless that itch is verra strong indeed."

Fiona asked Mab if she wanted some cider, then rose to get them each a drink. She thought over all Mab had told her as she filled two goblets with the highly spiced cider. If she believed all Mab said, then she could yet again believe Ewan pushed her away out of a sense of honor, perhaps even some personal fear. What made her reluctant to believe that again was a deep fear of further rejection from Ewan. One taste was enough. It hurt too much.

Before Menzies had slithered into her life, she had never known rejection. Men had appreciated the way she looked, had flattered her and complimented her on her beauty. She did not think she was vain, but she had enjoyed their appreciation. The first time she had faced the loss of that appreciation, realized the scars had changed how men looked at her, she had been hurt. She had finally accepted what Gilly and others told her, that such men were shallow fools and not worthy of one tear, that she would soon find a man who had the wit to look deeper. She had thought Ewan was that man. A part of her still wanted to, but she did not trust it.

"Ah, Mab, I am a coward," she said as she handed Mab her drink and sat down beside her. "I believed I had found a mon who could see beyond my scars, but he threw me aside."

"Foolish child." Mab took a sip and murmured her appreciation of the brew. "He didnae throw ye aside."

"It certainly felt that way."

"I am sure it did, but I am also sure he didnae do that. Nay, he is trying to protect ye from his desires. Mayhap he also seeks to protect himself."

"From me? I am no threat to him."

"Oh, but ye are. Many men see women as a threat, most certainly those women who make them feel things they dinnae want to feel. I believe ye make Ewan feel things he doesnae want to feel."

"Lust."

Mab shrugged. "Nay doubt of that, but I think 'tis more. After all, the mon has shown admirable restraint over his lusts for many years. In truth, Ewan has always shown admirable restraint in all his emotions." Mab frowned and sipped her drink. "In many ways, Ewan remained so e'en when he was besotted with Helena."

"Then how do ye ken he was besotted?"

"He took her to his bed and it wasnae his birthday. He was a wee bit distracted. She could actually turn his attention away from his work. Wee things. Verra wee things. Now that I think upon it, Ewan didnae bed her. *She* bedded *him*. It says a lot about a mon that people can think him besotted simply because he can be seduced into bed by a beautiful woman. That did put him in what, for Ewan, passed for a cheerful mood. It quite unsettled his brothers."

Fiona smiled. "I understand. My brother was a verra restrained mon once. Still is in many ways. I remember the first time our Gilly made him laugh. We were all quite shocked. A few women e'en got teary o'er it. Connor had carried the weight of all of us for years, our survival all-important to him, and he had hardened himself. It was all too much to set upon the shoulders of a lad of but fifteen. He shouldered it weel, but it robbed him of his youth and made him bury all softness. Our Gilly helped him see that he could show a wee bit of those softer feelings and still be the strong laird he felt he needed to be, could still hold the respect and obedience of his clan."

"And who did ye think has shouldered the weight of Scarglas and its people?" Mab said softly.

The revelation prompted by Mab's question came upon Fiona so quickly she gasped. There were indeed many similarities between Ewan and Connor.

Of course, Connor had not restrained his manly passions much at all, but she suspected he might have if he had had a father like Sir Fingal. Despite that, it was the sins and follies of the parents which had formed each man. Fiona was not quite sure how this sudden understanding would help her, however.

"Ewan was a mon grown when he became the laird," she said, fixing her attention upon the first clear difference she could see between her brother and Ewan.

"He was laird in all but name years before that. Ye have been here long enough to ken the mon Sir Fingal is. If the old laird isnae making us a new enemy, then he is off rutting with some lass making another bastard. Matters such as food for his clan, finding the coin he can spend so freely, or making sure his people have shelter, ne'er held his interest for long. He liked to call himself the laird, but he has ne'er much liked the work that comes with the honor."

"So Ewan did the work. As I have said, I have gotten the strong feeling that Sir Fingal is verra much like a spoiled child."

"Tis exactly what he is. Tis why he is here, why he calls us MacFingals. He wanted to wed a lass but his father and hers said nay. She was wed to his eldest brother, the heir. Sir Fingal cursed them all and left, got his hands on this place, and formed his own clan. Now and then his kinsmen wander by to see if he is ready to mend the breach, but he is a stubborn old fool. And nay, I still willnae say the name."

Fiona laughed. "Come, Mab, I willnae tell anyone. E'en if 'twas discovered that ye told me, what
could happen?"

"Twould put the old laird into a rage and I find
that most unsettling."

"Ah, weel, never mind. Mayhap they will wander
by whilst I am here and I can find out this dark secret then."

"Oh, I think ye will be here for a verra long time."

"Nay, Ewan doesnae want me here. I begin to
think I will just tell him who I am and let him send
me home."

"E'en if he truly did wish ye gone, he will still ask
a ransom for ye."

"I shall have to trust in my brother's wit and
guile to make it a wee one."

"I hadnae thought ye would be one to give up so
quickly," Mab said.

"Tis verra hard to fight when he willnae let me
near him."

"Weel, I do believe I willnae be about when 'tis
time to remove those stitches."

The sly look Mab wore sat so ill upon her sweet
face that Fiona had to bite back a smile. She knew
Mab was suggesting that she do more than just get
close to Ewan and hope he would reach for her
again. There were several problems with a plan that
included seducing Ewan. Fiona was not exactly sure
how to do such a thing as, aside from the rough as-
saults she had endured at Menzies's hands, her experience with men was limited to a few stolen
kisses. There was also the unease she felt over trying to make Ewan do something he obviously did

not wish to do. The consequences of such a thing were numerous, and none of them pleasant. The worst was that he might succumb to temptation only to turn about and reject her. Fiona was not sure she would be able to survive that, at least not in spirit.

"If I guess right, and ye hint at seduction, I am nay sure that is wise," Fiona said finally.

"Why? Ye want him and he wants ye. Ye just need to make him see that the world willnae end simply because he gives in to that want."

"Fine. So, he beds me. Then what? He would be appalled by his weakness and run away again, farther and faster. Or he could feel he must wed me because he stole my innocence. Or others could force him to the altar for the same reason."

"Isnae kneeling before the altar where ye want him to be?"

"Aye, but I would like him to go there willingly."

Mab smiled in understanding. "I am nay sure many men go willingly, and those who do are usually thinking of good bloodlines, heirs, and dower lands. Exactly why would ye be kneeling there, lass? Because he makes your blood run hot?"

Fiona blushed. "He does do that, but I ken he is my mate. I kenned it the first time he kissed me. I foolishly thought that I could make him see that."

"If ye had the time, ye might. Considering how stubborn Ewan can be, that could take a verra long time, however, and I dinnae think ye have that. If ye were wed to him, ye would have a lot of time."

"But if he is forced to wed me, by his own sense of honor or the demands of others, he willnae be feeling verra kindly toward me. All the old problems will still be there, but a few more will certainly be added."

"True, but ye will be close at hand to try to sort them out." Mab held up her hand when Fiona started to speak. "I ken what worries ye, but ye must think hard on this. What we speak of here isnae a good way to get a husband, but what other choices do ye have? Ye have a few days to weigh the matter in your mind and heart ere ye decide. But keep this in mind. His birthday is in but ten days and he will be healed enough by then to go to the village. If he sates himself on some whore, ye might weel find that he gains a renewed strength to resist ye."

The very thought of Ewan in another woman's arms, even a whore he cared nothing for, was almost too painful to endure. There was also the flicker of anger at the thought that he would flee what they could share, yet pay some woman for a soulless rutting. The mere thought of it was enough to make her consider Mab's plan. How much worse could it be? It would hurt to know he was an unwilling groom, but at least he would not be giving some other woman what she herself craved.

Fiona looked out the window and all thought of seduction, forced marriage, and consequences fled her mind. "Jesu, Mab, there must be nearly two dozen men out there now."

Mab peered out the window. "Some of the younger men have joined the dance. That often happens. The lads have a few tankards of ale and think that nonsense looks like fun. It does improve the view, however." Mab laughed along with Fiona, then gasped. "Oh, dear, the women are coming."

"Are they going to—" Fiona squeaked in surprise when a large, calloused hand was placed over her eyes.

"Ye ladies should be ashamed of yourselves," scolded Gregor, biting back a grin over the way Mab and Fiona blushed. "Come away from there."

"I think ye are calling the wrong people to account," mumbled Fiona as Gregor tugged her away from the window.

"There is naught I can do about those fools. I can but stand amazed that none of them get the lung fever. Simon sent me to find ye, Fiona. He was wondering if ye would play a game of chess with him ere ye sought your bed for the night."

For a brief moment, Fiona hesitated. She was not really in the mood for a game of chess. Simon was still new to the game and that meant there was more teaching than challenge. Then, she inwardly sighed. Simon was undoubtedly bored beyond bearing. Her sympathy stirred, she nodded and left to go to Simon.

"She seemed in better spirits," Gregor said as soon as Fiona was gone. "Did she say aught about Ewan?"

"Now why would the lass talk to me about the laird?" Mab kept her back to Gregor as she sorted through the gowns she had chosen for Fiona, trying to ignore Gregor and decide which gown to sew first.

"Dinnae play that game, Mab."

"What game do ye mean, lad?"

Gregor laughed at her supremely innocent expression, then grew serious. "My idiot of a brother was unkind to her, Mab. When she left him, she was upset. Women like to talk to other women when they are upset. Since ye are the only woman at Scarglas she spends much time with, I thought she might have spoken to ye about it."

"Aye, she spoke to me, but 'tis none of your business what she said. What was said was personal, confidences she entrusted me with. Ye must ask her your questions."

Seeing how nervous Mab was, Gregor wrapped his arm around her and kissed the top of her head. "I have but one question: Does Fiona-of-the-ten-knives want our dour, monkish Ewan?"

"Ah, weel, I dinnae think I will be breaking any confidences in answering that. Aye, she does, but she isnae certain he wants her." She peered up at him a little warily. "I tried to explain how matters stand at Scarglas, to make her see why the laird is the mon he is. I think she does understand some of it for she spoke of her brother Connor." Seeing the keen interest in Gregor's handsome face, Mab told him all Fiona had said about her brother. "Tis my opinion that she has dealt with a mon much akin to our laird, that she would understand him verra weel."

"Aye," agreed Gregor. "Tis *my* opinion that she would make a verra fine lady of Scarglas, and so say my brothers. The problem is how do we bring it about when Ewan is so determined to toss aside this gift?" He grinned when Mab blushed. "Aha! Is a plot already afoot then? Can ye nay share it with me? I may be able to help."

centrate on studying the scar left behind, but failed. She had to clench her hand into a tight fist to stop herself from stroking Ewan's long, well-shaped leg. Smoothly muscular and lightly dusted with black hair, the leg looked beautiful to her. Fiona inwardly shook her head, amazed and a little amused by how besotted she was.

Then again, stroking his thigh might be a way to seduce him, she mused. Mab had made it very clear that, if Ewan was determined to be a gentleman, seduction would be necessary. A slight nudge in the right direction, Mab had called it. Praying she was not about to embarrass herself, Fiona put her hand on the top of his strong thigh.

A swift inhale from Ewan caught her attention. She was just turning her head to look at him when he grasped hold of her braid. Fiona did not resist when he used her braid to tug her closer. She shivered beneath the look he gave her, his eyes darkened with desire. If he could look at her like that yet still send her away after one kiss, Fiona felt it would prove that her quest was utterly hopeless.

"I told ye that 'twould be best if Mab tended to me," Ewan said.

"Mab isnae here," Fiona said, "and I cannae see what difference it makes if 'tis Mab who removes your stitches or me."

"Nay? If 'twas Mab here, I wouldnae feel compelled to do this."

A soft gasp escaped her when he caught her up beneath her arms and pulled her on top of him. It was such a swift, abrupt motion that the slightly large shoes she wore fell from her feet. She placed her hands against his broad, smooth chest to steady herself and he growled softly. Then, he kissed her.

His kiss was fiercer, more demanding, than the others he had given her. Fiona hoped that meant he had finally lost his iron grip upon his passion. There was such need, such hunger, in his kiss that Fiona found it increasingly difficult not to succumb blindly to her own soaring desire. She struggled to keep a few of her wits intact, for she wanted to be alert enough to sense when he might begin to regain some control over himself. Although she was not sure what she could do to stop him if he started to withdraw from her again, she wanted to maintain enough presence of mind to give it her best try.

She smoothed her hand over his chest and felt him echo the shiver that went through her. The feel of warm skin, taut muscle, and even the light feathering of hair in the center of his chest made her heart race. Her hands itched to touch all of him, to find every ridge, every hollow. Fiona soon became irritated by their position despite the fever his kisses were infecting her with. The way he had his arms wrapped around her, holding her on top of him, made it difficult to satisfy her need to touch him.

As if in answer to her prayers, he turned so that they were lying on their sides facing each other. She took swift advantage, slipping her arms around him to stroke his back. A whispery moan escaped her when he began to kiss her throat. What few wits she had clung to were rapidly melting away beneath the heat of the desire he was stirring inside of her.

"Ye should run, Fiona-of-the-ten-knives," Ewan said even as he unlaced her gown, desperate to see her, to touch and taste her soft skin.

"Why?"

Fiona could feel him tugging at her clothes. A brief unease chilled a little of the heat in her blood, for she feared how he would react when he saw her scars. She ruthlessly buried that fear, shifting to make it easier for him to remove her clothes. If the sight of her scars repelled him, it was best if she knew now. It would mean he was not the man she thought him to be, that she had given her heart to an illusion.

Staring down at Fiona, who was now wearing only a thin chemise that revealed far more than it concealed, Ewan fought hard to cling to a few fragile strands of control. "Because ye have unleashed the beast."

"Och, weel, that sounds intriguing."

He opened his mouth to try to explain himself better, but she stroked his hip with one of her soft, pretty hands and all he could produce was a low groan. It was too late for her to save herself. Although she did not seem particularly inclined to do so, he thought as he unlaced her shift with badly trembling fingers. Her apparent willingness was making it impossible for him to think straight. He pulled off the thin linen garment, tossed it aside, and looked at her. One look was all it took for him to know that nothing short of death would stop him now. Just once he was going to take what he wanted, what he needed, and damn the consequences.

The tension that had entered her body as Ewan

looked at her fled swiftly beneath the heat of his
gaze. "Is the beast still unleashed?" she asked in an
unsteady whisper.

"Och, aye. Unleashed and on a rampage."

She was not sure what he meant, and a heartbeat later, she did not care. He placed his big, long-
fingered hands over her breasts and the heat that
flared to life inside her was so intense she was surprised she could not see the glow of it beneath his
hands. Certain that he would not be pushing her
aside again, Fiona released the last threads of her
control and let passion rule.

Ewan followed each caress of his hands with
kisses and slow strokes of his tongue. Fiona found
herself on her back. There was the soft sound of
something tearing as he yanked the covers away,
freeing his body from their hold. She got only a
brief glimpse of his body. He was a very big man
and Fiona decided it was probably for the best that
she did not get a really good look at him just now.
Then he took the aching tip of her breast into the
heat of his mouth and she lost the ability to think
at all.

Ewan was trying desperately to hold on to some
small scrap of control, but it was impossible. The
soft cries she made, the way her lithe body moved
beneath his, pushed him blindly onward. His lovemaking grew fierce, nearly frantic, but she seemed
to be equally enflamed. It was not until he thrust
himself inside her, crashing through her maiden's
gate and hearing her cry out, that he regained a
brief glimmer of sanity. He was just struggling for
the appropriate words and the breath to say them
when she wrapped her strong, slender legs around

him. The way she arched her slim hips pushed him deeper inside her tight heat and he was lost. He was aware of nothing but his body's screaming need.

Fiona stared up at the ceiling above Ewan's bed. She idly stroked his broad back as he lay weak and breathing raggedly in her arms. The feel of their bodies united, the knowledge that she had given him pleasure, gave her pleasure. Yet right beside that warmth, that tingling delight, was a vague sense of dissatisfaction.

Her eyes widened as she realized what ailed her. Ewan had not made her yell. She could recall Gilly stumbling to explain what one could feel in the arms of the man one loved, the sort of feelings that made Gilly notorious for her bellowing when Connor made love to her. Ewan had not given that to her.

For a moment, Fiona feared there was something wrong with her, then shook aside that concern. She had felt passion, had been wild with it. The need within her had reached almost painful heights. Even the sharp pain of losing her innocence had barely dimmed it. With each thrust of Ewan's strong body within hers, she had felt herself climbing toward some precipice. Then he had finished, flooding her womb with his seed before collapsing in her arms. And there was the problem, she thought. *He* had finished, but she had not. Ewan had brought her to the gates of paradise, then stepped through and left her behind.

She opened her mouth to inform him of this

failing, then quickly closed it again. Instinct told her that any comment, even the smallest hint of criticism, real or imagined, would be a serious error. Whether the knowledge came from things she had heard, or things Ewan had said, she knew that Ewan had very little confidence in his attractiveness to women. A man like her brother Connor would see any hint of criticism as a challenge to be met. Ewan would take it as a hard blow to his confidence.

It did not matter if he made her yell, she told herself as she felt him grow calm in her arms. There was all the dizzying joy of his kisses and caresses to savor. There was pleasure to be found in giving him pleasure. It could also be that, since he satisfied his manly lusts only once a year, he was simply too needy, too hungry, to satisfy her needs just yet. That would pass and then he would give her that bliss Gilly had tried to describe. At the moment, her biggest concern should be stopping him from trying to retreat again. As she felt him tense slightly, she braced herself for a confrontation.

Ewan grimaced as his senses returned. He had lost all control. Worse, he was fairly sure he had left Fiona unsatisfied. He was not sure how to mend that, either, for she drove him wild. The way she warmed to his caresses pushed him past all control and, obviously, all consideration. Since there was no turning back now, he was going to have to find a way to hold that madness back until she found her pleasure.

Sitting up, he picked up a square of linen from the table by the bed and dampened it in the bowl of water there. He ignored her blushes as he gently bathed away all signs of her lost innocence. As he did the same to himself, he frantically searched his mind for the right words to say.

He settled himself on his side, propping his head up on one hand, and smiled faintly when Fiona hastily pulled the sheet over their bodies. It puzzled him that she said nothing about his poor performance as a lover. Helena had always been quick to complain if he failed to give her pleasure. Of course, Helena had not been a virgin. There was a chance that Fiona, being an innocent, had no idea that he had failed her.

"That was ill done of me," he said and wondered why she frowned at him.

"I dinnae believe ye were the only one doing it," she snapped. "There is naught to feel guilty about."

There was, but he would not argue about that now, nor would he risk hurting her feelings by voicing his regrets or fears. "I didnae satisfy ye. I did a poor job of it."

"Oh, nay. Twas verra fine."

"Fiona, ye dinnae need to lie. I ken that I didnae satisfy ye, that ye didnae find your release."

"Ye mean ye didnae make me yell." Suddenly aware that someone might walk in on them at any moment, Fiona picked her shift up off the floor and tugged it on.

Although his body was already demanding more, Ewan did not stop her from getting dressed. He had briefly considered bringing her to release with his hand, but knew he would not be able to stop there. He would have made love to her again, given in to the craving to feel her tight heat around him once more. It was for the best if she put herself out of reach for now, if only so her body could recover from her first bedding.

"Make ye yell?" he asked as he watched her dress.

"Aye. Our Gilly yells when my brother loves her. Fair shakes the walls. She says 'tis the bliss which makes her sing out. She put thicker doors on their bedchamber." Fiona smiled when Ewan laughed.

He grasped her hand as she started to move away from the bed. "When we are married, I will make ye yell." Ewan watched her closely as he spoke.

It was what she wanted, Fiona told herself. It was what she and Mab had planned for. Fiona could not help but feel guilty, however. It was wrong to trick him, to entrap him, no matter how good her reasons for doing so. She had to give him a choice.

"Ye dinnae have to marry me," she said.

"Aye, I do. I just took your maidenhead."

"'Twas mine to give away as I pleased."

"Mayhap, but 'twas my duty to resist temptation. I may nay ken exactly who ye are, but I have no doubt that ye are of good blood. Your brother is a laird." He almost smiled when she grimaced and mouthed a curse as she realized she had given something away. "My honor demands I make this right."

"I dinnae want an unwilling husband, one brought to the altar for only reasons of honor."

He kissed her palm. "'Twould nay be just honor. Can ye deny that there would be passion?"

"Nay," she replied softly, "but ye dinnae want to get married."

"A mon can change his mind. Am I such a poor choice of husband?"

"Dinnae be an idiot. Tisnae if ye are a good choice or nay, is it, although ye are. Tis whether or not ye truly wish to be chosen."

"Mayhap I didnae, but I do now. Do ye think your kinsmen will just pat me on the back and say what a braw lad I am when they learn I took your innocence? I need no more enemies."

Her heart told her that was a poor reason to get married, but good sense silenced it. Connor would soon drag the truth from her once she was back at Deilcladach, and she could not be sure she could talk him out of his anger. The very last thing she wanted was for Connor and Ewan to come to sword-point because of her. Her besotted mind quickly latched on to the thought of how wonderful it would be to gift Ewan with one alliance, and she inwardly cursed. Since it was certain they would be married, she was going to have to stiffen her spine or she could find herself being twisted into painful knots trying to please him.

"And I left my seed inside of you," he said, encouraged to add more sound reasons for marriage by the way she was thinking over what he had already said. "Ye could, e'en now, be carrying my bairn."

Fiona pulled her hand free of his grasp and held it up to silence his words. "Enough. Ye dinnae need to bury me in reasoning. In truth, if ye state any more good, practical reasons to marry, I could turn stubbornly contrary."

Ewan inwardly winced as he sat up. He should have tried to say a few sweet words, but he was unskilled in flattery and wooing. The only clear thought he had in his head at the moment was how badly he wanted to get her back into his bed. Telling her how badly he wanted to be back inside her was probably not something a woman considered proper flattery. He vowed he would think of some sweet words to give her on their wedding night. She deserved some for the pleasure she gave him, and a few flatteries would not make her think him weak and besotted.

"Good. Then we shall marry in two days' time," he said.

"Two days?!"

"Aye. That should give ye time to heal and me time to become more steady on my feet." He grabbed her by the wrist, tugged her close, and gave her a quick but heated kiss. "I will be faithful and I will make ye yell."

As Fiona hurried out of the room, she wondered if she should see that second promise as more of a threat. Meeting Gregor and Mab in the hall, she grabbed Mab by the hand and dragged the woman off to her bedchamber. She was still blushing from the intense look Gregor gave her once she got Mab into her room.

"He didnae push ye away this time, did he?" Mab said, grinning widely.

"Nay." Fiona sighed and sat down on the edge of her bed. "We will be wed in two days' time."

"Ye dinnae sound as pleased by that as I thought ye would be."

"Oh, a part of me is verra pleased indeed, that foolish, ever hopeful part that thinks she can simply make Ewan care for her. The rest of me is a little stung by his lack of any sweet words. Nary a one, nay e'en the smallest, silliest of flatteries."

Mab sat down next to Fiona and patted her on the back. "They will come. Ye ken that ye have his passion. With many men that doesnae have to mean so verra much, but with our Ewan it means a great deal."

"I would like to think so."

"*Do* think so, for 'tis fact. Whate'er ye stir in that young fool, 'tis strong enough to make him forget his own rules, lose his legendary restraint. Tis more than many a wife begins with. Tis up to ye to make it into something deeper and richer, into what ye want and need."

"Ye are right. I have my chance now for he willnae be able to run away, might no longer see any need to. Tis up to me to make this marriage a good one. I just wish I felt more confident in my ability to do so."

"Heed a wee bit of advice from a woman who has had a wee bit of experience with men. Aye, Fingal was an error in judgment, but I was married once. It wasnae a love match, few are, but I made it one."

"There is a secret to it, is there?"

"Aye, although a mon has to have a heart ye can reach. Howbeit, I have known Ewan for years, and trust me in this, the lad has a verra big heart indeed for all he tries to bury it deep inside. In the beginning, ye must learn to nay take everything to heart. E'en a mon who dearly loves the lass he weds is going to speak wrong or step wrong. Men need a wee bit of training, ye ken."

Fiona grinned and nodded. "Our Gilly had to

train my brother. He had some verra strange, but firmly set, ideas about ladies and wives."

"As most men do. From what ye have told me of those two, I think it would serve ye weel to think on all your Gilly did to make her marriage a good one. My feeling is that truth and trust are essential. And by truth I mean ye must say what ye think and feel. Tis the only way the fool can come to ken ye as more than a body in his bed. A mon cannae care about a lass he doesnae ken weel or understand, can he?"

"Nay. Twill be easier after Ewan and I are wed, too, for I willnae have to weigh my every word." She grimaced. "I just hope he doesnae have any enemies amongst my kinsmen, the ones of blood or marriage."

"Just who *are* ye?" Mab placed her hand over her heart. "I swear I shall tell no one and let it be your truth to tell."

"I am Fiona MacEnroy of Deilcladach. My brother is the laird. He married Gillyanne Murray, the daughter of Sir Eric Murray of Dubhlinn, the niece of Lady Maldie Murray of Donncoill, and the foster sister of James Drummond, laird of Dunncraig. My brother Diarmot is laird of Clachthrom and recently married Ilsa Cameron, only sister of Sigimor Cameron, laird of Dubheidland. And by the look upon your face, Mab, I think I have already found a problem."

"Nay. Weel, mayhap. Still, so many strong alliances may ease the way, soften the blow. Aye, and those Drummonds are kin to my late husband's clan. Ah, but 'tis the Camerons, m'dear."

"They are enemies of the MacFingals?"

"Nay—kinsmen."

"Oh, nay, dinnae say 'tis *those* kinsmen, the ones Sir Fingal hates."

"Weel, it may nay be the same ones. There are many different Cameron families. Sigimor may be a common name."

"Nay, it isnae, and weel ye ken it. A Sigimor who is laird of Dubheidland is e'en more rare. A big mon, red hair, odd humor? Has thirteen brothers? All red-haired?"

"Oh, dear. Tis him. Fingal's nephew. The son of the woman Fingal feels was stolen from him. Weel, 'tis no matter. Ewan holds no grudge, has simply left it in his father's hands. In truth, I think the lads have begun to think it all verra silly when they are in such desperate need of allies. And most of the ones Fingal argued with are dead now. His brother, the woman, and both their fathers. So, it isnae as if he will have to deal with the ones he thought wronged him. If Ewan had been here, oh, three years past, when Sigimor stopped by, I suspect he would have welcomed the mon."

"I pray ye are right, Mab. E'en if those Camerons are only kin to me through marriage, they are still kin and I should hate to find myself caught between them and my husband." Fiona sighed and shook her head. "And here I had convinced myself that Ewan would be pleasantly surprised by who I am and all of my connections."

"Weel, he will most certainly be surprised."

Chapter 10

"I cannae believe ye havenae demanded that she tell ye who she is," said Gregor as he helped Ewan into a heavily embroidered black and silver doublet. "Ye will be marrying her in but an hour."

"She will tell me when we marry. I think she is a wee bit afraid that I might change my mind and try to ransom her if I ken who she is ere we say the vows."

There was no chance of that happening, Ewan thought. He had made no effort to convince Fiona of that, however. To do so would have required the type of soft words he had no skill with, and for all his effort over the last two days, he had not thought of any. He had also feared that any attempt to get her to trust him with the truth might have him stumbling into confessions of feelings he did not want her to know about.

Passion was safe. Passion was something he could give her in abundance, knowing she would see no

more in that than a man's natural lust. All other
feeling he would keep to himself. Helena had taught
him the danger of giving heart and soul to a woman.
It might be unfair to treat Fiona as if she were yet
another like Helena, especially when there had
been no indication that she was, but he could not
help but be wary. He might desire Fiona, but he
did not really know her well. Helena's betrayal had
left him hurt and cautious. A betrayal at Fiona's
hands would devastate him. Ewan was not sure
how he knew that, and he did not wish to peer too
closely into his heart to learn why it would be so.

Ewan ruefully admitted that he did not fully trust
the passion Fiona revealed in his arms. Women
rarely felt passion for him. Helena's had been a
lie. The whores in the village simply did what they
were paid to do. The few maids about Scarglas who
tried to flirt with him were stirred by his position
as laird, tempted by what that might gain them.
Over the past two days he had constantly thought
about the lovemaking he had shared with Fiona,
recalling her every sound, every touch, every movement. He could not detect any falsity in her passion, but since he loathed the mere thought that
her sighs and kisses had been lies, he could not really trust his own judgment.

"Ye dinnae look too happy," murmured Gregor.
"Ye are wedding a bonnie lass. I would think ye
would at least smile o'er the knowledge that she
will soon be in your bed every night."

"Aye, I should be," replied Ewan, "and I am a
wee bit, inside. Yet, weel, she is verra beautiful."

Gregor cursed and shook his head. "And so ye
wonder why she wants you. Ye are hardly an ogre,

Ewan. Aye, your face has been scarred and knocked about, but 'tisnae one to give the bairns nightmares. Tis clear to see that Fiona comes from a place that has kenned its share of strife and war. I suspicion she isnae troubled by a scar or two. And she has her own, doesnae she?"

"Wee ones. Barely noticeable. Mine are nay so neat and small." He looked down at the finery he wore. "This is much akin to gilding a nettle and trying to convince everyone 'tis a rose."

"Curse it, Ewan, is this the legacy that bitch Helena left behind?"

"She was beautiful and she claimed a passion for me, but 'twas only a trap. A lie. She made that most clear when she handed me over to Hugh Gray. Her true feelings were revealed then, in word and deed."

"And ye believed her, believed a woman who would go to a mon's bed one night and lead him to the slaughter on the next? Ewan, ye were but one-and-twenty. Aye, a mon, but due to your own somewhat monkish resolve, nay verra experienced with women. S'truth, none of us would have fared any better. The rest of us were e'en younger, and although we had more experience in bedding the lasses, we had none in how to deal with a woman like Helena. The lasses about here are simple and direct. Some say aye and some say nay. E'en the whores in the village are without deceit. Ye give them a coin and they let ye take your ease. Oh, some of them may groan or cry out or flatter a mon as he ruts on her, but 'tis a harmless deceit, meant to keep the one paying the coin happy. But Helena was a whore steeped in treachery and weel practiced in the sort of deceit that can cost a mon dearly. None of us were ready for her."

"I have always wondered why she didnae pursue our father, who was the laird."

"Because she recognized that he had the same lack of a heart she did. He would have bedded her, but she wouldnae have gained anything from it. He couldnae be wooed. The rest of us were too young, nay the heirs, and had little to do with training the men or all of the rest of the work here. Our father held the title, but e'en back then, ye held the reins." Gregor poured them each a goblet of wine and handed Ewan one.

"And ye dinnae think Fiona is any more than what she seems—a wee bonnie lass who got lost?"

"Nay, I dinnae. She has been here for a fortnight yet has done naught that would make me think her anything other than what she says she is. She doesnae ask suspicious questions or roam about the keep studying everything. Nor does she flirt with any of us. I can see it will take ye a while to believe that, however."

Ewan thought over all Gregor had said as he drank his wine. There was a lot of truth to his brother's words. It was also true that it would take him a while to accept them.

Shaking his head clear of all his confusing thoughts, he finished his drink and said to Gregor, "Best we wander down to the great hall. I hope Nathan has kept a close guard on that priest. I want him sober."

"He will be," Gregor assured him as they started out of the room. "I think e'en our father will see to it."

"The old mon is still boasting that this is the result of his clever planning, is he?"

"Och, aye. The way he tells it, ye would think he himself had set the lass down in your path that day." Gregor watched Ewan carefully. "He does grow humble in confessing that his choice for ye might nay be the best, that a lass with more meat on her bones and no scars would have been better."

A soft growl escaped Ewan. "The fool. He best guard his tongue before Fiona. He best nay insult her."

"True. She might hurt him." Gregor grinned when Ewan briefly chuckled.

Ewan paused just before stepping in front of the entrance to the great halls, avoiding the wide-open doors. "I may nay ken exactly who Fiona is, but I am verra sure she could do better than me. Mayhap . . ." he began.

Gregor shoved him in front of the open doors, and several men called out a greeting to Ewan. "Nurse your doubts all ye wish, but ye willnae shame the lass by abandoning her at the altar."

Although the ferocity of Gregor's tone surprised Ewan, he nodded. His brother was right. Ewan presumed that many of the people of Scarglas either knew or suspected he had taken Fiona's innocence. He had not even thought of hiding that fact until the maids had changed the linen on his bed and he had caught a glimpse of the small bloodstain on the sheet. Since the maids had arrived but moments after Fiona had left, he also suspected even the dullest amongst them had guessed what had happened. A suspicion given more weight by the announcement that he would marry Fiona in two days. Giving in to his cowardice now not only would be dishonorable, but would indeed shame Fiona before everyone. It troubled him a little that the latter bothered him far more than the former, but he shook aside that problem and stepped into the great hall to accept congratulations he did not feel he really deserved.

"Fiona, stop your wriggling," said Mab, "or Bonnie will be pinning those flowers on your left ear."

After a brief grin at the giggling Bonnie, Fiona stood very still. "Ye are getting verra bossy, Mab."

"Aye. After today ye will be the lady of Scarglas so I thought I best get it all out of my blood right now." Mab laughed along with the other women. "Twill be nice to have a lady of the keep again. It has been a long time. In truth, I am nay sure we ever really had one."

"Sir Fingal has had five wives, Mab."

"That he did, but do ye see their mark anywhere save for the lads cluttering up the keep?"

Fiona looked around the bedchamber she had been given. It was comfortable, surprisingly free of drafts, and rather plain. It was clean, as was the rest of the keep, but Fiona knew that was Clare's doing. The gardens and the herb shed were Mab's doing. The great hall was very fine, but that was mostly the work of the previous laird. Thinking of the things Gilly and Ilsa had done when they had moved in with her brothers, Fiona realized Mab was right. Sir Fingal's wives had left little mark behind save for their sons.

"How odd," she murmured. "Not e'en Annie Logan?"

"Nay," replied Bonnie. "My mother said the woman was run ragged trying to keep her husband out of the arms of other lasses. The other wives didnae last as long. Died, save for the last one, who ran away."

"Weel, at least that last one put an end to Sir Fingal marrying again," said Fiona. "Cannae find himself a new wife when he is still wed to the one who ran away, can he."

"Nay so sure that would stop him," said Mab. "I think 'tis that he doesnae go anywhere now, ne'er leaves Scarglas, so cannae find a woman who doesnae ken the truth about him. Fool has eleven legitimate sons and near to two score of bastards. Tis time and past someone tied a knot in it." Mab blushed, but smiled when Fiona and Bonnie giggled.

"Ah, m'lady, ye do look fine," Bonnie said as she stood back to look Fiona over carefully. "Such pretty hair."

Fiona touched her thick hair, which had been left to hang loose in long, rippling waves past her hips. "Thank ye, although I am nay sure I ought to be attired as if I am a maiden bride."

"Near a one as the laird will find about this place," Mab said as she gave a last brush to the skirts of Fiona's deep blue gown. "There, ye are ready."

"I will go to tell the others," Bonnie said even as she hurried out of the room.

"Ah, Mab, I do worry about this. I surely do," whispered Fiona, frowning after Bonnie.

"Weel, cease your fretting," ordered Mab. "Do ye think all Ewan's brothers would be so pleased if they saw aught wrong with this? Every one of them, legitimate and bastard, is fiercely loyal and protective of Ewan, though I am nay sure he is fully aware of it. If any of them feared ye would harm Ewan, in body or heart, they would try to stop this."

"They might if they kenned there was a plot to get Ewan to the altar."

"Wheesht, do ye think they dinnae ken? Gregor did. S'truth, how do ye think I was able to be lost that day? I was only in the herb shed, but e'en the youngest of them was suddenly too blind to see me." Mab hooked her arm through Fiona's and started to lead her out of the room. "In fact, the lads have chosen ye for their laird so cease your frowning. There will be problems aplenty in the days ahead so why dinnae ye just enjoy yourself today?"

"I will try, Mab. Twill be easier once the revelation of who I am is done and whate'er stir that news causes has passed."

"Twill be fine," Mab reassured Fiona, but could see that the younger woman did not believe it any more than she did.

"Fiona-of-the-ten-knives?" Ewan said, interrupting the priest to scowl at Fiona. "Ye cannae use that name in the vows. Ye have to use your real one."

"Nay, I dinnae," Fiona argued, wondering how the man could still look so big when he was kneeling at her side. "The priest said that as long as I sign my proper name to the papers, it doesnae matter."

"That is silly. Use your real name."

"Nay, not until we sign the papers and ye will sign them first."

"Ye are my wife. Tis your duty to obey me."

"Aye, lad, ye tell her how it is," said Fingal, only to back up a few steps when both Fiona and Ewan briefly glared at him.

"Now, tell the priest your real name," Ewan ordered Fiona and almost grinned at her dark scowl.

"Ye arenae my husband yet, and if ye expect blind obedience once the vows are done, mayhap we best pause to have us a wee talk."

"Och, nay. Considering how stubborn ye are, we could still be arguing o'er the matter whilst ye are birthing the bairn I have probably set to growing in ye." He nodded when she gasped and blushed. "We will discuss it later." He scowled at the priest. "Weel? Get on with it."

Since she had gotten her way, Fiona did not argue and dutifully repeated her vows. The kiss Ewan gave her while his brothers cheered and hooted left her breathless and dazed, but she quickly regained her senses when the quill was set in her hand. She could feel the others crowding in behind her and Ewan as she stared down at the document she was supposed to sign. Ewan had already scrawled his name there in bold letters. She took a deep breath and added her own.

"MacEnroy?" Ewan asked, ignoring the muttering of his family behind him. "Of Deilcladach?"

"Aye, I am the only sister of the laird, Connor MacEnroy," she replied.

"Lass, they are nearly four days' ride from here. Ye cannae be a MacEnroy."

"Four days?" she whispered in shock. "God's tears, how long was that cursed horse toting me about? I had thought myself only dazed, but I must have fallen unconcious. But I *am* a MacEnroy." She pulled her ornate silver eating knife free of its sheath at her waist and handed it to Ewan. "Read what is etched upon the hilt. Connor gave me that upon my sixteenth birthday. He said that I deserved such a fine gift now that we had coin to spare because I was a good wee lass who had the grace to survive whilst under his care." She smiled faintly at the memory.

"To wee Fiona, a MacEnroy to the bone. Connor," read Ewan, then stared at Fiona as he handed the knife back to her. "Who is this Gilly ye keep talking of? His wife, aye?"

"Aye. Gillyanne Murray, daughter of Sir Eric Murray of Dubhlinn, niece of Lady Maldie Murray of Donncoill, and foster sister to James Drummond, laird of Dunncraig. We MacEnroys are allied with the Dalglish clan of Dunspier and the Goudies of Aberwellen. My brother Antony holds Ald-dab-hach to the south of us." The muttering amongst the others in the great hall grew louder, but Fiona kept her gaze fixed upon Ewan. He appeared increasingly stunned. "My other brother, Diarmot, is laird of Clachthrom. He was recently wed"—she took a deep breath to steady herself—"to Ilsa Cameron, only sister to Sigimor Cameron of Dubheidland." The loud gasp of those around them was followed by such a complete silence that Fiona briefly wondered if anyone had remembered to breathe out.

"Through Gilly's kin, the Murrays, there are ties to the MacAlpins of Cairnmoor, the Armstrongs of Aigballa, the MacMillans of Bealachan, the Drummonds of Dunnbea, the Kirkcaldys, the Kinloches, the Lucettes of France—" She stuttered to a halt when Ewan pressed faintly trembling fingers over her mouth.

"A cursed Cameron," snarled Sir Fingal as he pushed through the others gathered around Ewan and Fiona to glare at her. "I kenned it. She is naught but a spy sent here by that fool Sigimor."

Struggling to think clearly despite the shock Fiona had dealt him, Ewan put his arm around her shoulders and pulled her close to his side. "She isnae a Cameron. The tie is but one of marriage—her brother's."

"Tis close enough. We should send her back to Sigimor."

"Ye arenae sending her anywhere," Ewan said, his voice cold and hard as he fought his anger over his father's blind hatred of his own blood kin. "She is my wife now. She may already be carrying my bairn."

"I wish ye wouldnae keep saying that," muttered Fiona, then pressed her lips closed when Ewan gave her a brief, hard squeeze.

"The Camerons ye feel wronged ye are all dead anyway," Ewan continued. "Sigimor is no threat to us. S'truth, I dinnae ken why he keeps coming here only to listen to ye rant and get the gates shut in his face."

"I willnae deal with one of those cursed Camerons!"

"Then dinnae deal with them. If there is a need,

I will tend to it. Tis past time we cease turning away the only ones within miles who dinnae want to kill us. They are blood, for sweet Mary's sake."

"Nay mine."

"Please yourself." He sighed when, after one last glare at Fiona, his father moved away, calling for ale.

"Do ye think that will be the end of it?" asked Fiona.

"I suspicion he will brood o'er it for a wee while, but nay more than that. Tis an old grudge he clutches like some holy relic, but 'tis a bloodless one. The worst he will do is insult Sigimor if he appears at our gates again."

Fiona could not fully suppress a smile. "I wouldnae fret o'er that. Sigimor willnae." She realized everyone was still staring at her with an unsettling intensity. "What ails all of ye? Have I grown another head?"

"Nay, just an army," drawled Gregor. "We suspected we would finally gain an alliance through ye, but Jesu, lass, we didnae expect ye to have ties to half of Scotland."

"They arenae verra large clans," she murmured, and frowned when Gregor laughed.

"Come, a feast has been set out," said Ewan. "I suggest we all set our teeth to it."

Ewan's words broke the silence and everyone moved to the tables. Fiona studied Ewan carefully as he led her to her seat, and then sat down beside her. For a man who had been striving for years to make some alliance, he did not seem terribly pleased with the ones she had brought him. While it was true that many of them were Gilly's kinsmen, Fiona knew they all considered her kin as well. During the times she had gone to train with Lady Maldie, she had met many of them and knew they considered all the MacEnroys part of their very diverse family. Even if one counted only her family's alliances, it was still a fine gift she gave him. Yet, he sat there silent and distracted.

"Are ye angry, Ewan?" she asked finally, speaking softly so the others at the table could not hear her.

"Nay." Ewan lightly stroked her hand where it rested upon the table. "Shocked. Due to my father's skill in making enemies, we have been alone all of my life. After years of work, I have eased close to an alliance with many of those my father angered, but havenae made any true alliances. Still, only the Grays are a real threat to us now. The others may nay be true allies until my father passes from this earth, but they arenae truly our enemies any longer, just an occasional irritant. Yet suddenly, after kneeling before a priest for a wee while, I find myself fair smothered in alliances. E'en if one only counts your family's direct allies, 'tis still far more than I had ever considered."

"My brother was a wee bit shocked when he discovered exactly who Gilly was. We had long seen ourselves as mostly alone, as weel. It wasnae until after Gilly arrived that we discovered the Goudies and the Dalglishes were closer allies than any of us had thought, including them."

He shook his head, slowly coming to grips with the massive change in his circumstances. Ewan inwardly grimaced when he realized Fiona was, indeed, far above his touch. For the sake of his people, he was pleased with the alliances she brought to their marriage, but such a rich prize should have gone to a richer, more powerful laird than he ever could be.

It was done, however, he thought as he watched Fiona laugh at something Simon said. He had touched her, had taken her innocence, and had married her. There was no turning back now. Considering her connections, even thinking about turning back could prove unhealthy, for him and his clan. Ewan did not really think Fiona was the sort of woman to call down a vengeance upon him if he cast her aside, but she might not have any say in the matter. It would not surprise him if he faced a tense confrontation with her kinsmen anyway, because he had held her for ransom, bedded her, and married her. It might be possible to keep the ransoming and bedding a secret, but he did not hold out much hope for that.

As they ate and suffered through increasingly ridiculous toasts offered by his brothers until he threatened them with slow dismemberment if they did not cease, Ewan asked Fiona about her family. There was more light than dark in her tales. It also troubled him a little that she probably knew his kinsmen the Camerons better than he did. One thread wove itself through it all, however, and that was the tight bond of blood and clan. That bond could stretch out to new members of the family, as it had to the Murrays and to his cousins the Camerons. Ewan wanted it to reach out to him and his clan.

He grimaced when somebody began to play music. Goaded by his brothers, Ewan forced himself to dance with Fiona once. Feeling big and awkward, he soon left her in the more willing care of his brothers. He sat and watched her, the swirl of her glorious hair and the movement of her lithe body heating his blood. She laughed and smiled, dancing with each of his brothers, including a blushing, awkward Simon. Once she even did a strange but lively dance with the children, bastards all, before they were hurried off to bed by their nursemaids.

A spark of guilt stung him as he realized he was not simply enjoying the sight of his bride heartily enjoying herself. Ewan admitted to himself that he sought signs of deception and betrayal, but he saw none. She did not flirt, smile too long or too welcomingly at any one man, or treat one man more favorably than another. In fact, if he dared trust his own judgment, she treated them all with a friendly ease. No more. No less.

She acted, he realized, like a woman who had been raised by men, treated as just another brother, exactly as she had claimed. Fiona displayed no fear and not one drop of submissiveness. Ewan suspected she would give a man her respect only if he earned it and that she would never be blindly obedient. It appeared that, in marrying him, Fiona had made his brothers, her brothers, too. It pleased him more than he could say to see that his brothers and his men had not only accepted Fiona as his wife, but welcomed her. If only his father would do so.

Pushing aside that thought, Ewan stood up and began to walk toward his wife. He was still riddled with doubts and fears, but for the moment, he decided to banish them all to the far corners of his mind. Fate had blessed him with a beautiful wife, one who set him afire. It was time to stop brooding about her and start enjoying her. He did not intend to do that by galloping around the great hall to the tune of some badly played music, either. When she skipped past him, he caught her by the arm to halt her dance.

"Oh, Ewan, have ye—" began Fiona, only to screech in shock and surprise when he picked her up and tossed her over his shoulder. "Ewan, put me down!" she ordered, blushing as his brothers and too many others began to offer a great many somewhat crude suggestions as to what Ewan should do next. "What about the celebration?"

"The celebration can continue without us," he said as he walked out of the great hall. "Tis time."

"Time? Time for what?"

"Time to make ye yell."

Chapter 11

It was difficult for Fiona to decide which was most responsible for the flush in her cheeks and the slight dizziness she suffered when Ewan set her down—being carried up the stairs like a sack of oats or Ewan's talk of making her yell. She was gathering enough breath to scold him when he shut and latched the door, then turned to look at her. That newly gathered air left her lungs in a rush. Ewan's storm gray eyes were nearly black with desire.

"I am glad we didnae have to suffer through a bedding ceremony," she said, wondering why she felt so nervous.

Ewan moved to stand in front of her and removed the flowers from her hair. "I told my brothers that they would find themselves missing precious parts of their bodies if they e'en considered it." He combed his fingers through her hair, savoring the rich, silken thickness of it. "Why are ye afraid?"

"I am nay afraid," she replied, silently cursing the slight tremor in her voice. "A wee bit nervous, mayhap."

"Why? Ye arenae a virgin. There will be no pain this time." He began to unlace her gown.

"There wasnae much last time." She shivered as he tugged off her gown, but did not stop him. "I dinnae ken why I am nervous. Mayhap 'tis because this time it isnae, weel, sudden, but planned." She blinked when she realized he had already stripped her down to her shift. "That was quick."

"This will be even quicker," he said as he began to remove his own clothes.

It certainly was, she thought dazedly as she watched Ewan's clothes fall away from his body. She was a little surprised she did not hear anything tear. She barely had time to consider the fact that she was about to see Ewan naked when he was.

Her breathing grew ragged as she looked at him. The glimpses she had gained while nursing him and the one time they had made love had not really prepared her for this. He was all lean, hard muscle and smooth, dark skin. There were a lot of scars on his body, large and small, from the new one on his leg to one that cut slantwise across his taut stomach. She looked him over from his broad shoulders to his long narrow feet before her gaze became fixed upon his groin. Fiona decided it was a good thing she had not gotten a close look at that when he had pulled her into his bed two days ago. She was certain she would have turned craven, become foolishly terrified that he would tear her apart. Her eyes widened when she noticed a scar that ran perilously close to that proud display of manhood.

"Jesu, Ewan, ye were nearly gelded."

"Aye." He knelt to remove her shoes and stockings. "Eight years ago I was betrayed by a woman to my worst enemy—Hugh Gray. It did not seem to matter to them that she had crawled into my bed in her eagerness to entrap me. They both felt I ought to pay for soiling her pure white skin with my touch." Tossing aside the last of her stockings, he ran his hands up and down her long, slender legs and heard her gasp softly. "That scar is from the cut they made to taunt me with what was to come, to make me afraid."

"Did it work?" she asked as he picked her up and carried her to their bed.

"Och, aye, verra weel, although I believe I was able to hide it." He savored the sight of her in his bed for a moment before unlacing her daintily embroidered linen shift.

"What stopped them?"

"Gregor and a great many of my brothers, as weel as my men. Unfortunately, Gray and Helena got away. It was felt it was more important to get me help than to chase them down. I was bleeding rather heavily. Several of the smaller scars and the one upon my face are also from that time."

"Torture," she whispered as he tugged off her shift, and she clenched her hands against the urge to cover herself. "For pleasure or for information?"

"A bit of both," he replied as he climbed into bed beside her and tugged her into his arms.

Fiona trembled when her body touched his, the

heat of his flesh seeming to enter her very blood. She did not think anything had ever felt so good, so right. This was where she belonged, but as he gently placed his hands on her cheeks and tilted her face up to his, she had the feeling it was going to take a lot of work to make him see that, too.

"This time, lass, ye will ken the full of it," he said and kissed her.

By the time Ewan ended the kiss, Fiona could hear herself panting softly. She ran her trembling hands over his broad back as he kissed his way down to her breasts. A whispery moan escaped her when he took the hard, aching nipple deep into his mouth and suckled her while he tormented her other breast with his hand and long, skillful fingers. She tried to wriggle her body into a better position beneath his, needing to feel him pressing against her, but he held her firmly in place.

His manhood pressed hot and hard against the side of her leg, but he held her down in such a way she could not move that leg against him. When she slid her hand over his hip then toward his groin, he grasped her by the wrist and pulled it away. Fiona was not quite sure what she should think about his apparent wish not to be touched. When she tried again, he pinned her hand to the bedclothes.

"Nay, lass," he said, his voice hoarse and unsteady. "If ye touch me there, ye willnae be having a chance to yell."

The thought that her touch would be enough to break his control made Fiona's desire soar. She wrapped her arms around him as he kissed her again, and could feel the barely leashed ferocity in him. For now she would find solace and hope in

the fact that she obviously enflamed his passion
enough to strain his legendary control.

When he slid his hand between her thighs, she
flinched slightly, still unaccustomed to such a shock-
ing caress. It took only a few strokes of his long fingers to banish that pinch of embarrassment. Fiona
soon opened to his touch, arching her hips slightly
to move against his hand with a rapidly growing
hunger.

A soft cry of need and welcome escaped her as
he settled himself between her thighs. She wrapped
her legs around him as he slowly joined their bodies. He moved within her as if he feared he would
break her and it made Fiona desperate for more.
When she stroked his buttocks, he growled and
pinned her hands to the bed. Then he took her
nipple deep into his mouth and she felt herself
reaching for those heights again.

Just as she thought she could bear no more of
his carefully measured thrusts, he released her
hands. With his mouth still feasting upon her breasts,
he reached between their joined bodies and stroked
her. Fiona was just wondering what he had touched
that could send such a fierce wave of delight through
her when he did it again, and she shattered, crying
out his name. Yet, even as she fell into that paradise she had only glimpsed before, she felt him
leave her. She clung to him as he groaned and
pressed his face against her breasts, but right there
next to the blinding pleasure rippling through her
body was a sense of loss.

It was not until her senses began to return that
Fiona realized what he had done and a chill entered her heart, banishing the lingering warmth of

desire. He had pulled away, denying her his seed. Fiona told herself not to let the hurt and anger she felt cause her to make any hasty judgments. When he moved to lie at her side, she looked at him, but could find no answer in his expression. He simply looked sated, content, and a little smug. When he met her gaze, he began to frown, and she wondered if her expression revealed her feelings all too clearly.

"Why?" she asked, praying that his explanation would soothe her pain.

"Why what?" he asked cautiously.

"Why did ye leave me?"

Ewan inwardly cursed, but decided it had been foolish to think she might not notice his withdrawing from her. "I dinnae want any children." He cursed aloud when he saw the look of pain that crossed her face, but when he tried to pull her into his arms, she wriggled free of his hold.

"Why?" she demanded, fighting to keep calm enough to try and understand.

"Fiona, ye have been here long enough to ken what my father is," he began, struggling for the right words.

"What does your father have to do with ye denying me your child? Ye didnae suffer this reluctance two days ago."

"I was careless then. I can but pray that my seed doesnae take root. There is madness in my blood," he confessed.

"What madness? What are ye talking about?"

"My father, the way he acts, the things he does, he—"

"Ye think your father is mad?"

"Aye."

"Your father isnae mad. He is naught but a spoiled child," she snapped.

"Ye dinnae understand—"

"Nay? Ye think not?" She grabbed his hand, bringing it to each of her scars as she spoke. "*This* is madness, Ewan. I ken madness verra weel indeed. I have seen it. I have been marked by it here upon my cheeks, here in this mark o'er my heart, here in this scar o'er my womb, and here in each of these scars upon my thighs. I have seen madness in the eyes of the man who did this, a mon who could speak of love as he inflicted pain. I have felt the chill of madness as I heard each word he said as he strung me up like a fresh kill and tried to decide where to leave his mark next, as he prepared himself to rape me. I have been dealing with madness for almost two years now so dinnae tell me I dinnae understand what it is.

"Your father isnae mad. He is a spoiled, selfish mon, one so arrogant it makes one's eyes cross, but he isnae mad. He doesnae have fits or spells, he has tantrums. The only thing wrong with your father is that he doesnae care for anyone or anything, only for what he wants."

She flopped down on her back and covered her eyes with her arm, fighting back tears. There was some comfort in the knowledge that Ewan had not been rejecting her when he had denied her his seed, but himself. He thought his blood was tainted by madness. It would take a while for reason to soothe the hurt she had suffered, however.

Ewan cautiously slipped his arm around her small waist and pulled her up against him. Her words had chilled him to the bone. She had told him about Menzies's pursuit, and how the man had captured her four times, but he had never really considered how it must have been for her, how the man had actually put the marks upon her lovely skin. She was right. There was madness, pure and terrifying. Although he was not quite ready to accept that there was not some hint of madness in his father, he knew there was none of the sort of poison she had dealt with for far too long.

The hurt he had seen in her face when she had realized he had denied her his seed still pained him. To his shame, it also pleased him, stroked what little vanity he had. Fiona wanted to bear his child, had been devastated by the thought that he would deny her that chance. The thought of Fiona growing round with his child was a sweet, heady one, despite his fears about childbirth. Ewan was just not sure he dared gamble on her being right about his father.

"Fiona," he said as he nuzzled his face into her thick, tossled hair, "I couldnae taint your womb with the blood of a madmon."

Sighing, she pulled her arm away from her eyes and looked at him. "Your father isnae mad, Ewan."

"He sees enemies everywhere. His moods can change in a heartbeat. He can be in a rage one moment, then in the blink of an eye, be thinking of naught but how to lift some woman's skirts. That isnae the way a grown mon, a laird, should behave."

"Nay, it isnae," she agreed, "but it isnae madness, either. If he sees enemies around every corner, 'tis probably because they are there and he kens he put them there." She took a deep breath, reminding herself that they spoke of his father and that Ewan's fear of madness was real. "Try, for but a moment, to think of your father not as a grown mon and your sire, but just as some small child."

Ewan was a little dismayed at how easy that was to do, and he realized he often thought of his father as childish. "I will confess that he often acts as if he forgot to grow up, to accept the responsibilities of a mon."

"That is because he did. Everything I have seen that mon do or say is, weel, much like a child, a verra spoiled child. Someone neglected to teach him how to behave or he refused to heed his lessons. He wants what he wants when he wants it, just like a child. He gives no thought to consequences or the future, just like a child. He becomes enraged when denied, just like a child. He leaps from interest to interest, just like a child. In truth, about the only differences I can see between your father and a spoiled child are that he can make bairns and, because of his size, he could hurt or kill someone whilst having one of his tantrums." She frowned. "Has he hurt or killed someone whilst in a rage?"

It took a moment before Ewan could reply because he had to think back a very long way. "He can be bloodthirsty in battle, but nay, I can recall no time when he killed anyone whilst in a rage. Dealt out a few bruises if one didnae get out of the way fast enough, but he usually just rants, tosses out a few bloodcurdling curses, and occasionally breaks things. He has ordered us to do some rather cruel things to people he was angry with, but we didnae do it."

"And I would guess that he didnae punish ye for disobeying him, either."

"Nay. He seemed to forget that he had given such an order."

"Has he e'er raped a woman who told him nay?"

"Nay, although he is verra angry that ye have taught the women here to do so," he replied, smiling a little.

"And yet, here I am, unpunished and unbruised."

Ewan blinked and stared at her. Even warning himself that he should not allow his own hopes to steer his beliefs, he could not deny the truth she was showing him. The more he thought of his father as a spoiled child, the more he saw that Fiona was right. His father might not be exactly *right*, but he was not mad.

"He isnae mad," Ewan whispered.

"Nay," replied Fiona, feeling a pang of sympathy for the torment Ewan must have suffered over the years.

"He *is* naught but a spoiled child in a mon's body."

"Aye, I fear so. Think, Ewan, if your father was mad, if it was something in the blood, surely that madness would have appeared in at least one of the dozens of children he has bred, or in one of your brother's children. It hasnae, has it?"

"Nay." Ewan dragged his hand through his hair. "For so long I have feared there was madness in the blood, 'tis difficult to accept that I was wrong."

"Aye, ye were." She met his scowl with a soft smile.

"I wasnae the only one who feared it."

"Och, nay, I am certain many another wondered on it. Tis probably why some whisper that he killed his wives. Tis difficult to accept that a grown mon would act as he does. He is big, strong, and virile so one doesnae look for the child who still lives in the mon."

"So, he doesnae need to be locked in the tower. He needs his backside walloped."

Fiona giggled at the image of Ewan paddling his father's backside. "Too late, I fear. Just be glad he was willing to let ye take the reins."

Ewan sighed. "I suspicion he simply grew tired of that game. E'en he could see that hard work was needed, if only to fix all he had set wrong and he didnae want to do it. His vanity was stung for he liked being the laird, but when everyone still called him that, he was fine. Nay too fond of the *old* they put in front of the title, but he pays no heed to it now."

Fiona slowly ran her hand down the side of his body to caress his hip and felt him tremble slightly. "At least he no longer rules, making new enemies for ye to deal with." She watched his stormy gray eyes darken as she stroked his thigh. "And, I think, he has just given ye leave to accept the Camerons."

It took Ewan a moment to clear the encroaching fog of desire from his brain and consider her words. "Aye, I think he has. He didnae say I couldnae, did he? He just said he wouldnae have aught to do with them. Allies," he whispered, savoring the sweetness of the word and the hope it carried for the future.

"Sigimor will make a strong ally. Tis odd that he and his family are all so red and ye and yours are all so dark."

"Different mothers. My father was born of a second wife, Sigimor's of the first. My grandsire was red-haired. All of my father's wives were dark haired, all of his brother's wives had red or fair hair. We bred it out. They bred it in." He frowned at her, recalling that Sigimor looked to be a big, strong, handsome man. "Do ye ken Sigimor weel?"

"Nay verra weel. My brother wed his sister but a year ago and I have spent a great deal of that time cowering behind the walls of Deilcladach."

"To keep oneself safe whilst hunting a madmon isnae cowering."

"Mayhap, but there were times when it truly was cowering. After each attack it would take a while for the fear to ease."

"I am nay surprised. I will kill him for ye," Ewan vowed, meaning every word of the promise.

"Thank ye," Fiona whispered, smiling faintly.

Ewan sucked in a breath through clenched teeth when she began to caress his stomach. He felt himself grow hard as he stared down at her small, pale hand moving over his dark, scarred skin. Even Helena's practiced touch had not stirred him so completely. The need Fiona bred inside him was deep and greedy. It was not going to be easy to savor the passion while sheltering heart and soul, but he would try. The safest thing for him to do would be to turn away from her completely, but he knew he could never resist another taste of the passion they shared. He had been right to think that once he got her into his bed, he would never let her leave it.

"Touch me," he ordered, not surprised to hear the hoarse tone of his voice for he was nearly desperate to feel those long, delicate fingers stroke him.

Fiona curled her hand around his erection. He was hot, hard yet silken soft at the same time. She watched him as she caressed him. His eyes were almost closed, but his gaze was fixed upon her hand. A light flush rode high on his cheekbones and his breathing was slightly unsteady. There was so much passion in the man yet he kept a tight rein on it. Although she understood what made him do so, she was determined to free him of those restraints, if only here in their bed. She slid her hand between his legs to stroke the sack hanging there and, an instant later, found herself on her back with Ewan crouched over her.

"I made ye yell, but then I ruined it," he said as he fought to regain a little control over his desire.

"Ah, weel, I wouldnae say it was ruined. Dimmed a wee bit, mayhap, once I realized what ye had done."

"It wasnae because of ye," he began, but she touched his lips with her fingers and silenced him.

"I ken it. I want your child, if God in His grace blesses us with one. Tis true, I dinnae wish to bear a child a year like some ewe, but Lady Maldie showed me a way to prevent that."

"So I wouldnae have to pull away?"

She almost smiled at the delight he could not fully hide. "Aye. What I ken will work just as weel."

"Then use it as ye wish, but if it fails too often, I will practice restraint. I have seen too many women sent to their graves worn out by constant child-bearing. Ye willnae be one of them." He kissed her, pleased beyond words by the dazed look she wore when he ended the kiss. "And now I will make ye yell again."

"Mayhap I will make ye yell," she said.

"Nay doubt ye will though I doubt 'twill be heard above your screams of pleasure."

Before she could respond to that teasing arrogance, he kissed her again and she was soon caught firmly in the grip of the passion he roused within her. She readily gave herself over to the sweet bliss he inspired with every kiss, every caress. As she felt her release tear through her, she heard herself loudly call out his name. It only enhanced her pleasure when she felt him bury himself deep inside her body and heat her womb with his seed as he bellowed out her name.

"I think ye were louder," she murmured later as, after they had washed away the remnants of their passion, she curled up against his side and rested her head against his chest.

"Nay, 'twas but a whisper compared to the noise ye made," Ewan said.

He grinned when her only response was a soft grunt before her body slackened in sleep against his. Ewan could not help but feel a pinch of male pride over how he had obviously exhausted her. And made her yell, he thought, grinning even wider. There was pure delight to be found in hearing a woman cry out his name as she shivered with passion.

The fact that Fiona found pleasure in his arms amazed him, yet he could no longer doubt that she did. He found he had no doubt about the honesty of that passion, either. Over the years he had seen enough of false passion, in the beds of the village whores and in Helena's arms, to recognize the difference. He could even feel the difference in the way Fiona moved, in the look upon her face, in the sounds she made, and even in the way her body held his deep within hers when her release swept over her. For some reason Fiona's desire was stirred by his touch and he was humbled by that gift.

Ewan idly combed his fingers through her thick hair, enjoying the feel of her soft, slender body so close to his, and the lingering warmth of sated desire. He had finally heard a woman cry out his name as his touch brought her to that sublime peak of pleasure, and he knew he would be greedy to hear it again and again. Big, dark, and scarred though he was, he could make the small, lovely Fiona scream. It was enough to make him vain, he mused as he pressed a kiss to the top of her head.

He felt almost cheerful, light of heart and mind. Some of that was due to the fact that he no longer feared madness lurked in his blood. It was embarrassing to have a father who was more a child than a man, but that was a great deal easier to accept than madness. Fiona had given him that gift, too, and his gratitude ran deep. He had not wanted a wife, but after only one night as Fiona's husband, he was glad that he had married her.

The only shadow on the horizon was that he knew it would be easy to love her. A part of him wanted to, wanted to place heart and soul into her small hands and trust her to treat them well. Ewan knew it was cowardly, perhaps even unfair to Fiona, but he could not bring himself to do that. Years of protecting himself from feeling too deeply, trusting too much, were not so easily cast aside. He found it somewhat amusing, in a sad way, that he who could endure wounds to his body yet never shy from battle could cower so at the thought of a wound to his heart.

Wrapping his arms around his slender wife, he rested his cheek against her hair and sighed as he closed his eyes. Ewan greatly feared that she was already holding his heart in her small hands despite how hard he tried to fight her allure. He could only hope that he had the strength of will to keep her from knowing it.

Chapter 12

"A cursed Cameron in my house," grumbled Sir Fingal. "I ne'er thought I would see the day."

Fiona rolled her eyes as she sat down across from him at the laird's table. She had faced the morning with a smile, her body still warmed by Ewan's loving, and her appetite keen. After a bath, she had made her way to the great hall to break her fast. Even the sight of Ewan's father seated at that table had not dimmed her good mood. Unfortunately, he had spoken to her and Fiona wondered how long it would be before he soured her mood. In the two weeks she had been Ewan's wife, Sir Fingal had revealed a true skill for making her angry.

"I am nay a Cameron," she said for what she felt had to be the thousandth time. "I am a MacEnroy by blood. I am a Cameron only by marriage." She filled a bowl with porridge and poured a little dark honey on it.

"Ye are a MacFingal by marriage."

"Fine. I am a MacFingal. That still means I am nay a Cameron, doesnae it?"

"What ye are is an insolent lass."

"Aye, I am." She began to eat her porridge, disappointed to see that Sir Fingal had obviously not finished his meal and so would be her companion for a while yet.

"My son needs to take a firmer hand with ye." Sir Fingal filled a large bowl with porridge and smothered it in honey. "Ye need him to teach ye respect and obedience. Ye need to be brought to heel."

"I should like to see him try," she muttered.

Sir Fingal shook his head as he shoved a piece of bread into his mouth. "Weel, at least ye serve some purpose. Ewan isnae behaving anymore as if he doesnae ken what a mon's parts are for. Ye may be able to give him a few sons, though ye look too thin and small. And ye have reminded me why I havenae taken another wife."

"Ye havenae taken another wife because ye are still married to the one who fled from here." She could tell by the brief look of confusion on the man's face that he had completely forgotten the woman.

"Och, aye, *her.* Faithless bitch," he grumbled. "She only gave me one son, then betrayed me with a cursed Gray."

Since pointing out to Sir Fingal that his complaining about another's faithlessness was the height of hypocrisy would be a complete waste of time, Fiona ignored his words. "Another son, eh? Did ye ne'er breed a lass or two?"

"Aye, three. I wed one to a Guthrie and one to

Kinnaird. Thought it would gain us an alliance or two, but nay, the lasses were quick to stand with their husbands against their own father. One wee mistake and all my hard work was for naught. The other lass ran off with a Gray. Women always betray a mon in the end, e'en when that mon is their own loving father." He sniffed and looked near to tears.

Fiona snorted with contempt over that show of an emotion she knew was utterly false and was not surprised when he was quickly glaring at her again. She hoped the daughters' husbands had proven to be better men than their father. She also sincerely doubted it was only one wee mistake that had ended an alliance sealed with a marriage. Since it was doubtful Sir Fingal would tell the truth, she did not bother to ask what that wee mistake had been. There was little doubt in her mind, however, that those marriages were helping Ewan mend some of the damage his father had done. Unfortunately, there had been no marriage between a Gray and a MacFingal. Just a lot of seduction or poaching of the MacFingal women.

"Why do the Grays keep taking your women?" she asked.

"They dinnae have many of their own," replied Mab as she sat down next to Fiona and helped herself to some porridge. "They have a lot of enemies, too. One of those enemies got into their keep when the men were nearly all absent, oh, near to fifteen years ago it was. They were brutal." Mab shivered. "They killed old and young, mon, woman, and bairn. Verra few escaped and, praise God, most of them were the bairns. Some women were taken, but I dinnae think they were e'er reclaimed."

"So the bastards go about helping themselves to everyone else's lassies," added Fingal.

"Aye," agreed Mab. "They have become quite notorious for that."

Sir Fingal nodded and looked hard at Fiona. "So ye best keep yourself within these walls." He stood up and started to walk away. "Ye may be all bone and scars, but a Gray cannae be too particular."

Fiona glared after the man, strongly tempted to go and kick him. "That mon is enough to make a lass want to scream and tear out her hair," Fiona muttered, then noticed that Mab was looking at her a little oddly. "Do I have porridge stuck between my teeth?"

Mab smiled and shook her head. "Nay, 'tis just that, weel, I think the old laird is growing fond of ye, as fond as he e'er feels about anyone."

"Fond? The mon does naught but glare at me, grumble, and insult me. That is fond?"

"He talks to ye, Fiona, almost as he talks to the lads. Fingal doesnae talk to women that way."

"He talks to ye much the same as he talks to me," Fiona said even as she realized that Mab was right in a way, that Sir Fingal did not speak to women as he did to men.

"Why so he does. It must be because I have been here for a long time and have nursed him through a few wounds and injuries. Tis different from how he speaks to the other women, though. With the other women he either tells them what to do, ignores them, or tries to flatter them out of their shifts. I sometimes think he doesnae e'en ken most of their names. At least, not unless he wants something. Then he recalls it or just calls the woman lass or wench."

"I am nay sure I want ye to start me thinking that there is more to the mon than I had thought."

"That *would* take some getting accustomed to, but I begin to wonder if there just might be a bit of depth to the old fool. Nay much, but a wee bit. He does have feelings for his sons."

"Nay, I saw how he was when Simon was wounded. He didnae blink an eye when he thought the lad was dead or ask about his wounds when he found out the boy wasnae dead after all."

"Of course he didnae. Ye were standing there with all the men. Fingal couldnae show any feeling o'er one of the lads there. But he did go to Simon each day whilst the lad was healing, to tell him wild tales or read to him. He also visited Ewan whilst he was healing. I thought on it and realized he always comes to see the lads if they are sick or injured. I discovered he visits the young ones, as weel, his own and his sons' bairns. Then there is the fact that he provides for every child he has sired. Two of his children died and he visits their graves every sennight."

Fiona was a little shocked. That did seem to indicate that Fingal had some glimmer of affection for the children he bred so recklessly. It would explain why none of his sons seemed to dislike him or hold any anger or resentment toward him. That would also imply that, despite the man's weaknesses and oddities, he had formed some sort of bond with his children.

"Does he ken the names of all his children?" Fiona asked.

Mab nodded. "All their names and all their ages. He isnae always sure who their mothers were, though."

That was very telling, Fiona mused as she took a drink of cool cider. Sir Fingal might not be a very good father and was an abysmal laird, but perhaps he was not as thoroughly bad as she had first thought. Of course, the fact that he had some trouble remembering the mothers of the children did not surprise her and suited the man she had thought him to be. His opinion of women was so low, it was appalling. Despite that, she knew she would be studying the man more closely now. A man who could recall the names and ages of so many children could not be all bad, could he?

As she and Mab finished their meal, they decided it was a good day to do some work in the garden. Fiona had discovered a true love for working in the garden. She had tended herb gardens before, but it was the flowers which interested her more. It was a little strange to find such an elaborate garden within such a formidable keep, especially one filled with big, dark, somewhat rough men, but they had given Mab free rein. And Mab had created a haven of beauty, Fiona thought as she moved amongst the flowers, pulling weeds.

As she worked, Fiona wondered what to do about her husband. The passion they shared was sweet and hot. They indulged themselves like greedy children every night and, often, in the morning as well. It would be easy enough to simply hold fast to that and leave matters well enough alone. Fiona suspected there were a lot of wives out there who would fall to their knees and offer up fulsome prayers of gratitude if their husbands could give them the bliss Ewan gave to her. It seemed selfish to want more, but she did.

What she wanted was love, she thought as she began to trim a wildly growing honeysuckle vine. She loved Ewan with everything in her and she wanted him to love her back. Naively, she had thought that, loving him as she did, he simply *had* to love her back. She had also felt that love had to lurk beneath all that fierce passion. That, too, had been naive, for it was well known that a man's passion could be a thing apart from love, or even the mildest of affection. It had taken her two weeks to wake up to the useless foolishness of that blind naiveté, but now she had.

The problem was, she did not know what to do now, or even if there was anything she *could* do. He was not cold toward her during the day, but there seemed to be a wall between them that she could not break through. Despite the passion they shared, once Ewan left their bed, he became the man he had been before they had become lovers. The only thing he no longer did was run away, at least not so obviously. He did not make her a part of his life in any real way, either. More and more she was beginning to feel as if she was nothing more to him than the woman who warmed his bed and could give him legitimate children. That was starting to stir up some very bad feelings inside her. She was beginning to feel more like his leman than his wife. Somehow she had to change that, for it was a wound to her heart that would certainly fester over time, producing bile and bitterness.

Hunger finally pulled her from her thoughts and

the garden. Mab had already left to visit a woman in the village who was about to bear a child. Feeling oddly alone despite all the people around her, Fiona made her way to her bedchamber, pausing on the way to ask for a bath to be prepared. She actually missed Nathan following her everywhere. And that, she mused, was a rather sad indication of the troubled state of her marriage.

Once the bath was prepared, Fiona sank down into the hot water and sighed with pleasure. Lost in her thoughts about Ewan and their marriage, she had worked a little too long and too hard in the garden. She rested her head against the rim of the bath and let the heat of the water soothe the various aches in her body. Closing her eyes, she sleepily wished a hot bath could also soothe the aches in her heart.

Ewan stepped into his bedchamber and stopped abruptly, his gaze fixed upon Fiona sleeping in her bath. Never taking his gaze from her slender form, he shut the door and latched it. He had just come from a quick swim in the river to wash away the sweat and dust of training the men and was seeking a clean shirt. The shirt could wait, he decided as he strode over to stand by the side of the tub.

Jesu, but she was beautiful, he thought as he stared down at Fiona. They had been married for two weeks and he still felt a tightening in his gut when he looked at her. There were far too many times during the day when he wanted to see her, talk to her, reassure himself that she was still there, but he always fought the urge. Trotting about after his wife like an unweened pup after his dam was no way for a grown man to act. It was certainly not dignified or restrained. If he chased her down to make love to her as often as he thought about it, he would be showing no control at all.

It was because it was all so new to him, he told himself as he knelt by the tub. He had never had such a beautiful woman welcome him into her arms and turn to sweet fire at his touch. Helena had been beautiful, but her warmth had been a lie, her welcome a trap. As he picked up the washing cloth and soap, he realized he could no longer make himself doubt Fiona's passion, but that only increased his astonishment.

He began to bathe her, starting at her small, rather pretty feet. Ewan smiled as a frown crossed her sleeping face and she muttered something. He had finished washing her legs and had begun to wash her left arm before she opened her eyes. The blush that colored her cheeks made him chuckle.

"Ewan," Fiona protested, "I can bathe myself now."

"Nay, I am enjoying this," he said as he began to wash her breasts. "Ye shouldnae sleep in your bath, Fiona. Ye could drown." Tossing aside the cloth, he soaped up his hands and returned to washing her breasts.

"I think they are clean now." Fiona was not surprised to hear a slight tremor in her voice for her desire was stirred by his touch. "I also think ye are doing a wee bit more than giving me a bath."

"Aye, I am, but be kind to your husband and let him finish his wee game. I have ne'er assisted a lass in her bath."

That statement silenced Fiona's last protest over

the intimacy. The idea of sharing something with Ewan that he had never shared with any other woman was too tempting to resist. As she banished the embarrassment she felt, the desire that had been stirring within her broke free. Then he slid one wet, soapy hand between her legs and she lost all ability to think, wantonly giving herself up to the searing pleasure of his touch.

Still tingling slightly from the pleasure of her release, Fiona peered at her husband through her lashes. He was wearing that faintly smug look again, the one she was beginning to see as a challenge. He was also looking highly aroused, proof that he could not touch her so without stirring his own desire. It was the only thing that kept her from wanting to slap that cocky look right off his handsome face. That left him open for an exquisite sort of revenge.

Fiona slowly stood up and watched Ewan swallow, hard. She smiled sweetly as she stepped out of the bath and murmured her gratitude when he quickly wrapped her up in the drying cloth. For some reason Ewan was not acting upon his obvious desire for her. Fiona did not ask why, suspecting she might not like his answer or would not understand it. Instinct suggested he was restricting their lovemaking to the night with an occasional tryst in the morning before he left their bed in order to maintain some sort of distance between them. He might even think making love to his wife in the middle of the day would shock her. Fiona was more than willing to disabuse him of that latter thought. The interlude in the bath had been exciting and satisfying, but not nearly as much so as feeling

Ewan's strong body joined with hers as ecstasy conquered them both.

Making no effort to hide her body, Fiona began to dry herself. Bending over, twisting her body about, and rubbing herself with the cloth, she hoped she was enticing Ewan. If his increasingly heavy breathing was any indication, she was succeeding despite her ignorance of the art of seduction. It amazed her a little that she was so wantonly displaying herself, but decided that a fortnight of enjoying Ewan's passion had made her far less concerned about her scars than she had been in the beginning.

"Fiona," Ewan said, vainly trying to clear the huskiness from his voice, "what are ye doing?"

"Drying myself," she replied, looking him over and pleased to see that he wore only his breeches, obviously having returned to their bedchamber to retrieve some clean clothes after washing away the dust of his morning's labor. "Taunting ye." She reached out to lightly stroke his erection. "Tis working, I think."

"Tis the middle of the day."

After glancing at the sun shining through the small window, Fiona smiled at him as she unlaced his breeches. "How perspicacious of ye, husband."

"Ladies dinnae care for a romp in the middle of the day."

Since he made no move to stop her, despite his words, Fiona tugged his breeches down. "Now, our Gilly ne'er told me that particular rule." She knelt before him and finished removing his short boots and breeches. "In truth, I do believe she and Connor were ne'er so constrained."

Ewan stared down at Fiona kneeling at his feet.

It was a sight that rent what little control he had regained after feeling her shatter beneath his touch. He trembled as she kissed the insides of his thighs while she stroked his hips with her hands. The way her soft hair brushed against him made the blood pound in his veins. When she placed her warm, soft lips against his aching manhood, he cried out in startled delight and a touch of shock.

"What are ye doing?" he demanded, thinking it a particularly stupid question even as he asked it, yet unable to believe that his delicate wife was planning to do something he had heard of but never dared ask for.

"I would have thought that was obvious."

"If 'tis what I am thinking of—but nay, ye couldnae ken about that."

"Our Gilly told me a great many things about what can occur between a mon and a woman."

Since she interspersed her words with kisses and slow strokes of her tongue, Ewan had to struggle fiercely to keep enough of his wits clear to continue the conversation. "She told ye about such intimacies?"

"Aye. Her cousins told her many things and she said the knowledge made it much easier to go from maid to wife. Dinnae ye like it?" She decided the hoarse groan that escaped him as she licked him was as good as an *aye,* then she kissed the scar that ran so dangerously close to his manhood. "I am so verra glad ye were rescued ere your enemies could carry out their threat."

"Ye cannae be any happier about it than I am."

"Mayhap we can agree to be equally pleased. I have certainly appreciated the stout lad, and mayhap 'tis time I gave him a wee reward for being so verra kind to me."

Ewan opened his mouth to tell her she was the one who deserved a reward for gifting him with her passion. The words he began to speak turned into a strange mixture of a gasp and a groan when she took him into the warmth of her mouth. He shuddered and threaded his fingers through her hair, blindly holding her in place even though she showed no inclination to retreat.

Despite all his efforts, despite all his years of practice in keeping a firm control of himself, Ewan knew he could not savor this delight for long. He watched her pleasure him until he feared his trembling legs would no longer hold him up. Briefly, he considered allowing himself the full measure of this ecstasy, then decided he dared not test her so. She might have knowledge, but she had no experience save what he had given her, and that could make her reluctant to gift him with this joy again.

Cursing softly, he grasped her beneath her arms, picked her up, and nearly ran to the bed. He dropped her on top of it, savoring her husky laugh as he threw himself on top of her. Ewan slipped a shaking hand between her legs and nearly prayed aloud in thanks when he found her ready for him. The fact that she had been aroused by loving him touched him in ways he dared not examine too closely. He kissed her even as he buried himself deep within her, determined to cling to the frayed threads of his control long enough to give her pleasure. To his relief and astonishment, it took very little time to fulfill that promise. The moment he felt Fiona's slim body tighten around his, he gave himself over to his own need, his release and joyous cry blending perfectly with hers.

Fiona clung to Ewan when he collapsed in her arms. Her whole body still trembled from the strength of her release. It pleased her that his did as well. How could he not see how perfectly they were matched, she wondered as she combed her fingers through his hair. Even if, in his man's mind, he did not connect passion with love, he had to recognize that what they shared was unique. It might simply require more time, she mused, but she was growing impatient and she was afraid that impatience might cause her to do things that would push him away instead of pulling him closer.

Ewan raised himself up on his forearms and brushed a kiss over her mouth. He felt overwhelmed, uncertain of what to do or say. Despite having softened, he enjoyed the feeling of being inside her for a moment longer, then eased away, rolling onto his side. When he saw the blush upon Fiona's cheeks and the way she cautiously eyed him, he began to relax. She was as uncertain as he was.

"Does your brother ken what sort of things his wife was teaching ye?" he asked, breathing an inner sigh of relief when, after a brief hesitation, she smiled at him.

"She told me a great many things," Fiona replied, "and if Connor kenned it, he did naught about it. Do ye object to your wife kenning a wee bit about such matters?"

"If I object, ye will cease, and I am nay such a fool as all that." He kissed her again and got out of bed. "Mayhap I need to be taught a few lessons," he said, winking at her as he began to dress. "I think I may have a few ill-informed ideas of what a lady wife should be and do."

"Ye couldnae have any stranger ideas than my brother did." Fiona slid out of bed and hurried to don her shift, suddenly a little too aware of her nudity. "He was fed lies all his life by our traitorous uncle, a mon who plotted the death of our whole family, who kept the feuds alive to do his killing for him, and who e'en tried to kill our Gilly." Seeing the curiosity on Ewan's face, she told him all about her uncle's treachery as she continued to get dressed. "It took our Gilly's arrival at Deilcladach to expose our uncle's vicious perfidy."

Ewan was so shocked by her tale, he silently tugged on his boots, and went to hold her in his arms. The thought of what her uncle had done, how he might have succeeded in his aim to see all his brother's family dead and buried if not for the stubborn courage of her brother, chilled him. He knew that the tale troubled him so deeply because, for a brief moment, he had considered what his life would be without her. Ewan was glad he had never plagued her with his suspicions about her. After what she had suffered, he suspected his doubts about her would have deeply insulted her.

"He is dead now," he said, responding to the touch of fear he had heard in her voice as she had told her story.

"Aye, murdered by my brother's whore." She tried not to see his impulsive embrace as any more than it was, a comfort offered for the hurt and fear roused by old memories.

"Your brother kept his whore close at hand after he was married?"

The shock on Ewan's face pleased her. She might be slow in discovering much about the man and his feelings, but she could count upon his faithfulness as she tried to puzzle him out.

"Aye and nay. She abided close by, but ne'er in his bed again. She was hanged once Gilly proved Connor didnae kill our uncle, that whore did."

"Such support from a wife is a good thing," Ewan said as he took her by the hand and started to lead her out of their bedchamber. "Tis her duty, but 'tis far sweeter when given freely. That stands true of all else, too."

And that, Fiona decided as he towed her down to the great hall, was probably the only compliment she was likely to get. When he ended those words with a light squeeze of her hand, which made her heart pinch with pleasure, she inwardly shook her head. It was going to be difficult to lead her husband down the path she wanted him to go if she could be so easily pleased. Unfortunately, she could no more tame her heart than she could her desire for him. Her goal to win his heart was obviously going to require a great deal more planning to reach.

Chapter 13

"Hmmm."

"Hmmm?" Fiona had to smile, for Mab looked at the moss by the tree as if it carried the secret of the Holy Grail. "Only a hmmm? And is it a hmmm of disapproval or one of questioning whether we need moss at all?"

Mab put her hands on her well-rounded hips and gave Fiona a falsely stern look. "Tis a hmmm that asks if I want this moss which looks badly trod upon and has a great many ants."

"The ants would certainly cause me to hesitate."

"Ye are in a verra lighthearted mood today," Mab said as she moved toward another clump of moss. "I must assume that all goes weel with your husband. Ah, good. Nary a single ant."

"Weel enough," Fiona replied as she knelt to help Mab collect some of the moss.

"After three weeks all ye can say is weel enough? Tis what ye wanted, isnae it?"

Fiona sighed, feeling her good humor wane a little. About the only change Fiona had seen in the week since Ewan had so delightfully interrupted her bath was that he had appeared once or twice during the day and made love to her. While it was true that he no longer remained almost completely unseen all day long, this was not the change she had been hoping for. It did mean there were a few more minutes of conversation between them, if only as they put their clothes back on, but she was the one revealing things about herself, not him.

"Tis what I wanted," she replied. "Tis *still* what I want. The trouble is, 'tisnae yet *all* I want."

"Ah." Mab nodded. "No love words, no whispered confidences. Ye meet in the bedchamber and make love and nay more than that. I assume *that* is fine, aye?"

"Och, aye, verra fine." Fiona kept her gaze upon the ground, looking for useful plants and hiding her embarrassment over the subject. Only Mab's practical tone of voice made her willing to even attempt such a discussion. "He does desire me. I have nary a doubt about that now. S'truth, he makes me feel beautiful."

"Tis no small thing that." Mab carefully inspected a low-growing plant, then shook her head as she muttered, "Too soon to gather it." She looked back at Fiona. "Many a wife would be happy with a lusty mon, one who holds fast to his vows and makes her feel beautiful."

Fiona grimaced even as she took note of the place where another useful plant grew so that she could find it again when it was time to gather it. "I ken it and I feel most selfish and ungrateful when

I find myself yearning for more. That doesnae stop me from doing so, however. I love him and I want him to love me," she frowned, "although there are days when I wonder why." She smiled when Mab giggled, then she sighed. "I want to be more to him than the woman who warms his bed and gives him daughters."

Mab stopped, frowned, and looked at Fiona. "MacFingals breed sons."

"I intend to break with that tradition. Weel, at least once."

"I see. Weel, it would be verra nice to have a wee lass about, but MacFingals breed sons. Scarglas fair swarms with the laddies. And ye have five brothers. Of course, Fingal did have three daughters."

"Aye, and my parents bore me. Our Gilly has given Connor a lass, too, and she feels the one she will bear next will be a lass." Fiona smiled a little when Mab looked confused. "Gilly can sometimes ken things. Her strongest gift is kenning how people feel, but now and again, 'tis as if she has a vision. She is certain that her next bairn will be a lass. I often wish she was here so that she could meet Ewan. She might be able to tell me why he holds himself away from me in so many ways. Och, weel, there are some people she cannae see into the heart of, such as my brother. I suspicion Ewan would be of his ilk."

"Ewan does keep his thoughts and feelings to himself. A quiet, restrained mon. A good laird." Mab turned to the east. "There is a small burn o'er this way. We may find some useful things there."

"There is a fair crop of thistles growing here," said Fiona as she followed Mab.

"Good, good. I think Ewan has lost too many people."

It took Fiona a moment to realize Mab had changed the subject, bringing it back to Ewan and Fiona's troubles with him. "What do ye mean *lost?*"

"His mother and three other women he was young enough to see as mothers. Fingal's last wife came when Ewan was too old and too hardened to seek a mother again. He cared for his sisters and they are now gone away. Then there was Helena. I think he reached for her, opened his heart a wee bit, and her betrayal cut him deeply."

"I am *not* Helena and I shouldnae be made to suffer for her crimes."

"Nay, ye shouldnae, but I fear ye must. At least for a wee while."

"Do ye think Ewan expects me to betray him?"

"Nay, I dinnae think so, but mayhap that alone troubles him. Then again, I am nay sure he trusts in the fact that ye are his, his wife, and that ye enjoy sharing his bed. Ewan has ne'er been the first choice of the lasses around Scarglas. That became e'en more true when his face was scarred."

"Weel, I dinnae understand it. He is strong, weel formed, and that scar doesnae twist his features, simply mars the skin." Fiona realized she was insulted on Ewan's behalf and nearly smiled. She was glad he had not known a lot of women, but obviously felt he should have been seen as worthy of their notice. "Tis probably because he isnae verra good at the wooing game."

"And ye want to be wooed?"

"Nay, I dinnae mind that lack. His words may nay be as sweet as what Gregor can spout, but Ewan has said things that please me. Tis just that I wish to be a true part of his life, to ken his thoughts, his plans, his feelings. He shares his body and his passion with me, but little else. I want him to love me as I love him, yet if he keeps this distance between us, I can ne'er reach his heart, can I?"

"Give it time, lass. Ewan has had nine-and-twenty years to build that wall round his heart, to grow into the mon he is now. Ye cannae expect him to change in but a month. Just keep reminding yourself that ye are the first lass he couldnae keep his hands off of, the first he pulled into his bed. Not e'en Helena could do that. She had to seduce him and it took more for her to do so than to just stand within his reach."

That reminder cheered Fiona immensely. She was just about to thank Mab for that when they stepped out into a small clearing. A carpet of violets was spread out before them, and the beauty of the sight pushed Ewan from her mind for the moment.

"We could make some lovely soaps," murmured Fiona.

"And scents," agreed Mab.

"Our basket isnae big enough and we could do with some help." Fiona realized Mab was not listening to her and had grown very tense. "Mab?"

"Someone comes," Mab whispered and slowly turned to look behind her.

Although she told herself it was foolish to be afraid, Fiona could not completely banish the flicker of alarm she felt. She had heard nothing, and even if someone was coming, it could easily be one of the MacFingals. Just as she turned to look in the direction Mab did, seven horsemen slowly rode out of the concealing shadows of the trees. When Fiona saw the man who rode a little to the fore of the others, her blood chilled so swiftly, she shuddered almost painfully.

"Greetings, my love," drawled the man, a cold smile curving his sensuous lips.

"Menzies," Fiona whispered as she struggled to shake free of the tight grip of fear. "When I say so, Mab, ye must run, verra fast, to the right of these swine," she told her friend in as soft a whisper as she could as she kept her gaze fixed upon the very handsome and very mad Sir Ranald Menzies. "Run. Now."

Fiona bolted to the left and was pleased to see Mab immediately bolt to the right. Her heart in her throat, Fiona ran as fast as she could, forcing aside all urge to see how Mab fared. She hoped Mab could hold to the same discipline. When she heard Menzies shouting and the sound of pursuit, Fiona tried to reach the cover of the trees. In the wood the men on horseback would be at a disadvantage. One of Menzies's men moved to block the way, however.

Cursing viciously, Fiona tried to elude the grasp of the men chasing her. She closed her ears to the voice in her head that kept saying it was a fight that was already lost. Suddenly, she saw an opening to the woods and she ran toward it. The curses of her pursuers told her that she actually had a chance of making it.

"Fiona! Ye had best stop! Now!"

Something in the way Menzies bellowed his command, the smug amusement behind his words, caused Fiona to halt. The fact that the men chasing her had already halted struck her as ominous indeed. Even as her mind ordered her to keep running, to complete her bid for freedom, she turned to face Menzies. Her heart sank into her boots when she saw Mab's squirming shape draped over Menzies's saddle.

"Let her go, Menzies," Fiona said. "She is of no use to you."

"Isnae she?" Menzies grabbed Mab by the hair, stilling her movements, and held a dagger to the side of her bared neck. "I think the cow might serve some purpose."

"Hurting Mab will bring the wrath of the Mac-Fingals down upon your head. She is verra important to them."

"Thus they allow her to roam about with only ye as her protector? And an unarmed ye, as weel, by the look of it. Threatening me with the wrath of such as the MacFingals, madmen and women-killers, isnae going to work, either. Do ye think they will use their witch's lore to bespell me?" Menzies laughed and his men dutifully did the same.

There was no way out of this trap, Fiona realized. Mab was staring at her and making little motions with her hands that told Fiona to flee. If Mab thought she would leave her in that madman's hands, then the woman was as insane as Menzies was. Fiona knew he would kill Mab just to spite her. Menzies knew he had her, knew she would never trade the woman's life for her own freedom. The gloating look upon his face made her wish dearly that she could be just so coldhearted.

"Release her, Menzies," she ordered again in a

cold, hard voice, determined to hide her fear of the man.

"Only if ye agree to come to me," Menzies said.

"I agree," Fiona replied and ignored Mab's muttered protest.

Then, to Fiona's utter horror, Menzies drew his knife across Mab's throat and tossed her body to the ground. Fiona screamed out a curse and pulled a knife from her sleeve, but one of the men grabbed her before she could bury it in Menzies's chest. Try as she might, there was no breaking free of the man's grasp. When he roughly turned her to face him, she watched him draw back his fist. An instant later, he swung that big fist and Fiona suffered a moment of blinding pain, then let the blackness swallow her whole.

An awareness of pain came to Fiona so quickly she gasped and heard someone laugh softly. Her head ached and Fiona slowly trailed that discomfort back to the sharper pain in her jaw. The pain in her arms confused her for a moment, but then she recalled Menzies. Her stomach clenched from the strength of her fear and the remembered sight of Mab's limp body hitting the ground, blood soaking the front of her gown.

Someone nudged her and she felt her body sway. It was clear that Menzies had hung her up by her wrists again. The brush of soft linen against her thighs told her that, this time, Menzies had at least left her shift on, and she tried to find some comfort in that. Slowly, she opened her eyes and glared at a faintly amused Menzies, hating him and savoring the way that bitter feeling pushed aside her fear.

"Ye will pay for killing Mab, ye bastard," she said. "I will make ye pay that debt. Blood for blood."

"With what?" Menzies pointed to where her daggers were set on top of the pile of her clothes.

"My teeth, if I must," she replied in an icy voice. "There was no need for ye to kill her."

"She tried to help ye run from me. That cannot be allowed." He idly brushed some dust from the front of his elegant doublet as he spoke. "Ye are mine and those who try to take what is mine, try to hold it out of my reach, must die."

He spoke as if Mab's life was of no more importance to him than the dust he flicked from his clothes. That was almost as frightening as the things he did to her, Fiona thought. Such a callous disregard for the life he had just ended might be acceptable upon the battlefield, but it revealed his insanity when he spoke so of a woman he had just murdered. She had to wonder just how long he would let her live once he had laid claim to her.

The thought of this man touching her made bile sting the back of her throat. That he had tried to rape her several times had caused her trouble enough before she had learned the joy of Ewan's embrace. She did not want to even consider how she would feel if Menzies succeeded in raping her this time. Or even more terrifying, how Ewan might feel. There was so much Menzies could destroy this time, it made her feel like weeping, but she fought that urge. She refused to show this man any weakness.

She knew from past confrontations that Menzies

loved to talk about himself, his skill, his cleverness, his daring. Although she had no idea of how much help it would be, she decided to start him talking. It would buy her some time. It might simply delay the inevitable horror at his hands, but it might also produce a miracle. Someone at Scarglas might have noticed how long she and Mab had been gone and search for them. One of the men in the watchtowers might have seen something despite how far away she and Mab had been. It was a small hope, but she clung to it, finding strength in it.

"How did ye find me?" she asked.

"It wasnae easy," replied Menzies, giving her a look of irritation. "Then I heard that ye had disappeared, were lost."

Was there a spy at Deilcladach? Fiona wondered. Menzies was certainly handsome enough, with his long fair hair and light blue eyes, to seduce some woman into telling him MacEnroy secrets. It was possible enough of a stir had been caused by her disappearance that it was no secret at all, but she had difficulty believing that. Since the trouble with Menzies had begun, Connor had kept the business of Deilcladach a close secret. Fiona could tell by the look upon Menzies's almost beautiful face that he wanted her to ask him how he had learned she had left the keep. She subdued the stubborn part of her that wished to deny him that little pleasure by reminding herself that she was buying herself some precious time.

"Ye have found some fool to tell ye what happens at Deilcladach, have ye?" she asked, nearly gagging at the way he preened.

"A bonnie wee lass she was. Sweet and besotted,

eager to please me with her knowledge of all that happened at Deilcladach from day to day."

"Was?" Fiona's mind had fixed upon that word, and although she had little sympathy for a traitor, she could feel some for a foolishly besotted woman who might not have known who she was consorting with.

"Weel, I couldnae let her cry out a warning once she had kenned who I was. Twas her own fault for lighting that candle. I had told her that it was dangerous for her to ken too much, that secrecy was verra important." He shrugged. "She obviously didnae think that included her getting a close look at her lover's face. I couldnae have those cursed brothers of yours guess that I had been close at hand."

"And ye dinnae think the murder of some poor deluded lass will make them suspicious?"

"Nay. I am nay such a fool as to leave a body behind. She rests at the bottom of the river, tied to a sack of rocks to hold her there. So, dinnae think your brother has scented my trail. He willnae be hieing to your rescue this time."

"That still doesnae answer the question of how ye found me."

"Trailed ye, didnae I? Several people recalled seeing that horse of yours. Then I met with a fine group of men called the Grays. They told me the laird of Scarglas had a woman with him near to a month past. This woman killed one of their men, had long golden hair, dressed like a lad, and handled a sword like a mon. Twas easy to guess whom that might be."

"Easy, was it? I *have* been here a whole month, ye

ken." She tensed when a look of anger tightened his features.

"Aye, and so ye have." He poked her in the side with the tip of his sword. "Some of the things the Grays told me made me verra angry."

"And why would ye believe all they had to say? They are the enemies of the MacFingals."

Fiona could see him thinking that over. She used his distraction to try to gain some laxity in the ropes binding her wirsts. After the first time he had hung her up by her bound wrists, she had had Connor do the same to her and the two of them had worked hard on finding ways for her to free herself or, at the very least, offer some resistance. Fiona was a little surprised that, after the bruises she had inflicted upon him and his men last time, Menzies had yet again hung her from a tree branch. She then noticed that his men kept their distance from her and she almost smiled.

"Nay," Menzies said after a moment of deep thought, "there was no deceit or trickery behind their words. In truth, they were curious when they realized ye were the woman I sought. But their interest in ye matters naught. All that matters is what they told me about ye and the laird of Scarglas."

"Since there is naught to say about me and the laird of Scarglas, I cannae guess what they told ye."

Menzies sighed and shook his head before he looked at her with an expression of such condescending recrimination that she sorely wanted to kick it off his face. It was a very similar look that had caused her to turn aside his request for her hand in marriage. She had been as stunned and blinded as many another woman by his angelic looks, but then she had seen that look. It was one that said she was only a poor, dull-witted woman who was in sad need of the guidance and wisdom of a man, that she was to be pitied for her lack, but then forgiven and cared for. Fiona had often wondered if the fact that she, a mere pitiful woman, had rejected him was what had twisted him so, then told herself not to be so vain. The man had already suffered this madness. Her refusal had, at best, simply made it stronger and clearer to see.

"Ye have been the laird's captive for o'er a month," Menzies said in a tone of voice that implied he was trying to explain a simple fact to a person who had all the wits of a flea. "Despite all my efforts, ye are still lovely enough to stir a mon's lusts." He scowled and cast a suspicious look toward his men, who were smart enough to appear completely uninterested in her. "I have also heard that the laird is a dour mon, dark of looks and horribly scarred."

Fiona bit back an instinctive urge to defend Ewan against that slur. The sly look upon Menzies's face warned her that he had set a trap for her. Instinct told her she would suffer if he suspected she cared for Ewan. Worse, Menzies would then want Ewan to suffer as well. The last thing Ewan needed was another man hunting him, and Menzies seemed to have the wit and skill the Grays lacked despite his madness. She met his gaze calmly, as if she merely waited for him to continue speaking.

"Such coarse hands should ne'er touch ye," Menzies said after watching her closely for a minute. "That would be a crime, a sin I would have to see punished. The question would be—who deserved

to be punished more, him or ye. Did ye let the
mon touch ye, Fiona? Did ye give him your maidenhead, mark his sheets with your innocence as ye
refused to mark mine? Have ye let him make ye his
whore? The Grays claim ye have."

"The Grays also claim they have a right to Scarglas
e'en though the previous laird was cousin to the
new," she said. "I wouldnae put much weight behind the words of a clan that believes it should have
a better claim to something than a mon's own blood
kin."

She tensed when he slowly walked around her,
touching her as if he had the right. Even though
good sense told her it was impossible, she began to
fear there was some mark upon her that would tell
him she was no longer a maiden. Silently talking
away her rising fears, she met his gaze directly when
he returned to standing in front of her. There was
now a glint in his eye that told her nothing she
could say or do would convince him that the Grays
had lied. He had been convinced of her loss of innocence before he had come after her.

A chill slithered down her spine as he flicked
the ribbon tying her shift closed with the tip of his
sword. There would be no more time, no more
talk. Fiona was surprised she had held him off for
as long as she had. It was difficult to see just how
his belief that she was no longer pure had affected
him.

"Ye do understand that for each mark ye make
upon my skin," she said, "my brother will make ye
pay for it tenfold. He counts each bruise, each pain,
as a debt that must be repaid in blood and agony.

Each time ye capture me and torment me, ye add another week to the length of time he will make ye suffer." Although Menzies appeared unmoved by her threats, his men shifted on their feet a little uneasily. "Connor has made a close study of all the ways he can hold ye tight in the bonds of agony yet not lose ye to death's grasp."

"Your brother hasnae caught me once in all this time. I dinnae think he is such a great threat."

"Nay? Do ye think he will give up if it takes too much time to chase ye down? Mayhap ye should pause a moment and think upon the mon my brother is, remember for a minute the tales of his becoming laird at but fifteen, of all he endured and all he accomplished. Hunting ye down, e'en if it takes years, will be as naught to him. Ye will ne'er be able to run far enough or fast enough, ne'er be able to cease looking o'er your shoulder to see if he is there. One day he will be and then ye will begin to suffer, long and hard. Aye," she added in a near whisper, smiling coldly, "then ye will begin to scream."

The way he stared at her made Fiona think she might have, finally, scared him. Then he laughed and she felt her heart sink down to her toes and her courage waver. Time had gained her nothing. Threats had not caused Menzies to feel any hesitation or fear. She grit her teeth against a cry when he cut the ribbon of her shift with the tip of his sword. He was not even drawing near enough for her to kick him.

She prayed. She prayed for the courage to endure whatever Menzies did without flinching. She prayed for some miracle, for the hand of fate to reach down and yank her to safety. She also prayed that, having been rescued from this man four times already, she had not run out of second chances or small miracles.

Chapter 14

"Where is your wife?"

Ewan sheathed his sword, waved away the men he had been training with, and looked at his father. "I am nay sure. With Mab in the herb hut? Visiting the sick? Why do ye expect me to ken where she is?"

"Because she is your wife." Fingal scowled at his eldest son. "Have ye lost her, then?"

"Nay, I havenae lost her. I just dinnae ken where she is. I dinnae keep her leashed to my side, do I? What do ye want her for?" Ewan frowned and studied his father closely. "Are ye ailing?"

"Of course I am nay ailing! Do I look as if I am ailing?"

"Then what do ye want with her?"

"Tis the nooning," Fingal muttered, crossing his arms over his chest.

"The what?"

"The nooning. Time for a meal, ye ken."

"Oh. Da, the church calls it—"

"I dinnae care what the church calls it. *I* call it the nooning. Tis a fine name. Better than what the church says. Those are prayer times and I am nay praying. I am eating."

"Of course." Ewan took a deep, slow breath as he struggled to remain calm, even patient. "And Fiona has to do something about this *nooning,* does she?"

"Aye, she sets down with me and we have us a fine meal spiced with a verra fine quarrel. Weel, I went to the great hall, set myself down, and she didnae come in. She always comes in. And ere ye start asking, she isnae in the keep or the herb shed or the garden. Thought ye might have taken her off to sow an heir, but nay, for here ye stand. So, why cannae your wife be found, eh?"

Ewan looked around him a little blindly, then looked back at his father. This was beyond strange. It was also a little disconcerting. He had thought his father disliked Fiona, did not want anything to do with her because of her Cameron connections, yet they had obviously been taking meals together. It did seem that that was something he ought to have been aware of.

What was even stranger was that his father had missed her, though Ewan suspected the man would never admit it even upon pain of death. In the weeks Fiona had been at Scarglas, she had clearly wriggled her way into his father's affections. Ewan knew his father had some, but they had never been given to a female before as far as he knew. If Sir Fingal's scowl was any indication, the man also felt

Ewan was sadly remiss because he did not know where his wife was.

Then, abruptly, the importance of that sank into Ewan's mind. His father had looked in all the places Fiona was usually to be found yet had not seen her. Ewan struggled to subdue a sudden urgency and a flare of alarm. Just because his father said he had looked everywhere did not mean he had.

"Did ye look in the solar?" he asked.

"I told ye, the lass isnae inside the keep," Sir Fingal snapped. "I may be old, but my wits are still keen, as are my eyes. I also sent the women in the keep to hunt her down and they couldnae find her. Spoke to young Ned and he said he hasnae seen Mab since they broke their fast together."

"Mayhap Fiona and Mab went to the village." Ewan's alarm grew when his father shook his head.

"A mon just came from the village asking for the lass and Mab. Got a sick bairn he wanted them to come and see. Ye *have* lost her, havenae ye."

Before Ewan could respond to that, a cry went up from the men upon the walls, followed quickly by another from the men guarding the gates. Ewan ran to the gates, his father close at his heels. Just as he reached them, Mab staggered through them and fell to her knees at his feet. Ewan felt himself sway a little only to be brought to his senses by the painful grip of his father's hand upon his upper arm.

It took several slow, deep breaths this time for Ewan to regain some sense of calm. It was difficult to hold firm to it as he crouched by Mab. All he could think of was that Fiona was gone, that Mab had returned to Scarglas bloodied and alone. He took a quick look at the woman's wound and was relieved to see that it appeared to be a shallow one. Later, he knew, it would please him for Mab's sake alone, but right now, he was only glad that she would be able to answer his questions. He waited with taut impatience as Mab struggled to catch her breath.

"Mab, where is Fiona?" he asked her as the woman finally began to breathe more evenly.

"Menzies," Mab replied, nodding when she saw how Ewan paled. "We were searching for healing plants and he found us."

"Ye and Fiona went outside these walls unguarded?"

"Here, lad," Sir Fingal said as he lifted Mab into his arms, ignoring her protests, "the woman needs tending to."

"Mama!" cried Ned as he ran up to Sir Fingal and tried to reach his mother.

"Hush, laddie," Sir Fingal said. "Your mother has but a wee scratch. She will be fine."

"Aye, Ned." Mab reached down to stroke her son's fair hair. "Do ye remember what I told ye one needs to tend a cut?" When the boy nodded, she smiled at him. "Weel, ye go get what I need and bring it to me."

"Bring it to the great hall," Sir Fingal ordered, then the moment the boy dashed off, he started toward the keep again. "That lad has verra fair hair. Are ye certain he is mine?"

"Of course he is, ye old fool." Mab groaned and rubbed her thigh. "That bastard threw me to the ground."

"Now, dinnae fret, woman. Ye can tell Ewan everything in but a moment."

"Da," Ewan protested as he hurried after his father, "Fiona is out there in the hands of her enemy."

"Aye, and we will fetch her back soon. She has been in the mon's hands before and wriggled free. As soon as we get Mab tended to, we will go after your impertinent wife and kill that bastard. We need answers first, though, aye?"

Ewan knew his father was right, but that did not make it any easier to accept the delay. He paced the great hall as Bonnie tended to Mab's wounds, Mab reassured her son that she was fine, and Sir Fingal scowled down at Ned's fair hair, occasionally muttering vaguely insulting remarks to Mab.

"Get over here and ask your questions, lad," called Sir Fingal.

"Och, Ewan," Mab said the moment he reached her side, "we were just standing there talking about what we could do with all the violets we had found and there he was. She called him Menzies."

"He is the mon who chases her, the one who gave her those scars," Ewan said. "What happened?"

Stroking her son's hair as if she needed that touch to calm herself, Mab told Ewan all she could remember. "Poor Fiona must think me dead, that she gave herself into her enemy's hands for naught."

"She will soon learn the truth. Did ye see which way they went?"

"Nay, I fear not. I dinnae believe I was unconscious for verra long, though. It should be easy to see where we were, where they caught her as they chased us about on their horses for several minutes ere they took her." She carefully told him where she and Fiona had discovered the violets. "The ground is quite soft there so whate'er marks they left should be clear to read and follow."

"Then we shall do so," Sir Fingal said even as he started out the door of the great hall. "Help your mother up to her bed, Ned," he ordered the boy as he left.

Ewan picked ten men from the dozens who offered to ride with him. Although he was surprised that his father was coming with him, he realized he was glad of it. At the moment Fingal had the calm and control he himself lacked. He knew what little he had grasped hold of could easily be lost depending upon what he found when he tracked down Fiona's enemy.

As he led his men to the place Mab had described, Ewan tried to banish the fear that was twisting his insides. He told himself, over and over, that Menzies did not want Fiona dead. The man wanted her for his wife. Ewan prayed Fiona had the wit to keep her marriage to him a secret, for there was no guessing how such news would make a madman like Menzies react. Then he reminded himself that Fiona had proven herself very clever indeed time and time again, and he relaxed a little.

It proved easy to follow Menzies and his men. Ewan had to wonder why. Was the man simply unaware of such things, or did he think no one would try to rescue Fiona? Or worse, was this a trap? From all Fiona had told him of her brother Connor, Ewan knew that man had both strength and intelligence, yet he had failed for almost two years to catch Menzies. That would seem to imply that Menzies was clever yet this easily read trail was the act of a clumsy fool. Ewan quickly halted his men and explained his concerns.

"I will go ahead and see what I can find," said Gregor, and he left the moment Ewan nodded his agreement to that plan.

"Do ye really think this Menzies is clever enough to hide his trail?" asked Sir Fingal.

"Aye," replied Ewan. "This is as good as a clearly drawn map. Either it is a trap or the mon has become too certain of success this time. Mayhap his madness has grown so strong it has overcome whate'er cleverness he once had." Ewan shook his head, then dragged his fingers through his hair. "Tis hard to ken how to step when dealing with a madmon."

Sir Fingal scratched his chin. "The mon wants your wife. He has spent near two years hunting her down and cutting wee bits off her. Aye, 'tis a madness. Howbeit, mayhap he was so caught up in his pride o'er finding the lass when no one else has that he wasnae thinking. Mayhap he didnae realize that, in his rush to ride away with his prize, he didnae kill Mab."

"Possible. Are ye sure he meant to kill Mab?"

"Aye. He but hurried it, cut too quick, and didnae pay any heed to the wound he gave her. The mon was so certain he had cut her throat that he ne'er looked back. Tis the way our Mab bled so freely which saved her. Menzies cut her, saw the blood flow, and tossed her aside." Sir Fingal looked down at the tracks they would soon follow. "Why should a mon hide his trail when he believes no one else kens he has stolen something?"

That made sense, Ewan realized, and he tried to hide his surprise. It was not quite fair. His father was old, made more problems than he solved, and had all the sexual restraint of a goat, but he was not stupid. He had also always been skilled in battle, in both the fighting and matters of strategy. Ewan knew he should heed the man's words, then he tensed when he saw Gregor riding toward them.

"They are just beyond that line of trees," Gregor reported as he reined in before Ewan. "There is a small clearing there and they have set up camp. Menzies and six men, no more, and all are within the camp."

"And Fiona?" Ewan felt his blood chill when Gregor snatched his reins from his hands before answering.

"She is alive. She is wearing naught but her shift, her wrists are bound, and he has strung her up by them to the branch of a tree," Gregor replied, watching Ewan closely and keeping a firm grip on his brother's reins.

"She said he liked to string her up like a fresh kill," Ewan whispered.

"Then best we slip up on them and steal their catch away," said Sir Fingal. "We plan a raid, nay a battle."

Ewan nodded as he fought down a fierce blood-lust. A direct attack would put Fiona in danger, especially since she was so helpless. Stealth was needed, the sort of stealth they used when they deprived a man of his cattle or his horses. Once Fiona was safe, however, Ewan had every intention of casting aside all stealth and killing Menzies.

Glancing at Simon, Ewan was now glad that he

had allowed the youth to accompany them despite his inexperience. Simon owed his life to Fiona and had desperately wanted a chance to repay that debt in some small way. Now the boy would have that chance, for there was one thing Simon did very well. Simon could move through a wood without disturbing a single leaf upon the ground. He could also climb trees silently and quickly, his skill a wonder to behold. Looking the youth over very carefully, Ewan decided Simon was strong enough to pull Fiona out of harm's way and he gave the boy his orders.

It took another few minutes to make their plans before they rode toward the trees. When Ewan spoke of needing a diversion, Gregor assured him that Menzies and his men were already well diverted and Ewan did not ask what held their interest. He knew. Any man with blood in his veins would be unable to resist staring at Fiona dressed only in her delicate shift.

They left their horses at the edge of the wood. Ewan gave Simon a few moments to get into position, then signaled the other men on their way. With his father at his side, Ewan crept up to Menzies's camp. The moment his men silenced Menzies's men, he and his father would go after Menzies. He was not surprised when his father grabbed his arm the moment the camp came into view. One look at Fiona hanging there, Menzies's sword pointed at her, roused the bloodlust in him so swiftly and fiercely Ewan knew he was in need of the restraint.

"Your wee wife has a clever way with a threat," whispered Sir Fingal as Fiona told Menzies what her brother would do to him.

Ewan was a little hurt that Fiona did not threaten Menzies with him, then told himself not to be such a fool. Fiona had indeed had the wit to know it would be dangerous to let Menzies know she was no longer an innocent maid. Menzies already knew her brother hunted him and why, so that was the man to speak of.

A cold smile curved Ewan's mouth as he watched his men slip in behind Menzies's men and silence them. The fact that each one of them needed only a knife to his throat to remain still and quiet as they were all disarmed told Ewan that their loyalty to Menzies probably ran very shallow. The moment Menzies's men were disarmed, Ewan nodded to his father and they began to stealthily work their way toward Menzies's unprotected back.

"I dinnae fear your brother," said Menzies.

"Then ye are a fool," said Fiona. "And 'tis nay just Connor ye must watch for, but all MacEnroys, all their allies, and all of Gillyanne's kinsmen. Ye are naught but a walking dead mon. Do your worst. I will ne'er pledge myself to ye. I will say nay and keep saying nay until ye breathe your last and I but pray that that will be soon."

"Ye *are* mine!"

"Nay, fool, she is mine."

Fiona could not believe what she was seeing. It seemed impossible that Ewan could be standing there right behind Menzies, that his men now held Menzies's men captive. She had seen and heard nothing. It was obvious that neither had Menzies or his men. Then she felt strong hands grasp her wrists and she shook aside the shock gripping her so tightly. She glanced up to see Simon grinning at

her as he pulled her up. The moment she was able
to, she swung herself up onto the branch with him.

"Your wife is a nimble lass," said Fingal as he
watched Fiona follow Simon down out of the tree.

"Your wife?" Menzies stared at Ewan, his eyes
widening when he realized he faced this threat
alone.

"Aye, *my* wife," said Ewan. "It tends to irritate a
mon when some fool steals his wife."

"Nay! She is mine! I had first claim!"

"Ye ne'er had a claim to her. She told ye nay."

"I will go help your wife dress," said Fingal as he
started to move away. "Cease talking and just kill
the bastard."

Ewan just nodded since that was what he intended
to do, what he had promised Fiona he would do.
He pushed aside the strong urge to make this man
suffer for what he had done to Fiona, to torment
him with little cuts for a while. That, he knew, was
the bloodlust talking, the anger and fear this
man's actions had roused in him. It was best to just
end this, swiftly and cleanly, and get Fiona back to
Scarglas.

The sudden clash of swords startled a cry out of
Fiona. She started to turn toward the fighting, but
Sir Fingal grasped her by the shoulders and stopped
her, keeping her face turned toward the woods. A
part of her bristled, wanting to argue, but she silenced it. If she watched Ewan fight Menzies, there
was a small chance she might do something foolish like cry out and dangerously distract him. Despite having been well taught the danger of
distracting a man who was in a battle, Fiona could
not be certain she would remember those lessons if

she saw the man she loved fighting Menzies, a fight that could only end in the death of one of them. She told herself firmly that it would be Menzies who died and set her mind to the task of getting ready to leave when Ewan was done.

A soft curse escaped her when she fumbled with the laces of her gown. Her hands were shaking badly. She suspected some of that was caused by the strain of hanging by her arms. The rest was caused by a wealth of emotion she was struggling to hold back, relief at being saved as well as all the fear, anger, and grief she had fought to hide from Menzies.

"Here, lass, I will do it," muttered Sir Fingal as he pushed her trembling hands aside and began to lace up her gown. "Dinnae ken why ye are so clumsy now when, a minute ago, ye were climbing down the tree with near as much skill as Simon."

"I am just a wee bit shocked that ye are here," she said. "How did ye ken Menzies had found me?"

"Mab staggered into Scarglas, all blood and bruises, and told us."

"Mab is alive?" Fiona felt a few of the tears she was fighting to hold back slide down her cheeks.

"Here, now, dinnae ye start that. Aye, Mab is alive. Yonder fool didnae cut hard enough or straight enough. Nay sure whether she will be needing stitches or nay, but ye can see to her when ye get back to Scarglas." He looked her over. "Did he give ye another scar? I thought I saw a wee bit of blood upon your shift ere ye pulled on your gown. Ye will start to look too much like your mon if ye arenae more careful."

"Nay, no scar this time. He but scored my skin once with the tip of his sword."

Sir Fingal was being remarkably kind to her, Fiona realized. That he had even joined in her rescue was a bit of a surprise. The man was such a bundle of contradictions she doubted she would ever understand him. Even now he grumbled, spoke somewhat insultingly, but tended to her with a surprising gentleness.

"Ye moved like the mists," she said. "I heard nary a whisper and didnae see ye until ye were there right in front of me."

"Aye, we are good. We can steal a mon's leg of mutton right off his table and be gone ere he kens we were there," he boasted. "None are as skilled at rieving as me and my laddies."

Fiona was about to tell the man that a skill at thievery was not something to be so proud of when a scream cut through the air. For one brief moment, doubt about Ewan's skill caused Fiona to fear Menzies had just killed her husband. Then knowledge overcame emotion. She had seen Ewan fight and knew Menzies had never had a chance of winning. Although Sir Fingal allowed her to turn around to face the camp, he kept a light grip upon her arm and she accepted the restraint. Menzies sprawled dead upon the ground and Ewan looked unhurt. It was all she needed to know for now.

Ewan cleaned his sword on Menzies's elaborately embroidered doublet as he studied the man he had just killed. Sir Ranald Menzies was the sort of man that women made fools of themselves over. Ewan had to wonder why Fiona had not been besotted with the man, for Ewan doubted Sir Menzies's madness had always been so clear to see. Realizing what sort of man had courted Fiona in the past, Ewan simply could not understand what she was doing in his bed. He shook away such unsettling thoughts and moved to face Menzies's men.

"Do I need to worry that ye will be troubling me and mine again?" he asked the men, and all six quickly said nay. "Are any of ye Menzies?" Two nodded. "Good. Tell your clan exactly what happened here. I dinnae wish to be beset by angry kinsmen who dinnae ken the truth and think I must pay for killing the fool."

"None will come after ye, m'laird," said the biggest of the six men. "He has always been a sore trial to his kinsmen."

"They kenned that he hunted my wife, but did naught?"

"What could they do but cage him or kill him, and his mother . . ." The man sighed and shook his head. "Tis done, naught else matters, does it?"

"Nay, mayhap not. Take him with ye. I willnae have his body souring my ground."

Letting his men see to the removal of Menzies's body and the retreat of his men, Ewan turned to face Fiona. She looked steady upon her feet and he saw no obvious wounds. Ewan prayed he had reached her in time, before Menzies was able to do any more than frighten her.

The way he had felt when he had thought she was lost to him troubled him deeply. He knew what it meant. All of his efforts to keep a distance between them, to shield his heart, had utterly failed. When he had seen a bleeding Mab return from the wood without Fiona, the truth had hit him like a sound blow to the side of his head. He cared.

He inwardly cursed. He more than cared. He loved. He loved Fiona deeply, with his whole heart and soul. That brief moment when he had thought her lost to him had been complete hell, a dark, cold, lonely hell. Long, empty years had stretched out before his mind's eye, the chill of them quickly entering his bones. Now that she was safe and returned to him, he was fighting the urge to drag her behind a tree and make love to her, marking her as his own like some beast marks his territory. Steadying himself, he walked over to her.

"Did he hurt ye, lass?" he asked, unable to resist the urge to brush his fingers over her cheek.

"Nay," she replied and, casting aside all efforts at restraint, flung herself against him, wrapping her arms around him. "He was still boasting about his cleverness in finding me." When he wrapped his arms around her, she felt her riotous emotions begin to calm and told him how Menzies had tracked her to Scarglas.

"I thank God we found ye ere he could do all he planned. He will ne'er hunt ye again, Fiona."

"Tis a sad waste of a mon so weel loved by his family, but the madness had worsened, and there was blood upon his hands." She leaned back a little, saw how Menzies's men were gone and had taken his body with them, and then looked up at Ewan. "May we go home now?" she asked quietly.

"Aye, lass," he replied as he led her to his mount, deeply moved by how she had called Scarglas home.

Holding her close as they rode, Ewan wondered what he was to do now. He was not such a fool that he thought he could kill the feelings that had taken root inside his heart. That battle had been well and truly lost. Fiona was as much a part of him as the blood in his veins. It felt both glorious and terrifying.

What caused his greatest concern was that he did not know what Fiona felt for him aside from passion. Until he did, he cringed at the mere thought of letting her know or even guess at his feelings. Somehow, despite the fact that these strong emotions were now free and flowing within him, he had to hide what he felt until he could win Fiona's heart. Hiding his feelings for her might not be too difficult. He had hidden them from himself for weeks, after all. It was winning Fiona's heart that worried him the most. That would prove a battle he felt ill equipped to wage.

Chapter 15

Fiona nearly hurled her boots at the bedchamber door as it shut behind Ewan. If she could have reached them without getting out of bed, she would have. Even better, she thought, would be to hurl them at Ewan's thick head. It had been one week since Menzies had captured her and died for it. One very long week, for Ewan was still treating her as if she were made of precious glass. That restraint she had thought she had weakened in him was back in full strength.

She sighed as she cautiously sat up. It was probably for the best that her attempt at seduction this morning had succeeded only in making Ewan flee the room. She was feeling somewhat nauseous, and if he saw her become ill, she feared he would lock her in the bedchamber and have Mab drown her in healthy potions.

A cold sweat broke out on her skin and she dove for the chamber pot. Once she was sure the retching had ended, she cleaned her teeth, rinsed her mouth, and crawled back into bed. She breathed in and out very slowly until her stomach calmed and the weakness caused by her illness had passed.

There was little doubt in her mind as to what ailed her. She was with child. She had not bled once since her marriage. Fiona would not be surprised if she had gotten with child that very first time. No one could question the potency of a MacFingal man. Or a Cameron, she mused, thinking about all of Sigimor's brothers and cousins.

Resting her hand over her womb, she felt both elated and troubled. She wanted to bear Ewan's child, yet a part of her wished his seed had not taken root quite so quickly. Their marriage still needed work to be a good one and her feelings were still unreturned. What sort of life was that to bring a child into?

Fiona eased herself up into a sitting position again, pleased to find that her stomach held steady. She decided she would keep the child a secret for a while. Not only did she want to be sure the child was set firmly within her womb, but there was always the chance that something else ailed her. She also wanted more time with Ewan without the presence of the child confusing matters. Fiona did not want to be put into the untenable position of trying to decide whether whatever Ewan said or did was simply because she was carrying his child. Trying to understand the man was difficult enough already.

Although she was tempted to crawl back into bed and sleep for a few more hours, Fiona got dressed. Ewan had finally come up with a plan to send word to Connor about where she was, how she fared, and their marriage. It had been difficult to wait so long to let Connor know that she was safe, but she understood the reasons for the delay. Any MacFingal leaving Scarglas had to cross the lands of their enemies and such journeys required very precise planning. She certainly did not want someone to die just to deliver a message to her family. Before the men left, however, she had a message of her own she wanted to send to Connor.

By the time Fiona reached the great hall to break her fast, she was feeling much better. She knew she was eating a lot more than she usually did, but ignored Sir Fingal's looks of surprise and curiosity. It was a little harder to ignore the sharp looks Mab kept giving her. Mab was a good enough healer to easily guess Fiona's condition, and she decided she would have to have a quiet word with the woman. Although Mab was not quite as scatter-witted as many thought, Fiona knew it was possible the woman could blurt out the wrong word at the wrong time all too easily unless counseled beforehand.

"Wheesht, lass," muttered Sir Fingal as Fiona helped herself to a fourth chunk of bread heavily covered with butter, "ye will be as big as Mab if ye keep stuffing food down your gullet like that."

"I am nay big," snapped Mab.

"Nay, ye arenae," Fiona said, patting Mab's plump arm as she frowned at Sir Fingal. "And why are ye complaining about how much I am eating, Sir Fingal? Ye are the one who is always complaining that I am naught but bones. Mayhap I but decided to heed your words and try to put some more meat on my bones."

Sir Fingal snorted. "Ye wouldnae heed my advice e'en if I held a knife to your pretty throat. And concerning your bones, it appears my son likes them just fine. He may nay want ye putting any meat on them."

He isnae going to have any say in the matter soon, Fiona mused, and nearly smiled. "When do the men leave to take word to my brother?" she asked him.

"Soon. An hour, mayhap a wee bit more. Why?"

"I just thought I would send a wee message of my own."

"Why? Ewan said all that was needed, didnae he?"

"Aye, but my brother may have a doubt or two left after he reads Ewan's message. He doesnae ken who any of ye are, does he? So, I thought just a word or two of assurance from me, something he would ken as a message only I could send, would ease those doubts and aid him in welcoming the men ye send." She gave Sir Fingal her most innocent look and held it firmly even when he gave her a long, narrow-eyed stare.

"Clever, lass," he murmured, revealing his doubts about the truth of her claim. "Weel, do as ye wish. Ye ken your brother better than any of us do. Do ye think he will come here?"

"Oh, aye, but nay for a wee while. Tis a busy time of the year. I suspect Gilly will insist upon coming, too, and that will require some verra careful planning. And Connor may feel a need to brood o'er the fact that 'twas Ewan who killed Menzies and nay him."

When Sir Fingal nodded in solemn understanding of that last statement, Fiona had to stuff some bread into her mouth to keep from grinning.

Connor was going to enjoy Scarglas, she thought as she watched Old Marta talking to her unseen friends while she cleaned the hearth. Peter sat in a far corner eating porridge, his stench keeping all others away. Although, she mused, he did look a little cleaner since the men had tied him to a post in the bailey and left him out in the rain two days ago. The more Fiona came to know the odd people Sir Fingal had allowed into Scarglas, the more she began to think that, despite his many faults, he was actually a very nice man. Underneath all that grumbling might actually be a very large heart. Someday she would find out why it did not beat quite so warmly for the women he bedded.

As soon as she felt pleasantly full, Fiona hurried out of the great hall, Mab close at her heels. Mab followed her to her bedchamber, where she collected the letter she had written to Connor, then back down the stairs. The moment Fiona stepped outside, she turned to frown at her silent guard.

"Why are ye following me?" she asked Mab.

"Because ye are hiding something, I think," Mab replied.

"Are ye sure Ewan didnae tell ye to watch o'er me?"

"Nay, why should he do that?"

"Because he seems to have gotten it into his thick head that I need to be watched and coddled like some puling invalid. I told him naught happened whilst Menzies held me captive, but I begin to think he doesnae believe me. Ah, there is Brian."

Mab followed Fiona as she hurried over to Ewan's younger brother. "What do ye want with Brian?"

"He is one of the men going to see Connor," replied Fiona, "and I want to give him this letter."

"He will tell Ewan."

"Nay, he willnae."

Fiona stopped before Ewan's twenty-three-year-old brother and smiled at him. It never ceased to amaze her how much the brothers resembled each other. They were all big and dark like their father. Some had softer, more handsome features, some had different colored eyes, but there was no mistaking their heritage. Brian had eyes of a slightly darker shade of blue than Nathan's, and although his features were very similar to Ewan's, they were not as harshly drawn.

"Why are ye smiling at me like that?" Brian asked, looking both amused and suspicious.

"I have a letter from me that I wish ye to deliver to my brother Connor." Fiona handed him the letter.

"But Ewan has already written one," Brian said even as he tucked her letter into the small leather pouch hanging from his belt. "Do ye want Ewan's back?"

"Nay. Give both to Connor."

"Ah, and I suspicion Ewan doesnae ken ye wrote one yourself, does he?"

"I will tell him about it after ye are gone." She rolled her eyes at the look of suspicion that darkened his face. "Tis no plot, nothing to anger my brother. S'truth, it will make him much calmer."

"I dinnae think I ought to be helping ye keep secrets from my brother. My brother who is also my laird."

"There are no dark secrets in that letter, only a

few things I havenae told Ewan yet. *Personal* things."
She held his gaze for several minutes, then breathed
an inner sigh of relief when he nodded. "Oh, and
ask Gillyanne for her receipt for a morning tonic.
She will understand." By the sharp look Brian suddenly gave her, she had the feeling he did as well.
Mab's soft *aha* undoubtedly confirmed his suspicion.

They all watched as Old Marta walked by them
carrying on a vigorous, one-sided argument, and
then Fiona looked to Mab for an explanation. Before
Mab could reply, however, Ewan strode up to them
and frowned at Fiona. She inwardly sighed, preparing herself for the lecture he had grown fond of giving her for the last week. The man seemed to have
convinced himself that Menzies's attack had turned
her into some frail creature who needed to stay in
bed and drink a lot of vile potions to strengthen
her blood.

"Ye should be resting," Ewan began.

"I was just giving Brian a few greetings to pass
along to my family," Fiona said as she hooked her
arm through Mab's. "Now I must go and help Mab
make some soap. God's speed, Brian," she said as
she pulled Mab toward the herb hut.

"Why should she be resting?" Brian asked Ewan.

"She needs to rest after the travail she went
through whilst in Menzies's hold," Ewan answered,
frowning after his wife, who appeared to have fled
his presence.

"She looked hale to me. Menzies didnae cut her
again or rape her or e'en beat her badly. I dinnae
think she suffered so direly that she needs to still
be resting. It has been a full week."

The way Brian was looking at him made Ewan nervous. There was an uncomfortable mixture of amusement and understanding in his brother's expression. Ewan knew he was, perhaps, being too cautious about Fiona's health, but just when he would begin to think that, he would vividly recall seeing her dangling from that tree limb, blood on her shift and a bruise upon her jaw. He would also recall that icy fear which had gripped him at the thought of losing her.

"She isnae a verra big woman," he muttered. "She is just a wee, delicate lass."

Brian laughed. "A delicate wee lass who can wield a sword like a mon, wrestle Clare into shutting her bitter mouth, kill a mon, swing herself up into a tree whilst her hands are still bound, and climb down it almost as swiftly and silently as Simon, run like a hart—"

"Enough," snapped Ewan, but then he cursed and rubbed the back of his neck. "I rather like having a wife. Tis my duty to see that she takes care of herself."

"Of course it is. Then again, one must be careful that one's duty doesnae start to smother a person." Brian glanced toward the herb shed. "Or make them flee one's presence."

Ewan winced. "Noticed that, did ye?"

"Twas hard not to. Ewan, I think the verra worst thing ye could do to a woman like Fiona is to try to wrap her up in soft blankets and make her sit quietly in a corner. E'en if, by some miracle, she allowed it, I think she would soon wither and die like a cut flower." He shrugged. "I have heard some of the tales of how she spent the first thirteen years of her life. I am certain ye have heard the same, and more. Ye may try to remember some of them from time to time. And remember that your wee, delicate wife survived." Brian slapped Ewan on the back and started toward the horses that had been readied for his journey. "Time to leave. Pray to God that we get to the MacEnroys without meeting any trouble on the way. I begin to think I will need all my wits and strength to deal with Fiona's family."

When Brian and his six companions were gone, Ewan turned to stare at the herb shed. It was not comfortable to have one's younger brother guess at one's fears, he mused, but that moment of embarrassment had given him some very good advice to heed. He was letting his fears turn his wits to warm gruel. Fiona might look delicate, a fair and frail flower, but she was pure steel beneath that soft skin. He had felt the strength in her often enough to wonder how he could have forgotten it.

What Brian had not guessed (and Ewan thanked God for that small mercy) was that, in his effort to coddle Fiona, he had been denying himself the joy of her passion. Fiona had made it very apparent, especially this morning, that she was willing and able to make love, yet he had stoutly ignored her invitations. That was a self-imposed punishment he did not intend to suffer any longer. For a moment, he was sorely tempted to go and get her, carry her to their bedchamber, and thoroughly feed the hunger that had been knotting his innards for a week. He shook away that tempting plan as he started toward the training fields. Tonight would be soon enough, if she was not still angry or offended over his hasty rejection of her this morning. Ewan wondered if there was any way a man could grovel without actually appearing to do so.

"I ought to make him grovel," Fiona muttered as she viciously ground some poppy seeds in a stone mortar. "I ought to make him get down on his knees and plead most prettily. Then I could kick him."

"Fiona!" Mab snatched the pestle out of Fiona's hand and glanced warily at the fine powder in the mortar. "If ye were imagining this was your husband, I must assume that he has angered ye." She looked at Fiona. "Is that why ye havenae told him that ye carry his bairn?"

"Tis too early to be certain of that," Fiona protested.

"Oh, I think ye ken it as weel as I do. Ye are with child. Kenning such a thing is something I have always been able to do, e'er since I was a wee lass. I can see it almost from the moment the mon's seed has taken root." Mab frowned. "I ceased telling women when I kenned they were with child for they began to whisper that I was a witch. I was seeing it *too* early, ye ken, ere they had e'en wondered on the possibility."

After dealing with Gillyanne and all her kinsmen, Fiona was accustomed to people with odd gifts, and she just nodded. "If ye kenned I was with child, why havenae ye said anything?"

"Twas the oddest thing, but I couldnae be certain, not until this morning. The feeling I get when a woman is with child was there, but 'twas e'er so slightly different. Then, this morning, when ye walked into the great hall, that feeling was as true and clear as it has e'er been."

"And then I began to eat a meal that would have done Ewan proud." Fiona grinned when Mab giggled. "Aye, I feel sure I am with child. I havenae bled since I married Ewan and the last two mornings I have been unweel. I havenae told Ewan because I want to be sure the bairn is here to stay and I want some more time alone with Ewan."

"The bairn willnae be here for eight months or so, Fiona."

"I ken it, but the moment I tell Ewan, I shall change in his eyes. I will no longer be just Fiona or just his wife, I will be the woman who carries his child. Weel, if Ewan is going to change in how he behaves toward me, I want to be able to ken for certain that the change is because of me alone and not because of this bairn."

"Ah, I understand. I willnae tell a soul. Is the bairn why ye wish to make Ewan grovel then kick him?"

"Nay, I am just angry o'er how he treats me as if I will shatter at the slightest touch. Not that he has tested that conclusion, for he hasnae touched me in a week." She nodded vigorously when Mab gasped. "Weel, enough is enough. He will cease this nonsense tonight e'en if I have to tie him to our bed." Fiona suddenly had an image of Ewan tied to the bed, completely naked, completely at her mercy. "Oh, my, that is a rather intriguing thought."

"Fiona!" Mab gasped in shock, but then she began to laugh. "Shameless lass. Ah, but ye are so good for our Ewan."

"Do ye truly think so?" Fiona asked quietly, suddenly very serious.

"Och, aye. Ewan has e'er been a serious lad, but tragedy and heavy responsibilities have made him e'en more so. He is a mon who could all too easily wake up one morn to find that he had protected his heart and hid his feelings so weel, he was now utterly alone. Ye willnae allow that to happen. Ye will keep him from slowly dying inside from wanting so much, but fearing to reach out for it. Just be patient. If ye could have seen how he acted when I told him Menzies had ye, ye would ken that he isnae so verra far out of your reach as ye might think. Now, I want to feel this bairn."

Fiona stood still as Mab placed her hands over her stomach. The woman closed her eyes, but Fiona could tell by the expressions upon her face that Mab truly felt something. A brief frown crossed Mab's face, and Fiona grew a little uneasy. When Mab finally opened her eyes and stepped back, Fiona watched her and fought back a twinge of anxiety.

"That wee devil doesnae want to give up his secrets," Mab said.

"Oh. Tis a lad then."

"I am nay sure. That is what I meant by his secrets. I can usually just feel if it is a lad or a lass, almost from the start, but your bairn obviously doesnae think 'tis any of my business. But he couldnae hide all the truth. Tis a healthy bairn. I dinnae think I have e'er felt such a strong sense of life." Mab grimaced. "Listen to me babble. Now ye ken why so many call me Mad Mab or a witch."

"Then they are fools. What I see is a true gift, a gift far more precious than a potion to clear up a

lad's spots or to grow hair upon some vain mon's
head." Fiona could see the glint of hope and interest in Mab's eyes.

"It frightens people, Fiona. My mother said 'twas
naught but the devil's work."

"Nay, 'tis God's gift. Ye have tried to ignore it, I
suspect, when ye should have been learning how
to use it. That is what we shall do. We will learn just
how great this gift is and how it can be used. We
will also learn how ye can use it to its fullest yet in a
way that willnae stir dangerous fears and supersti-
tions. Our Gilly's clan, the Murrays, has many people born with such gifts and I spent enough time
with them to learn how ye can protect yourself from
those dangerous fears yet use this wondrous gift
for the purpose God intended." She laughed softly
when Mab hugged her.

"How can I e'er thank ye?" asked Mab.

"Weel, ye could help me find something soft yet
strong enough to bind a mon's wrists to the bed."

Ewan blinked and stared up at the ceiling above
his bed. He could not believe he had fallen asleep
while waiting for Fiona to come to bed. Obviously,
all the hard work he had done in an attempt to keep
himself from chasing after his wife like a buck on
the trail of a doe in season had exhausted him far
more than he had realized. If he had been able to
make love to his wife as he had planned, he would
have stayed awake, but Fiona had claimed someone desperately needed her particular healing skills
and left him alone.

As he became more alert, an itch on his stomach drew his attention. He moved to scratch it only to realize his right arm was lashed to the bedpost. A quick glance revealed that his left arm was also secured to the bed. The bonds upon his wrists were thick ropes wrapped in layers of soft, dark blue wool. Ewan wondered why he was not immediately alarmed and searching for an enemy. Then he smelled a hint of lavender and Fiona stepped up to the side of the bed, and he knew why he was still calm. Some part of him had recognized that his wife was in the room and that he was not in any danger. Ewan suspected the ropes wrapped so carefully to protect his skin had been a clue. He also suspected her tying him to the bed had been what had awakened him.

"Why have ye tied me to the bed?" he asked her, feeling his body tighten with need at the sight of her in her shift.

"So that ye cannae run away from me this time," Fiona replied and she took one last, bracing drink of wine before climbing onto the bed. "I am going to show ye that I am hale and hearty, that I need no more time to heal from Menzies's attack."

Ewan opened his mouth to tell her about his change of heart, then quickly shut it when she settled herself astride him. It did not take a man of vast experience to guess what she planned to do. Only a complete fool would risk saying anything that might make her change her plans.

"It was a sad travail for ye," he murmured. "Ye being such a wee, delicate lass and all."

"True, it was an upsetting experience, but I intend to show ye that I am weel o'er it, that I dinnae wish ye to treat me as if I am some frail, swooning maid any longer."

He just quirked one brow at her, knowing she would see it as a challenge. She did and the way she met his challenge soon had him fighting the inclination to tear free of his bonds and grab her. The way she kissed and caressed every inch of his battered body had his blood running so hot in his veins, he was surprised parts of him had not begun to melt. He also felt honored, even cherished, and his hope that he might someday hold her heart began to rise. Ewan groaned and closed his eyes when she took him into her mouth, determined to savor the heady delight of this intimacy for as long as possible.

"Fiona," he groaned when he knew he was reaching the end of his endurance. "Take me inside ye. Now."

She straddled his body and he shuddered as she eased their bodies together. She was all tight heat and moist welcome. Ewan still found it difficult to believe that she could be stirred to passion simply by pleasuring him.

"Untie me, lass," he said in a hoarse whisper. "I need to touch you."

The moment she released him, he reached for her, and their passion for each other swiftly became fierce and wild. Release was mutual and devastating. Fiona collapsed into his arms and he held her trembling body close while they both struggled to recover their senses.

"Weel, mayhap ye arenae so verra delicate," Ewan said when he found he could finally breathe regularly.

"Nay, I am not." Fiona idly stroked his chest, wondering when, or even if, she would have the strength to move again.

"I dinnae think I have e'er been so pleased to be shown I was acting the fool." He smiled when she giggled, then kissed the top of her head. "I thought I had lost ye," he whispered.

Fiona felt her heart skip with pleasure and hope. There was such deep feeling behind his words, yet she resisted the urge to press for more. Instinct told her that pressing Ewan for more would only push him away.

"Nay," she whispered back, "ye will ne'er lose me. I was but taken away for a wee while, but I would have found my way back. I will always find my way back." She almost smiled when his only response was a soft grunt and a tightening of his embrace. It would do for now.

Chapter 16

"They are here again."

Ewan looked up from the ledger he was working on and frowned at his brother Gregor. "Who is here again?"

"The Camerons."

"Jesu, has our father seen them?"

"Aye. Tis difficult to miss about a dozen verra big redheads."

Cursing softly, Ewan hurried out of the small ledger room, Gregor close at his heels. He was just going down the stairs when he saw Fiona and Mab leave the great hall and run out of the keep. His father's bellows were clear to hear through the briefly opened door as the women passed through it. It was time this foolishness ended, Ewan decided as he followed the women. When he reached the bailey, however, it was to discover that his wife was already taking his father to task for his intransigence. He hesitated, tempted to let her handle the problem of his father.

"He doesnae sound quite as rabid as he used to," said Gregor as he moved to stand next to Ewan.

After listening for a moment, Ewan had to agree. "Mayhap he finally begins to see reason. Open the gates and invite our cousins in."

"What about our father?"

"He will have to endure or he can go sulk in his bedchamber. Instinct tells me this visit is too weel timed to be all chance. Our cousins are united with the MacEnroys through marriage, and it was barely a sennight past that Brian went to meet with the MacEnroys. Go, let them in so that I might satisfy my curiosity," Ewan said even as he started toward his father and his wife.

"Ye are being blindly pigheaded," Fiona told Sir Fingal, tired of trying to reason with the man.

"Ye shouldnae speak to your elders that way," said Fingal, looking slightly wounded.

"I will speak that way when 'tis but the truth."

"I—"

"Am being blindly pigheaded," finished Ewan as he stepped up next to Fiona and looked at his father. "If these were the ones who had wronged ye, Da, I would offer to cut them down where they stand. They are not. Aye, I ken 'tis a lot to ask of ye to accept the son of the ones ye feel betrayed ye, but the needs of the clan force me to do so. We cannae continue alone, Da. We need allies. When I go to treat with our enemies, I can do so from a position of greater strength if they ken others stand behind me. The best I can do now is to get some of our enemies to consider nay killing every MacFingal they see."

Sir Fingal put his hands on his hips and glared at his son, then at Fiona. He then turned to stare at the men riding in through the now open gates. Ewan watched his father very closely as the man who called himself Sigimor dismounted and walked toward them. Seeing that the man was indeed as handsome as he had appeared to be from a distance, Ewan draped his arm around Fiona's shoulders and stoutly ignored his father's snort of amusement.

"Ye look just like your father," snapped Sir Fingal after they had all exchanged somewhat terse greetings.

"I should hope so," drawled Sigimor. "I should hate to think that my mother had played him false."

"She played *me* false."

"Truly? Was that before, or after, ye put a bairn in her cousin's belly?"

Ewan joined Fiona in staring at Sir Fingal, who scowled at a faintly smiling Sigimor. The barest hint of a blush colored his father's cheeks and Ewan cursed. Although he hated to believe Sigimor, there was no doubting the look of guilt upon his father's face. It was Mab who broke the tense silence.

"So, ye were a *young* fool, too," said Mab and she shook her head. "And here I had imagined that ye had turned into what ye are because of some great betrayal of your heart. Twas just another instance of ye being unable to keep your breeches on, ye old fool."

"It *was* a great betrayal," protested Fingal. "I was

holding fast to the vows I shared with my lass. Then my brother found out that his promised wife loved me and had almost convinced her father to end their betrothal and let her marry me. He sent that woman to me. She visited me in my bedchamber whilst I still slept, like some cursed succubus she took me. It was o'er and done ere I was even full awake. Then she went crying to them all claiming I had seduced her. No one would heed me when I tried to tell them the truth. For a wee while, I thought I might have a second chance, that my lass was finally listening to me, but then that wretched woman said she carried my bairn and everyone said I had to marry her. I lost my temper, cursed the whole lot of them, and left. So, ye see, Mab, it was a great betrayal," he added quietly, looking and sounding very weary.

"Aye, Fingal, it was," Mab said as she slipped her arm through his and started to lead him toward the keep.

Fingal paused after a few steps and looked back at Sigimor. "I tried to get my bairn. That woman told me the lad had died. She said that she had been cast out because of me and that the bairn couldnae survive the hardship of it."

"She lied," Sigimor said. "The bairn was weel cared for by her kinsmen. He inherited their lands and has been wed for six years now. His mother died near fifteen years ago at the hands of a jealous wife."

Fingal nodded and let Mab lead him away. Fiona thought he looked as if he was suffering from that pain all over again. Her eyes widening, she looked around at all the MacFingal lads gathered in the bailey, at all the bastards Fingal had taken in to raise. She then looked at Ewan, who appeared to be as shocked as she was.

"Ewan," she began, faltering when he nodded and gently tightened the grip of his arm around her shoulders.

"One is left to wonder which hurt him the most," Ewan murmured. "I think he has blamed himself for the bairn's death all these years." Ewan looked at Sigimor. "Why was he ne'er told the truth?"

"By the time I kenned the truth, your father wouldnae speak with me. The others held fast to the lie for so long because the lad's grandsire was afeared of losing him. When the tales of how efficiently your father was breeding an army reached our ears, none of the elders felt he would e'en care. He didnae need the lad as they did."

"And what did ye think, Sigimor?" Fiona asked. "What did the tales tell ye?"

"That Sir Fingal had a true fever for the lasses," Sigimor drawled. "They also told me that he wouldnae have deserted the lad. The woman, aye, but ne'er the lad. His son kens it, too. He but waits for me to tell him when the gates are finally opened and if they will stay open for him to ride through."

"Aye, they will," replied Ewan. "Come, we can talk o'er some food and drink. Introductions may take hours."

"First, I have to give each of ye a message from Connor."

"I thought your appearance was strangely weel timed."

"Aye. Your lads arrived safely and will return within a few days," he told Ewan before smiling at

Fiona. "And now for the message your brother sent to ye, lass."

Fiona suddenly found herself in Sigimor's arms being heartily kissed. She was thinking that he was very skilled when she heard the sound of a great many swords being rapidly unsheathed, and she wriggled free of his grasp. The Camerons were now all gathered behind Sigimor with their swords drawn. Around them stood scowling MacFingals, and every man who had a sword now had it pointed at the Camerons.

"Jesu, Sigimor," muttered a voice from behind him, "do ye plan to get us all killed?"

Leaning to the right, Fiona peeked around Sigimor and smiled at his cousin Liam. "Hello, Liam."

"Greetings, lass," replied Liam.

She squeaked as a strong arm curled around her waist and she was yanked back against Ewan. "I dinnae think my brother told ye to do that, Sigimor," she said, hoping a little talking would ease this tense confrontation.

"Nay," replied Sigimor. "He told me to make sure ye are weel protected and cared for." He calmly looked around at all the MacFingals ready to cut him into small pieces for touching their laird's woman. "I would say ye are."

Liam stepped up to Sigimor's side to glare at him. "Ye did that just to see how they would react?"

"Actions speak louder than words."

"Ye are mad," said Ewan as he sheathed his sword, listening as everyone else slowly followed his lead. "Ye came verra close to being killed." Ewan understood his own swift reaction to another man kissing Fiona, but was a little surprised at how closely his clan's reaction matched his.

"I got my answer, didnae I?" Sigimor watched Ewan's gaze fix upon Liam. "Ah, now, dinnae mind Liam. He is your cousin, too, ye ken."

"Is he." Ewan found himself actually considering telling his far too handsome cousin to go stay in the village.

"He has that look, Liam. Ye ken, the one Diarmot and Connor get when ye are about."

"The one that says he would like me better with a crooked nose and a few scars?" said Liam. "And that he would be pleased to assist me with the change?"

"Aye." Sigimor grinned at Ewan. "Ye said something about food and drink?"

Gregor led the Camerons away and Ewan looked at Fiona. "Ye didnae tell me he was a lunatic."

Fiona laughed and nudged him to start him walking toward the keep. "He can be. My brother Diarmot says the mon looks at everything from a different direction than most people and that his humor takes some getting used to."

"I see. And the way he looks at things told him the best way to find out if we would protect and care for ye was to kiss ye in front of your armed husband and all his equally armed men?"

"Aye. I suspect it told him a few other things he was eager to learn, as weel."

"How ye taste?" he muttered.

"Nay. It told him that ye willnae blindly attack a mon. Every one of ye was ready, but not one struck out."

"He took a great risk with his life and those of his men."

"I wouldnae be so certain of that. S'truth, I wouldnae be surprised to discover that Sigimor kens a great deal about all of ye. If he doesnae make ye gnash your teeth or want to kill him, he will make ye a verra strong ally."

It did not take long for Ewan to understand what Fiona meant about his cousin. He wondered at various times during the evening's festivities if he had, perhaps, been a little too quick to cast aside the possibility of madness in his blood. It felt good, however, to have allies, even if they were a little odd. Glancing around at the MacFingals, Ewan had to admit that one probably needed to be a little odd to accept them all as kinsmen.

Then he saw Fiona and Liam seated closely together on a bench in the far corner of the great hall, their heads close together as they talked, and he decided one less kinsman would suit him very well. Just as he started to rise from his seat, a hand clasped his shoulder and pushed him back down. Ewan looked at Sigimor and idly wondered what would happen if he punched that look of amusement off his handsome face.

"Liam willnae try to seduce your wife," Sigimor said. "Your wife wouldnae let herself be seduced, either. I would say ye insult your wife by worrying, but a woman could be but one step away from sainthood and her husband would still fret if Liam drew near her. Poor lad is oftimes so maligned."

"That *poor lad* has to beat the lasses off with a stick," Ewan drawled.

"True, and he doesnae wield that stick as often

as he should. Howbeit, he doesnae trespass. I willnae say he ne'er has since he left the monastery
three years ago, but he does believe in the sanctity
of marriage. And of course, if he tried his wooing
on Fiona, she would undoubtedly give the lad that
crooked nose we all think he needs." Sigimor smiled
faintly when Ewan laughed, then looked around at
the people gathered in the great hall. "Your father
collects people."

Ewan blinked in surprise at that sudden judgment, then thought about it for a moment. "Aye, I
suppose that is exactly what he does. Some of the
older men and women were here ere my father inherited the place. Then there are all my brothers,
half-brothers, and nephews. And aye, my father allows others like Mab to come here, ones who are
cast out of their clans, but he is careful in choosing
them. When he used to go outside the boundaries
of our lands, he almost always brought someone
home with him. Someone lost, or alone, or cast
aside by their people."

"As he was cast off in many ways. As he believed
his bairn was cast off. Twas the lie told about your
father's bairn that troubled my father the most,
that drove him to confess it all to me ere he died.
My father was certain that lie would be the one
that struck your father the hardest."

"I believe that is so, although I hadnae seen the
truth of that until now. My father ne'er told me
the whole story of what had happened." Glancing
toward where his father sat with Mab, Gregor,
Nathan, and several Camerons, Ewan was pleased
to see that the man was scowling and arguing again.
"Seeing how simply telling the tale pained him, I

can understand. And yet, I think the telling of it may have bled out some of the bile in his heart and blood."

"Aye, it can do that."

"Did your father e'er think that what he had done was worth it?"

"Some days he did; some days he didnae. He loved my mother, but she ne'er loved him back, not as she had loved your father. As he said when he was dying, he lost a brother, but ne'er really gained the bride. Sad, but I cannae grieve o'er it too much. After all, if it hadnae happened, ye and I wouldnae be here."

"Ah, verra true. So, tell me, how do the MacEnroys fare as kinsmen?"

Ewan listened carefully to all Sigimor told him about his wife's family. Although he could foresee a few tense moments ahead with Fiona's brothers, everything Sigimor said pointed to yet another strong, worthy alliance. When he went to parlay with his enemies now, he would do so from a position of greatly enhanced strength. He tensed when his father joined them, but Fingal sat quietly gathering information about the MacEnroys just as he was doing. Ewan was too well acquainted with his father's rapidly changing moods to let his hopes rise too high, but he could not help but think a change for the better had come over his father.

"Ye dinnae think the lass's brothers will be wanting to toss my lad about for a wee while, do ye?" asked Sir Fingal.

"They may want to," replied Sigimor, "but they willnae. Unless, of course, Fiona gives them leave."

Sigimor winked at Ewan. "So, when ye see them coming, it might be wise to soothe any anger she may be feeling toward ye that day."

"Where is the lass, eh?" Fingal looked around and gaped when he saw Fiona and Liam talking. "Ye have left her with that bonnie lad?" Fingal stared at Ewan in shock. "Go get her."

"Nay," Ewan said. "She isnae doing anything wrong. She is just talking to the lad. What harm can there be in that?" Ewan had to bite back a grin when his father looked at him as if he needed some sense knocked back into his head.

"What harm? Have I taught ye naught o'er the years?" Sir Fingal stood up. "Ye are too trusting, lad, but I havenae the time now to explain the error in your thinking. *I* have to go pull the lass out of harm's way. I cannae believe any son of mine could be so witless as to leave his woman unguarded whilst *that* lad is about," he muttered as he strode off toward Fiona.

"That was weel done," murmured Sigimor as he watched Sir Fingal push his way in between Liam and Fiona.

Seeing no reason to deny his guilt in sending his father off after Fiona, Ewan replied, "Thank ye."

"The lass could have stood here listening to that whole conversation and ne'er been able to prove that ye sent your father o'er there apurpose." Sigimor raised his tankard in a brief, silent salute. "Liam *is* a good lad, ye ken."

"Nay doubt. Twould just be better if he was a good, *ugly* lad." Ewan smiled when Sigimor laughed.

* * *

Fiona scowled at Sir Fingal after a chuckling Liam walked away. "I was talking to him."

"Ye are a married lass," Sir Fingal said, crossing his arms over his chest. "Ye shouldnae be talking to such a bonnie, unwed laddie. Why are ye nay sitting with your mon, talking to him?"

"Because he doesnae ken anything about my brother Diarmot's children and Liam does. He was staying at Clachthrom for a wee while ere he traveled to Deilcladach with Sigimor. Liam gained a lot of knowledge whilst in the monastery and he was teaching Diarmot's children."

"If he was so welcome and helpful at Clachthrom, why did they let him leave, eh? Ha!" He nodded when Fiona blushed. "Your brother got tired of looking at that bonnie face. Wanted it far away from his woman."

"That is such foolishness. Ilsa and Gillyanne would ne'er betray their husbands, nor would I. Ewan, at least, has the sense to ken that. He wasnae troubled by my talking to Liam." Fiona inwardly admitted that she was a little disheartened by Ewan's lack of jealousy, a jealousy both her brothers had suffered despite knowing their wives adored them. "But enough of Liam. Have ye talked to Sigimor?" She almost smiled at the way Sir Fingal grumbled over the change of subject.

"A wee bit," he muttered. "A good lad, if a wee bit odd."

Sir Fingal complaining that someone was odd was a little like a fish complaining that water was wet, but Fiona just nodded. "He does take some getting accustomed to. He will be a good ally, though."

"Aye. Ewan is right to say we need them. Now he can face our enemies with two clans standing behind him. They will listen to him now. Mayhap next time one of my lads has to ride off somewhere, he willnae have to creep from shrub to shrub or take half a dozen weel-armed men with him."

And that, Fiona realized, had so troubled Sir Fingal that he had obviously become fully aware of his clan's precarious position at long last. The man must have kept a close watch on all of the careful preparations and intricate precautions, and seen what his actions and hasty words had brought them to. Some men grew more hardened in their ways as they aged and some grew wiser. For Ewan's sake, she prayed Sir Fingal was going to be one of the latter.

It was only an hour later when Fiona realized she was too tired to linger in the great hall any longer. She quietly informed Ewan that she was retiring and kissed him on the cheek. Laughing softly over Sigimor's protests that he was being neglected, she kissed his cheek as well. The way Ewan watched her so closely as she left the great hall warned Fiona that she might not be able to keep their child a secret for much longer. His frown had not all been caused by her kissing Sigimor. Her unusual weariness had caught his attention.

She softly cursed as she prepared for bed. There was just another reason she was reluctant to tell Ewan he would soon be a father. Considering how he had behaved after she had been rescued from Menzies, she dreaded how he would behave when he discovered she was carrying his child. His protectiveness would know no bounds and she would know no peace.

* * *

"Ye had best cease kissing my wife," Ewan told Sigimor as he poured them each some more ale.

Sigimor chuckled. "Twas more a giggle against my cheek than a kiss. And the lass needs a touch of flattery now and then, a wee bit of attention from a mon and all."

"I dinnae think Fiona has e'er suffered a lack of such things."

"Och, aye, she did. Nay before she got the scars, but after. Gillyanne told me. Many a mon who had wooed Fiona before she was scarred hied themselves off to find some other beauty to praise, a perfect beauty of course. Some fools acted as if she bore a mark akin to the one ye bear. The lass isnae vain or foolish enough to believe all the pretty words she might hear, but Gillyanne believes the way far too many reacted to Fiona's scars left the lass feeling as if those marks were far worse than they are."

"Fools, the lot of them," Ewan muttered, and Sigimor nodded.

Ewan knew the pain of watching people looking away after seeing his scarred face. How much worse must it have been for a beautiful young woman? In truth, he suspected the fact that Fiona was not vain had made it all the more difficult in some ways. She had been forced to see that very few people had ever really looked beyond the beauty she had been gifted with. She may not have fully believed all the pretty words said to her, but it had to have hurt to realize just how empty they had been. He was curious as to how much of that hurt still lingered, and he wondered sadly if he could ever find the skill to soothe it.

He was more than a little drunk by the time he sought his bed. It was probably for the best that Fiona was deeply asleep, he mused as he crawled into bed beside her, for he could easily embarrass himself if he tried to make love to her. He pulled her soft, warm body into his arms and sighed with contentment when she murmured his name in her sleep.

Everything was going so well, he felt distinctly uneasy. His father appeared to be growing up at last, or perhaps telling the full tale of what had happened in the past had bled away some of the anger and pain he had nursed for so long. Ewan was certain that hearing the child had lived had removed a heavy load of guilt off his father's heart, a guilt Ewan had never known the man had been carrying. A change in the man had begun after Fiona had entered their lives, and Ewan felt that change for the better had been strengthened by all that had been said today. He thought his father may have finally set the past aside.

Reuniting with the Camerons was a blessing, even though Sigimor would take some getting used to. Ewan was not sure he liked the idea of having so many big, strong, handsome men coming and going from Scarglas, but it was good to have allies. From what Sigimor told him, he would face that same two-edged sword when the MacEnroys came, they and all of their various connections. If Sigimor was right, the moment this Gillyanne accepted him as part of her family, so would all of the Murrays, which included a vast array of other names and alliances. It would not be the same sort of alliance as he would have with the MacEnroys and the Camerons of Dubheidland, but there was a great comfort in knowing how far and wide he could reach out for aid if it was ever needed.

This change also opened up new paths for his brothers to walk. Life at Scarglas was good and would be better once he could make peace a greater part of their lives. However, now there were other places his brothers could go, opportunities they could grasp. Perhaps even some advantageous marriages to make, ones that could bring lands or money into the family or strengthen tenuous alliances.

It was too much good fortune for him to accept easily. Never had things looked so promising. Ewan rested his cheek against Fiona's soft hair and told himself not to look for trouble. He had a beautiful, passionate wife, his father was changing for the better, the two halves of the Cameron family were together again, and he had the allies he had always hungered for. Life was good and he should simply sit back and enjoy it for a while. He closed his eyes, held Fiona close, and used his need for sleep to push away that faint tickle of forboding in the back of his mind.

Chapter 17

He should have heeded that pessimistic side of himself better, Ewan thought, as he stared at the poorly written message in his hand. Was it only last night that he had thought everything was so hopeful, that life was good? Now a ghost of the past had come creeping in to cast a shadow over it all.

Helena had given him a child, or so it was claimed in the message. That child was now residing with an old couple in one of the small crofter homes scattered over his lands. It did not surprise him that Helena would abandon their child. The question was, why had it taken her so long to do so?

Ewan left his ledger room to seek out Gregor. This sudden appearance of a child he had never been told about roused all of his suspicions. Helena was a Gray and had betrayed him once before. It was possible this was a trap, just another lie meant to draw him into danger.

He found Gregor in his bedchamber preparing

to have a tryst with one of the maids. After sending the girl away, Ewan looked at Gregor and shook his head. It might be time to try and put a stop to the use of the women who worked in the keep. If they were put out of reach, Gregor and the others would not be distracted from their work as often as they were.

"Ye grow pious, Ewan," said Gregor, smiling faintly at the look of disapproval upon Ewan's face. "She was more than willing."

"I ken it," replied Ewan. "Maisie is verra free with her favors. Tis why she has three bairns. Do ye mean to breed another bastard?" He realized his anger and worry had sharpened his voice when Gregor looked at him in surprise. "I have just received a message that causes me to be a little uneasy concerning the breeding of bastards." He thrust the note at Gregor.

A curse escaped Gregor as he read the message. "Do ye believe this?"

"Nay and aye. There is a wee chance that she could have borne me a bairn. Spilling one's seed upon the sheets doesnae always prevent a bairn."

"Then why did she ne'er tell ye? Why didnae she have it brought here? I cannae believe the Grays wanted your child about the place."

"Nay. If 'tis true, and if the child has spent the last—what?—seven years living amongst my enemies, one can only imagine how hard life was for him. In truth, one wonders why he wasnae killed at birth. The Grays see all MacFingals as vermin. I doubt his youth or the fact that he carried Helena's blood, too, would stay their hand."

"So, 'tis a lie, a trap."

Ewan strode to the window in Gregor's room and stared blindly out of it. "I fear so, yet I must be sure, aye? What if my child *is* at that cottage? I cannae just leave it alone now that the thought has been put into my head."

"Then send some men to go and collect the boy and bring him here," Gregor suggested.

"And present him to Fiona?"

Gregor cursed again. "I cannae think she would be harsh to the lad or cause too much trouble o'er something that was done eight years ago."

"Yet?" Ewan asked, turning to look at Gregor again. "Therein lies the problem. Those many *yets*. She has heard about Helena so there isnae any need to hide an old affair. But a child? Women can behave oddly o'er the fact that their mon has given another woman a bairn. To us, 'tis but an error, e'en if we care for the child. But women can see it as so much more, as proof of some bond between the mon and that woman. Mayhap ye cannae recall all the arguments between Da and his wives, but I can. A bastard bred on another woman always seemed to them to be some grand insult, more of a one than the unfaithfulness that bred the child."

Gregor grimaced at the painful memories Ewan's words aroused, then sighed. "Ye mean to go to this cottage yourself, dinnae ye."

"Aye. If 'tis a trap, I cannae knowingly send other men into it. If 'tis the truth, and Helena has left my son there, I must see him. I cannae really decide anything until I see the child and see if he is mine."

"Ah, but will ye be able to tell?"

"MacFingals tend to breed true. E'en wee Ned,

Mab's lad, looks like a MacFingal despite his fair hair. Father kens it despite all of his muttering. I but need to decide how to do it, how to go yet nay fall into any trap that might be waiting for me."

"I will go with ye," said Gregor even as he donned his boots. "If 'tis just the two of us, we can slip up to the cottage unseen and have a good look about to judge the danger. I ken the place, and there is cover aplenty for us to use as we approach. The trick will be in deciding just how far away we leave our mounts ere we begin our creeping."

Ewan nodded. "Aye, 'tis a plan and that was what I needed. I seemed unable to come up with one the moment the idea of a child got stuck in my mind."

Gregor clapped him on the back as they started out of his room. "We will sort this out. Of course, if there is a child of yours there, explaining it to Fiona is in your hands."

And that, Ewan decided, was what troubled him more than anything else. Instinct and knowledge told him Fiona would accept his child, care for it, and not give him too much trouble over the results of such an old affair. They were not strong enough to completely banish his fears, however. He worried that this could cause some breach between them, stir up a chill that would rob his marriage of all warmth.

Shaking aside all of those concerns, he concentrated on getting out of Scarglas without a half-dozen armed men trailing him and Gregor. If there was a trap waiting for him, the Grays would be watching for just such a group of men as no MacFingal traveled without such an escort. After feinting a ride

to the village to add veracity to the lie he had told
the others, he and Gregor turned their mounts the
moment they felt they could do so unseen. Once
they had reached the woods, he relaxed, knowing
that even the men in the watchtowers would not be
able to see them if they stayed within the shadows.

They were a goodly distance away from the cottage when they decided to dismount and continue
on foot. He and Gregor crept through the wood
and slipped across clearings with a skill Ewan knew
would have had his father smiling with gleeful pride.
They finally halted, using a crumbling stone wall
as a shield to closely watch the cottage.

"I see nothing," said Gregor. "Saw nothing all
the way here, either."

"Nor did I, and the Grays have ne'er been that
good at hiding," said Ewan.

"Nay, and if they were hiding weel enough for us
to miss them, we would be dead or captured by now."

Ewan tensed as a stooped, white-haired man came
out of the cottage. He left the door wide open behind him, and Ewan could see no men within. It
was such a small cottage that they would have been
easily spotted for there were no rooms for them to
lurk in, only one large room and a sleeping nook.
This particular cottage had no loft for them to hide
in, either.

"Old Robbie doesnae act as if there is anything
wrong, and I dinnae see anyone but the old woman
inside. I think there is a child seated by the table,
but 'tis too dark to be certain," said Gregor. "Do we
wait awhile longer or go?"

"Go. There is no one here but Old Robbie and
his wife." Ewan stood up, but hesitated.

"Changed your mind?"

"Nay, I have to go, dinnae I? I was but preparing myself. The problem is, I would rather there was-nae a child, yet now that the idea has been set in my head, I think I might be disappointed if there isnae."

"I think I understand." Gregor stepped over the wall and started toward the cottage. "There is only one way to settle the matter." He hailed Old Robbie as he approached the man.

Ewan took a deep breath to steady himself and followed Gregor. The moment he greeted the old man, Ewan felt his stomach clench with nervous anticipation. Old Robbie looked at him once and nodded as if a question had just been answered. Ewan knew that question had concerned the parentage of the child within the cottage. Stiffening his spine, he followed the old man into the cottage.

"There he be," said Old Robbie, pointing a gnarled, dirty finger toward a small boy sitting at a table eating an oatcake.

One look was all it took and Ewan inwardly cursed. He moved to the table and sat down on the bench opposite the boy. His eyes stared back at him out of a face that held Helena's beauty yet enough of his own features to keep the boy from looking too pretty. Thick black hair hung past the child's thin shoulders, further marking him as a MacFingal.

A wealth of emotions stormed through Ewan, and he gladly accepted the tankard of ale Old Robbie set in front of him, quickly taking a deep drink to try and calm himself. There was rage, strong and hot, and born of Helena's lies. She should have told him about the child, should have sent the boy to him years ago. Now this child was over seven years old and stared at him with a wariness that made Ewan's heart hurt. There was also a softness welling up as he looked at this child born of his seed, as much a part of him as his arm or leg. Underneath it all was worry. How could he tell Fiona? How could he bring this child home?

"What is your name, lad?" he asked as Gregor moved to stand guard at the door.

"Laddie."

"Are ye sure? Tis an odd name. Is there another that people call ye?"

"Bastard." He glanced at the old couple. "They call me laddie. I like that better than bastard."

Such anger welled up inside of Ewan that he had to take several deep breaths to push it aside. He could hear Gregor muttering curses behind him. The way the boy looked at him nervously told Ewan that the anger he felt was still too clear to see and he fought harder to banish it. Later he would set it free and aim it where it belonged.

"We shall have to find ye another name. Do ye ken if ye were christened?"

"Nay, I wasnae. I heard people speak of it, ye ken. I am unblessed and will go to hell and cannae be buried in holy ground and the devil will steal my soul if he hasnae already and—"

"Please, lad. Nay more. Tis enough. More than enough," Ewan added in a whisper, before looking into the boy's eyes. "I am Ewan MacFingal, laird of Scarglas. Does the name mean aught to ye?"

The boy nodded. "Ye are the mon my mother hates." He frowned. "I think a lot of people hate ye. Hugh does."

"That doesnae grieve me. Lad, I am your father." He sat patiently as the boy studied him closely, those all-too-familiar eyes slowly widening.

"Ye do look like me."

"Aye, I do, though ye are bonnier. The mon by the door is your uncle, Gregor."

"My mother said there were a lot of ye cursed MacFingals."

"There are. Did your mother say why she has sent ye to me?" He saw the tears flood the boy's eyes and almost went to him, but Kate, Old Robbie's wife, got there first, and Ewan decided that was probably for the best. He was a complete stranger to the boy.

"My mother said she was fair sick of me," the boy whispered. "I said I could go stay with Mary, who liked me, but my mother said she didnae want to see me about anymore and was going to send me where she would ne'er have to see me again."

"I found him on my threshold at dawn yesterday," said Old Robbie. "Just him, a thin blanket, and that piece of writing. Kate and I cannae read, can we, so we didnae ken what to do with the lad. Then he read a wee bit of it ere we put him abed that night and we kenned who he was to go to. Got the lad o'er the hill to take ye that writing."

"So, ye can read a wee bit, can ye?" Ewan asked the boy.

"A wee bit. Mary was teaching me."

"Who is this Mary?"

"Hugh's youngest sister. He doesnae like her, either. She limps, ye ken, because he tossed her down the stairs once and she ruined her leg. I told her I was sad for her, but she said I shouldnae be as she only broke her leg. She could have broken her neck, ye ken."

Hell, he thought. His child had spent seven years in hell. The Grays were far worse than he had ever thought. He wondered if some of them would be thankful if he rid them of their laird, as he fully intended to do. If naught else, he would be giving this kind woman Mary a gift.

"Do I go with ye now?" the boy asked.

Ewan grimaced. "Nay today. Ye are a surprise to me, lad. Your mother ne'er told me about ye. I wasnae sure ye were really here or really my son. Now I am and I must return to Scarglas and prepare for ye to come there."

"And think of a name for me?"

"Aye, ye will have a name and we will see that ye are christened."

The boy's eyes widened, the hint of a dawning hope within them. "May I sleep inside?"

"Aye," Ewan said, not surprised to hear the huskiness in his voice for he was very close to unmanning himself with tears. "Soon, lad. I promise ye, 'twill be soon."

After assuring the old couple that he would send them some supplies, Ewan briefly touched his child's head then fled the cottage. He could hear Gregor keeping pace with him as he nearly ran toward the wood. Once inside the shadowy shelter of the trees, he halted. He placed his hands on his hips and stared up at the glimpses of sun visible through the leaves as he fought for control of the emotions tearing through him, of the urge to hunt down Helena and Hugh immediately and kill them.

"Ye cannae kill them yet," said Gregor as he leaned against the trunk of a tree and studied Ewan.

A little startled at how closely Gregor had read his thoughts, Ewan looked at his brother. "She didnae e'en name him. How can a woman bear a child and nay e'en name him?"

"Weel, we all ken Helena is a bitch, cold of heart and treacherous. Ye cannae tear yourself to pieces o'er what was done, Ewan. All ye can do is make it better now. And of course, find a way to kill Hugh and Helena." Gregor grimaced. "I wince as I speak of killing a woman, but sweet Jesu, she needs killing."

"Who would be laird if Hugh died?"

"I think the next son is a lad named Wallace. Why?"

"I need to find out what I can about him. Hugh is dead. Tis but a matter of time. I but wonder if that will actually end our trouble with the Grays, if after that bastard is dead, we might be able to make peace with the new laird. Hugh has no sons?"

"Nay, none that I have heard of. Ye ken he wed Helena?" Ewan nodded and Gregor continued, "I wonder if that is why your son was so poorly treated. She hasnae given him a child from what I have heard. Nary a one, let alone the son he craves."

Ewan started to make his way back to where they had left their horses. "Tis time to find out all we can about our enemy. Since his sister Mary sounds a good woman, one has to wonder if the rot runs as deeply as we thought or if all these years 'tis mostly Hugh we have been fighting. I ken that his father was angered by the loss of Scarglas, but I dinnae recall that there was verra much fighting between us and the Grays in those early years."

"Ye may be right. Best ye talk to our father. All I ken is that the trouble with the Grays has been deadly and almost unrelenting since Hugh began to lead them. I was still a beardless youth when that happened. I hear a few rumors here and there, but nay much else. Thinking on it now, though, that slaughter which took place years ago, the one that killed so many of their women and all, happened after Hugh became the laird. The mon stirs up deeper hatreds and anger than our father e'er could, I think."

"He has certainly stirred such inside of me," Ewan said. "We have fought him mostly in defense of our lives and lands. Now, I want to destroy him. The first step is to try and find out all we can about the Grays."

"Agreed. And what do ye do about your son? Ye have promised him he will be brought to Scarglas."

"And I will keep that promise, but I need time. This isnae an easy thing to tell a wife. I have to do it right, if only for the boy's sake. When I bring him to Scarglas, I want him welcomed, I want Fiona to want him there, to become his mother. I feel that she would accept him, yet once the tale is told . . " He shrugged, his thoughts too confused to put into words.

"I think ye worry o'er naught, but aye, 'tis still a thing that must be gently and carefully done. Old Robbie and Kate will treat him weel and kindly. And I think ye must always approach that cottage carefully. A trap may yet await ye."

Ewan nodded as they reached their horses, and quickly mounted. "This must remain a secret for now. Just ye and I, aye?"

"Aye," agreed Gregor as he mounted and they started to ride back to Scarglas. "It certainly would-nae help your cause if Fiona heard about the lad ere ye could tell her. Dinnae wait too long, Ewan. That cottage isnae that close to the keep, but word could easily slip out from there and reach our gates."

That possibility was still troubling Ewan by the time he joined Fiona in their bedchamber that night. Since his return from the cottage, he had avoided her, struggling to sort out his thoughts and feelings as well as come up with a plan. He suspected she had sensed his odd mood, his distraction, for she watched him closely.

And she was not the only one, he thought, and inwardly grimaced. His cousin Sigimor had begun to watch him closely as well. The man was uncomfortably keen of wit and sharp of eye. It also proved that he was not very good at hiding secrets, especially ones as troubling as this, Ewan mused. He would have to come up with a plan soon.

When Fiona unbraided her hair, he moved to take over the chore of brushing it out. She had become so important to him, so great a part of his life and all of his future. There was a part of him that wanted simply to ask her what she felt for him, but he was a coward. If she did not say the words he wanted to hear, it would strike him to the heart and he shied away from the promise of such pain. Yet not knowing made the problem now confronting him an even knottier one. He simply could not be sure how she would take the news of his son, or if she felt deeply enough for him that it would not be sufficient cause to push her away.

"Is there some trouble brewing, Ewan?" Fiona

asked as he set her brush aside and began to lead her toward their bed. "Ye seem deeply lost in your thoughts."

"There have been so many changes around here, lass, that I find myself lost in my thoughts a great deal."

"Good changes," she said as she climbed into bed, quickly slipping into his embrace when he got in beside her. "A lot has been gained."

"A lot and all of it welcome. My father also seems to be changing for the better. I realized there is now a chance for some of my brothers to do better for themselves than stay here as little more than men-at-arms." He began to kiss her throat, enjoying her soft murmur of pleasure. "Tis simply that it is a lot to accept. We have gone from being all alone, to having allies. That was something I have wished for for so long that I hesitate to believe I have finally gained my wish."

He tilted her face up to his and kissed her. The way she so readily accepted his kiss, his touch, quickly fired his own passion. This was what he feared to lose, he realized. Here was where he feared the chill of anger or hurt could seep in. The mere thought of such a thing happening made him feel desperate and his lovemaking grew fierce.

Ewan pulled off her night shift and pushed her onto her back. He ignored her blushes as he looked her over thoroughly. The beauty of her made his breath catch in his throat, and the fearful part of him wondered how much longer he would be blessed to enjoy it. The threat of losing her freely given passion made him want to leave some mark on her, a fierce memory of heat and hunger, one that might make it impossible for her to cool to his touch.

As he kissed her, he gently captured her wrists in his hands and pinned them to the bed. Before the night was through, Ewan intended to smother her in his passion, to leave her so sated she could not even twitch a toe. The passion they shared was the only thing he was sure of, and he intended to use it to its fullest.

Fiona gasped as he moved his kisses to her breasts, stroking her nipples with his tongue and encircling them with light kisses until she was squirming beneath him. There was something slightly different in his lovemaking tonight, a touch of determination, even desperation. When he finally gave her what she ached for and drew her aching nipple deep into his mouth to suckle her with a tantalizing rhythm, she decided she would worry about his mood later. Whatever was tumbling about in his head and heart, the pleasure he was giving her was too delicious to interrupt with questions and concerns about why.

"Ah, lass, ye taste like the sweetest of honeys," he murmured as he kissed his way down to her silken stomach. "A mon could get drunk upon ye."

"Let me touch ye, Ewan," she pleaded.

"Nay, not this time. Ye touch me and what little control I have vanishes beneath those wee, soft hands."

Her eyes widened when he kissed the curls between her thighs. She tried to clamp her legs together, but his broad shoulders stopped her retreat. Shock held her very still for a moment, but with each stroke of his tongue, it faded. Passion forced it aside as he made love to her with his mouth and tongue. With a soft cry of acceptance and desire, she opened herself up to this new intimacy.

"Ewan," she cried out as she felt her release tightening her insides.

"Nay, hush, lass, give me this."

With a harsh cry, she did. She was still gasping from the wonder of it when he began to kiss his way back up her body. The first touch of his lips against her breasts renewed her desire, much to her astonishment. She wrapped her limbs around him as he eased their bodies together. For a little while, he moved within her almost tenderly, but then their need for each other grew too strong for such gentleness. Her last clear thought as he took them both to the heights they sought was that, for someone who claimed he had little experience, Ewan was proving to be a lover who could easily kill her with passion.

Weakly, Fiona stroked Ewan's back as he lay sprawled in her arms. She decided it might take days to recover from his lovemaking, then smiled to herself. After a little rest, she knew she would be more than ready for him to try and drive her mad with desire if he felt inclined.

She was glad he was not looking at her, though. It was going to take her a little while to quell the embarrassment she felt at the memory of what he had done, the deep intimacy of that kiss. Fiona knew it was a little foolish to suffer such an attack of modesty. She felt none when she loved him with her mouth and he certainly did not blush or hide his face afterward. There was no question that she had found pleasure in it, and if he did as well, then she

would learn not to suffer even that fleeting resistance that had afflicted her, nor would she trouble
him with the need to soothe her delicate sensibilities after the loving ended.

A little smile touched her lips as she realized he
had gone to sleep. She found herself wondering
yet again about the strange mood he had been in
since returning from his ride with Gregor. Something was troubling him; she was certain of it.
Fiona wished he would share it with her, let her
help him solve whatever problem he was fretting
over, but he would not do so. It hurt, but she told
herself not to take it to heart. Ewan had dealt with
problems and responsibilities all on his own for
too long to suddenly begin openly sharing them
with his still very new wife. She would just watch
and wait, keeping her eyes open for some chance
to help him. Touching a kiss to the top of his head,
she swore she would be patient. She decided it
might not hurt to pray that whatever the problem
was, it could be solved without bloodshed.

Chapter 18

Ewan laced up his doublet as he stood at the end of his bed and watched Fiona sleep. She looked exhausted, and he felt both guilty and pleased about that. For the last three nights, he had done his best to love her into a stupor. He was still a little surprised by how he had finally learned some control over his passion for her and by his ingenuity. If Fiona's cries of pleasure were any indication, he was becoming an accomplished lover, at least in her eyes, and that was all that mattered. Ewan just wished that part of his reason for such efforts and success was not because he had a secret he wanted to hide until he could feel more certain of her.

It was wrong, he decided as he left the room. In a way, he was trying to enslave her and using her own desires to do so. That not only was wrong, but could well be impossible. From what he had seen over the years, women were not the ones easily enslaved by passion. Men were. Women were ruled by their hearts. Making love to Fiona until she could not walk was not the way into her heart. At least not all on its own. The problem was, he had no idea of how to make a woman love him.

He paused at the head of the stairs and considered returning to his bedchamber, waking Fiona up, and simply asking her how she felt about him. It was an idea he had considered a few times before. Then, just as before, he turned craven. He knew she had to care for him in some way in order to feel such passion, but he did not want to hear her mouth only gentle words of affection. They could cut him as deeply as if she said she had no true caring for him at all.

Shaking his head over his own cowardice and confusion, Ewan hurried down to the great hall. He would eat and then go get his son. If nothing else, he could not keep slipping over to the cottage to see the boy. It had been only three days and people were already looking at him with suspicion. Such secretiveness was so unlike him, it was hardly surprising that it had been noticed and had roused the curiosity of too many.

An hour later, having been unable to find Gregor, Ewan started on the trip to the cottage on his own. There had been no sign of the Grays in all the time he had traveled back and forth to the cottage. It appeared that Helena had done exactly what she said she had—left him his child. Nevertheless, he followed the ritual he and Gregor had established, leaving his horse at the same place as before and walking the rest of the way to the cottage.

With every step he took, he tried to think of a way to present his child to Fiona. It would have been best to prepare her for the boy, but each time he had opened his mouth to say something, no words would come out. Now he had simply run out of time. He would have to be simple and direct and hope for the best.

Old Robbie answered his rap at the door and Ewan stepped into the cottage. His heart performed a strange, painful lurch in his chest when the boy looked up from his bowl of porridge and smiled at him. That faint glint of hope shone in the boy's eyes again and Ewan knew that, even if he had not already decided to do so, he would be taking the boy back to Scarglas today. He could not dim that hope again.

"Have ye thought of a name for me?" asked the boy as Ewan sat down opposite him.

Ewan shook his head when Kate silently offered him some porridge, but he gratefully accepted the tankard of cool cider she placed in front of him. "I have thought of several, but decided it would be best to wait until we get to Scarglas. Fiona should have a say in it, I think."

"Are ye sure she will like me?"

"Aye, she willnae have any trouble taking ye in. The lass has a good heart." *She just seems reluctant to give it into the care of her husband,* he mused.

"Did ye tell her all about me?"

"Er, nay. So, dinnae be bothered if she acts surprised or the like. And she might get angry, but 'twill be with me, nay you. Remember that."

"Mayhap ye should tell her about me first."

"I have tried, lad. Tisnae easy and I am nay good with words, ye ken. Tis nay an easy thing to be telling a wife, and ye will understand that weel when ye get older." Ewan grimaced, then smiled when he heard Old Robbie laugh.

Then he heard something else, a noise that made the hairs on the back of his neck stiffen. He was just getting to his feet when the door to the cottage was kicked open. Kate screamed and Old Robbie quickly wrapped his arm around her and dragged her with him into a corner by the hearth. Ewan drew his sword and put himself between the armed men near the door and his son.

It had been a trap after all. The Grays had baited it with his son and then waited with a patience they had rarely shown before. Since he was sure he and Gregor had missed nothing when they had come here that first day, the Grays must have left the boy and gone away, staying away in the hope of lulling their suspicions. It had worked. When no attack had come, when no enemy had been sighted, he and Gregor had relaxed their guard, ignoring their own advice. Now he was stuck, the only armed man between the Grays and three helpless people.

A man shoved his way through the others crowded near the door, and Ewan's stomach tightened with fury when he heard a soft whimper escape his son. Hugh, the laird of the Grays, was a good six inches shorter than Ewan, but his body was thick with muscles. His broad face was handsome enough, Ewan supposed, but he had to wonder what Helena found so compelling. Hazel eyes, nut brown hair, and somewhat ordinary features seemed ill suited for the brute Hugh was. There was a look in the man's eyes, however, and something in his smile that warned a person. At the moment, that smile held cold triumph and anticipation.

"Couldnae resist the boy, could ye?" Hugh said. Ewan shrugged. "He is mine."

"Aye, any fool can see he is a filthy MacFingal."

"I am curious as to why ye kept him so long if he troubled ye so."

"Thought the little bastard might come in useful someday and he has, hasnae he."

The thing that upset Ewan the most was that, unless some wondrous miracle happened, he was not going to have the chance to kill this man. "This has been a most pleasant visit," he drawled, "but I really must be on my way now."

"Och, dinnae spoil my fun. If ye take one step toward this wee door, I will have to have ye killed—quickly—and that wasnae my plan at all. Now, why dinnae ye just put down your sword."

"And just why should I do that?" He cursed when one of Hugh's men moved to hold a sword at Kate's throat. "Ye would kill an old woman who has ne'er done ye any harm?"

"Aye."

Ewan knew he had no choice. If he kept arguing, Hugh would kill Kate and Old Robbie. The man might even turn his brutal attention upon the boy. There was no guarantee that he would not kill them all anyway, but Ewan could not ignore the chance that his sacrifice might keep them alive. He tossed his sword at Hugh's feet.

Hugh chuckled and signaled two of his men to grab Ewan. As he was dragged outside, Ewan found some comfort in the fact that Hugh seemed to forget about the old couple and the boy. Even his men just turned their backs on them and left them alone in the cottage. He hoped there was some way they could take advantage of that and slip away. Once out in the clearing before the small cottage, Ewan looked toward a tall, stout post that had been erected. Standing next to it, and smiling sweetly, was Helena.

Sigimor cursed as he watched Ewan being stripped of his clothes and tied to the post, his arms stretched wide and lashed to the crosspiece nailed to the top of the post. He had been watching his cousin for three days and had decided the man was acting strangely. Due to the somewhat licentious nature of his newfound cousins, Sigimor had wondered if the man had a mistress. That being an insult to Fiona he could not tolerate, he had followed Ewan. At the moment, he rather wished it had been a woman.

The sound of someone behind him made him tense and he rested his hand on his sword. Then he heard a soft curse in a voice he recognized. When Gregor started to hurry by him, Sigimor lashed out with one arm, catching the younger man in the chest and knocking him to the ground. He stood over Gregor until the man caught his breath enough to glare up at him.

"What did ye do that for?" demanded Gregor as he rubbed his chest.

"I thought ye might wish to pause a moment and come up with a plan ere ye rushed off to face odds of ten to one."

Gregor cursed as he stumbled to his feet. "I cannae leave Ewan in the hands of that bastard Hugh." He paled slightly as he looked toward the clearing. "The mon is going to make him bleed."

"Aye." Sigimor frowned as he caught sight of movement at the rear of the cottage. "Ye cannae fight all those men by yourself. Even if I lend ye my awe-inspiring skill, the odds are still too great. We need to hie ourselves back to Scarglas and get some help."

"Then let us be on our way."

"In a moment. I want to see who is escaping from the cottage."

"Jesu, 'tis Old Robbie, his wife, and the boy."

"The boy?"

Gregor hastily explained. "We thought it might be a trap, but then days passed and naught happened."

Sigimor nodded. "They waited for ye to grow comfortable, to feel as safe as one can about this place. The first day, mayhap e'en the second, there probably was no one about. From what I have heard of the Grays, 'tis a remarkably clever plan for them to devise."

"Aye," agreed Gregor. "We should have suspected that they might actually get clever at some time over the years. That bitch Helena is down there, I see. She is as bad as Hugh."

"She will soon be as dead as Hugh. Come, those people are about to slip into the wood to our left. We will get them and take them with us."

"I hate leaving Ewan to suffer at Hugh's hands."

"Suffering is better than dead."

"He has a mistress."

Mab handed Fiona a linen square to wipe her tears and returned to making some lavender sachets for the linen chests. "Now why should ye think Ewan would have a mistress?"

Fiona frowned at her friend as she blew her nose. There was a distinct lack of sympathy in Mab's voice. "For the last three days he has gone somewhere and no one kens where."

"Weel, if no one kens where, then how can ye be sure 'tis a woman he goes to see?"

"Why else would he be slipping away without the guard he has always had?"

"To get away from the guard?"

"Possibly," Fiona conceded, then shook her head. "Nay, 'tis more than that, more than stealing a wee bit of freedom for himself. He is being secretive."

Mab leaned against her worktable, crossed her arms over her chest, and looked at Fiona. "That is odd, and many people have noticed it. Ye are the only one who has decided it is a woman, however."

"'Tis usually why a mon starts tiptoeing about, keeping secrets, and disappearing for hours with no one kenning where they are."

"Not here. The MacFingals make no secret of their, er, lustiness."

"Most of them arenae married."

"Fiona, I really dinnae think Ewan is being unfaithful. I cannae think why ye would wonder on it. Has he been less than enthusiastic in the bedchamber lately?" Mab's eyebrows rose when Fiona blushed bright red. "I gather not."

"I am sure he is keeping a secret, Mab. There is something troubling him, something making his mood turn somewhat odd. And, weel, he has become *verra,* er, enthusiastic."

"I would think that, if he is servicing a lass for

hours during the day, his enthusiasm would wane a little at night. E'en a MacFingal needs a rest now and again."

Although it surprised Fiona a little that she could do so when she was so upset, she giggled. "He did tell me he would be faithful when we got married."

"Then he isnae visiting some lass. Ewan is a mon of his word. I think ye are just being a wee bit sensitive, prone to frets and fears. Tis the bairn, mayhap. It can do that."

Fiona slowly nodded. It was possible that she was just succumbing to a surfeit of emotion, imagining problems where there were none. The fact that she was desperately in love with her husband and still had no hint of his feelings was certainly not helping her stay calm.

"I tried to speak to Gregor about it, but he is verra good at slipping away and staying out of sight."

"Why would Gregor ken anything no one else does?"

"Because he is the one who slips away with Ewan."

Mab rolled her eyes. "Listen to yourself, child. Gregor goes with Ewan. Do ye really think a mon would take his brother with him when he went to visit his leman?"

"I am being silly," Fiona whispered after a moment of thought. "Tis just that I am so in love with him yet cannae seem to get him to feel as I do. Tis making me witless and afraid."

"That and carrying a bairn. Why dinnae ye just tell him how ye feel, lass?"

"Pride, I suppose. I think on it, then think on how I would feel if I bared all and he couldnae say the same. Jesu, but that would hurt. And what if

kenning how I feel when he cannae return the
feelings makes him so uncomfortable he starts to
pull away from me? Not that he can pull away much
further than he has already. Oh, I am nay making
any sense."

"Aye, ye are," Mab said. "I wish there was some
advice I could give ye, some clever wifely thing ye
could do to make it all right for ye, but I ken nothing. All I can keep saying is that he is a good mon
and ye must be patient. Just keep reminding yourself of all ye do have. He is faithful, he is passionate, he will see all your needs met, he will protect
ye, and he will give ye children. They dinnae sound
warm and loving, save for the passion, but they are
verra important things."

Fiona smiled faintly. "I ken it. I was just suffering
a weakness. It is just that I ken he is troubled, but
he willnae tell me what it is, then he disappears for
a wee while every day, and from there I managed
to start imagining him rolling about in the heather
with some lusty, buxom maid."

"The lusty ones are always buxom, I fear." Mab
laughed along with Fiona, then shook her head.
"Trust him, Fiona. Just trust him and love him and
'twill all come right in the end."

As she left the herb shed and started back to the
keep, Fiona promised herself that she would repeat Mab's words several times a day. Gillyanne
had not been able to win Connor's heart very quickly, either, she told herself. She suspected her
brother's heart had been placed in his wife's hands
long before he had actually admitted it. If he had
not been faced with the very real chance of losing

her, Connor might have held silent for far longer than he did.

And Ewan is like Connor in many ways, she mused. That same hard outside with a soft inside that he fights to keep hidden from everyone. Ewan would probably never be a man of soft, pretty words and open affection. She was going to have to accept that. Fiona knew it would not be so hard if just once in a while he would whisper that he loved her.

She was sighing with pleasure over the image of Ewan whispering vows of undying love into her ear when a cry went up from the men watching the gates. Her eyes widened when she saw Sigimor and Gregor come racing into the bailey with an elderly couple clinging desperately to a third horse and a small boy clinging to Gregor. Then she recognized the third horse and her heart nearly stopped.

As soon as Sigimor dismounted, she raced to his side. "Ewan? Where is Ewan?"

Sigimor put his arm around her shoulders and gave her a light squeeze. "He is alive, lass, so ye can set aside that fear."

"Then why have ye brought his horse back without him?"

"Because he fell into a trap set by the Grays," said Gregor. "Ye explain it, Sigimor. I will get the men we need."

Fiona kept her gaze on Sigimor as Gregor hurried off shouting orders. "Explain."

Her eyes widened with each word he said. Here was the problem that had been gnawing at Ewan for the past few days. Helena, his first love, had returned to his life. She had given him a child, never told him, and then tossed the boy into his lap. And it had all been a trap set by Hugh and Helena Gray, two people who loathed Ewan. The same people who had captured him once before and tortured him, nearly gelded him. She felt the chill of her fear for him reach deep into the marrow of her bones.

"We were able to help the old people and the lad escape," Sigimor said, and added in a whisper, "The poor lad doesnae have a name. Just call him lad or laddie for now. Your husband can explain all that later."

"If he survives," she said.

"Oh, he will survive."

There was such cold certainty in Sigimor's voice that she felt compelled to believe him. Slowly she turned to look at the child. It hurt that Ewan had not told her about him, but she pushed that aside. The boy looked terrified and needed comforting. She suspected he also needed some assurance that he was welcome.

"Ye look like your father," she said softly and gently touched his hair. "His eyes and his hair."

"He was going to bring me here today," the boy said, rubbing away the tears on his cheeks with a dirty hand.

"I am glad. He should have brought ye here the verra first day, but I shall scold him about that when we get him home."

"Hugh and my mother are hurting him. They are always hurting people."

"I can fix his hurts. I am Fiona, his wife."

"He said ye were bonnie and would be kind to me, but ye dinnae have to if ye dinnae want to."

"Oh, I want to. Who wouldnae want to keep such a bonnie lad about, eh?"

"My mother. And Hugh. Tis because I am a Mac-Fingal."

"Aye, ye are," said Gregor as he stepped up beside them, his father at his side. "Lad, this is your grandsire and he is going to show ye your new home."

The boy cautiously gave his hand to Fingal to hold, then looked at Sigimor. "Ye will bring my father back here?'

"Aye, lad," replied Sigimor.

"My mother?"

"I am afraid ye will ne'er see her again."

He just nodded and let Fingal lead him away. Fiona sensed that Ewan's son was going to need a lot of gentle handling. The look in his eyes, his quiet, tentative nature, and the fact that he apparently had never been given a proper name told her that he had probably paid dearly for being Ewan's child every day of his short life.

She stood by, listening carefully as Sigimor and Gregor made their plans while the men and horses gathered. Their plans sounded good, their confidence in their success was comforting, and she felt her fears ease a little. She saw only one small problem. There was open space that needed to be crossed before they could reach Ewan and his tormenters.

"Ye are going to need something to divert their attention as ye draw near enough to strike them down," she said.

"I hope ye arenae about to suggest what I think ye are," said Sigimor, frowning at her.

"I fear your hopes are in vain."

"Ewan wouldnae be happy with us if we used ye, put ye at risk, just to save him," said Gregor. "One of the men can do something."

"The Grays recognize your men. The only diversion they could create is a brief fight, or a squabble amongst Hugh's men as to who will get to kill them. They willnae recognize me," said Fiona.

"Some of them did see ye the day Simon got injured."

"They saw a dusty lass in boy's clothing and that only during a fight for their lives." She nodded when they both looked a little surprised, then thoughtful.

"And what will stop them from squabbling o'er who will get to kill ye?"

"Simple curiosity. Mayhap lust. It doesnae matter what will make them hesitate to kill me, just that they will. E'en if they somehow recognize who I am, they willnae kill me for they will think I will be useful to torment Ewan with. Ye dinnae need much time to slip o'er that open ground and get close enough to be a real threat to Hugh and his men, do ye?"

"I fear she is making sense, Gregor," Sigimor said. "She can give us those few short minutes we need to cross the clearing and do so better than anything we could think of. The minute they glimpse a MacFingal, they will be alert and battle ready. A wee lass tripping up to them will just puzzle them. I also think most of the men will watch her, even the most conscientious of them needing a few moments to recall that they ought to be watching for a threat."

"And those few moments will be enough to put your swords at their backs," Fiona said.

"Ewan is going to flay me alive for this," Gregor said then asked her what her plan was.

Chapter 19

This was not going to be pleasant, Ewan thought as he stared down at a smiling Helena, who stroked the stout whip in her delicate hands as if it were a lover. He began to understand why she loved Hugh. They were of the same ilk. What he did not understand, had never understood, was why they had such a deep, abiding hatred for him. That he was laird of the lands Hugh coveted did not really seem reason enough.

"Ye should have given the lad a name," he told Helena, and almost smiled when he saw how his words startled her.

She shrugged. "I ne'er thought the little bastard would survive. Jesu, but he was stubborn. I couldnae clean him from my womb ere he was born, and after he tortured me with his birth, he just seemed to grow stronger. I thought once that a fever would take him, but Hugh's crippled sister Mary nursed him back to health."

"We MacFingals are hard to kill."

"I am pleased to hear it for I want ye to take a long time to die."

It was strange to hear such vicious words spew out of such a tempting mouth. Ewan could still look at her and see that she was beautiful, but that beauty no longer moved him. He could now see the rot beneath her fair skin. It ran so deep and was so strong, he was somewhat surprised that she could still be so beautiful to look upon.

He knew what true beauty was now. Fiona might be scarred, her form not so lush, but in all ways she was far more beautiful than Helena could ever hope to be. Fiona had the softness, the kindness, and the generosity of spirit that Helena lacked and would probably see as only weak and foolish. Ewan was a little embarrassed that he had allowed lust to so completely blind him to the sort of woman Helena truly was.

"I do have one wee question ere ye begin your play," he murmured.

"Weel?" Hugh pressed when Ewan said no more.

"I confess I am a wee bit curious as to what has stirred this hatred ye and Helena have for me. Except for the land ye wrongly believe was stolen from ye, Hugh, I cannae recall any particular sin I may have commited against either of ye."

"Scarglas should have been mine!" yelled Hugh. "Your mad father slithered into his cousin's good graces and took it from me. I should have been the one to inherit it, nay you. I should have been its laird, nay you. From the moment ye were born, the child of that fool Fingal and the old laird's daughter, we lost all chance of getting this land. Ye were the old laird's grandson. It didnae matter what Fingal was or what we did to him, ye are the rightful heir in the eyes of the king, the church, and the law. It wasnae to be borne."

"Ye dinnae need these lands. Ye are laird of your own."

"Miserable, useless stretches of rocky moor. With these lands added to mine, I could have been a verra powerful laird." He glanced in the direction of Scarglas keep. "'Tis a much finer keep, as weel. One more worthy of a mon like me. I could have been a respected, wealthy mon if I had that keep."

It still did not make much sense to Ewan. Hugh seemed to think he had become heir to Scarglas out of pure malice, and had robbed him of some glorious future that only existed in his mind, at least in part. Ewan still had the feeling that there was more to it, more twists to Hugh's thinking that probably made sense only to him. At some point in his life, Hugh had decided that the loss of Scarglas was the reason for everything that had gone wrong in his life, and since Ewan was the heir, he had to suffer. The fact that Ewan had bred a son upon Hugh's lover when he had been unable to had undoubtedly strengthened that strange reasoning and sense of grievance.

"And ye, Helena?" he asked.

"Ye killed my family," she replied. "My mother and sister."

"Nay, I didnae."

"Nay by your own hand, mayhap, but 'twas your clan who did the deed. They were slaughtered during one of your raids. My father found their savaged bodies and, in his grief, hanged himself. I lost everyone because of the MacFingals." She smiled at Hugh. "I was utterly lost and alone until I found Hugh."

"My men dinnae kill women."

"Ye MacFingals were raiding Hugh's lands. Your men were seen near my home. Ye just insult me with your denials. Who else could have done it?"

Your father, Ewan thought, but said nothing, just stared at her. Instinct told him that a part of Helena knew that, but rather than face that gruesome truth, she blamed his clan, thus him. It had been their ill luck to be close at hand on that dark day.

It was almost funny in some grim, twisted way. He had done no real harm to either of these people. He would be tortured and murdered for wrongs he had never commited, for crimes and hurts only their twisted reasoning could possibly have blamed upon him. He was their demon, the one they had chosen to bear the blame for their own faults, pains, and losses. For years he had been trying to reason with people who lacked all reason.

"Enough talk," drawled Hugh as he stepped nearer to Ewan, his dagger in his hand. "Tis but a waste of time."

"Killing me willnae gain ye Scarglas," Ewan said.

"True, but it will make me verra happy."

"Ye said I could go first, Hugh," Helena said, a slight whine in her voice. "Tis why I brought my whip. If ye start carving on him, he will be all bloody and senseless ere I can pay him back for touching me."

"Ye touched me," Ewan murmured. "I wasnae spitting out my secrets fast enough for ye, so ye crawled into my bed and tried to seduce them out of me. Ye can cease acting as if ye are some virtuous lass debauched by a filthy MacFingal. Twas quite the other way around."

And now she was not beautiful at all, Ewan thought, as he watched her face twist into ugliness with hate and fury. Now one could clearly see what was in her heart. It had probably not been wise to say what he had, but he was weary of being called a vile seducer by this whore.

"Let me make him pay for that, Hugh," she hissed. "Let me make him bleed."

"I will stop ye if ye go too far, my love," Hugh said as he stepped back. "I will let ye have your vengeance, but not at the cost of my own. Turn him round," he ordered his men.

And so it begins, Ewan thought as, despite his struggles, he was finally turned so that Helena could wield her whip upon his back. He prayed he had the fortitude to endure it without giving them the pleasure of seeing his pain. The longer he could endure, the more the slight chance of rescue grew as well. Someone would soon notice that he had been gone longer than ever before, that he had gone away alone. Gregor knew he would be here, something the Grays were obviously unaware of. As Helena's whip seared across his back, he gritted his teeth against a cry and began to pray that someone came looking for him soon.

"I want ye to kill them both," Fiona said as she stared at her husband, naked and bleeding, yet still attempting to struggle as the men turned him around upon their strange scaffold so that he was facing Hugh Gray.

"Tis what we intend to do," said Gregor.

"We could do it slowly," murmured Sigimor, watching her closely. "Give them a wee taste of what they deal out to your mon."

"Ah, how ye tempt me, Sigimor," she said, taking a deep breath to control the fury that had ripped through her at the sight of her husband. "But nay. E'en if it is weel-deserved justice in a way, we willnae act as they do."

"As ye wish. Ready?"

Fiona tugged her bodice down just a little and ran her fingers through her hair to make it look more tousled. "Aye, I think so. How do I look?"

"Delicious."

"Ye cannae see any of my daggers?"

"Nary a one."

"Then I am ready."

"Be verra careful, Fiona," said Gregor. "If ye e'en think they are about to grab ye, hurt ye, run. I have seen ye run and ye ought to be able to keep free of their grasp, at least until we can turn their attention away from ye."

"Agreed."

Fiona was glad of the rage that heated her blood, for it burned away her fear as she picked up her basket and started toward the Grays. Although everyone thought her plan a good one, she knew it could all go horribly wrong. None of them could be sure just how much the Grays may have heard about her. If they knew too much, she would be quickly recognized and that could put her in even more danger.

"Uncle Robbie," she sang out as she skipped toward the cottage. "Hallooo! I have brought ye cakes." She stumbled to a halt and looked at the Grays as if she had only just noticed them. "Oh, my, my, my. I hadnae realized Uncle Robbie was having guests. I would have brought more cakes."

Ewan blinked. That could not possibly be Fiona he saw standing there. His pain had made him delirious.

Then he looked at Hugh and his men, at their lusty expressions, and realized that it was indeed his wife standing there. His wife looking so sweetly confused, her beautiful hair swirling around her slender body, and her bodice pulled so low that he could see the slightest hint of her nipples. One deep breath or wriggle and her breasts would be bouncing about in front of everyone's eyes. When he was free, he was going to find out who had allowed her to do this and kill them—slowly.

Then she looked at him, and for one brief moment he saw rage and pain in her eyes before they turned somewhat cloudy. Her face held an expression of simple curiosity, not a glimmer of recognition to be seen. In fact, considering she was staring at a bloodied, naked man, her expression was so sweet and calm, one would have to wonder if she was in possession of all her wits. He idly wondered how many knives she had tucked away upon her person.

"Who the hell are ye?" demanded Hugh.

The way Hugh was staring at Fiona's breasts made

Ewan hope someone would come and kill the man soon. After a quick look around at the lust-filled expressions on the faces of Hugh's men, Ewan nearly told his wife to go home. Then he saw Helena's face. The woman looked from Hugh to Fiona and back again. The way her expression hardened and her grip tightened upon her bloodied whip made Ewan feel that she was the one who had to be watched closely.

He kept his gaze fixed upon Helena as Fiona played her game. If nothing else, it kept him from looking for the men he hoped were coming. Impetuous though she was, Fiona would never attempt to rescue him on her own. She was too intelligent for that and, he realized, too well versed in the ways of battle. Ewan struggled not to give in to his pain, to do his best to watch the Grays for any sign of a threat to Fiona or that one of the fools might suddenly remember that he ought to be keeping a guard.

"Why, I am Old Robbie's niece," Fiona replied, smiling at Hugh. "I oftimes come to see the mon and his sweet wife."

"He doesnae have any kin," snapped Helena.

"Weel, I am nay blood kin, but we still consider each other family."

"This is wrong, Hugh," Helena said, moving next to him and grabbing his arm, scowling when he barely looked at her but kept his gaze fixed upon Fiona's lithe body. "Send this skinny bitch away or kill her."

"Oh, how unkind!" cried Fiona.

Ewan watched as every man's gaze followed her hand when she pressed it against her bosom. If rescue did not come quickly, they would fall upon her like a pack of slathering wolves. Or a jealous Helena would attack her. Then Ewan almost smiled. Helena would be making a very grave mistake, perhaps even a deadly one, if she did that.

"But I forgive ye," Fiona said, "for I suspect those spots are verra uncomfortable and make ye ill humored."

"Spots?! I havenae any spots," said Helena, even as she ran her hand over her face.

"Oh, pardon. It must have been a shadow or two. My mistake." Fiona glanced at Ewan. "Ye really should put some clothes on this poor mon. Tis nay right for ladies to be subjected to such a sight. To see so much manliness displayed can sorely upset our delicate sensibilities."

"Ye are an idiot."

"Shut your mouth, Helena," said Hugh. "And ye, wench," he said to Fiona, "what do ye do here?"

"I wait," replied Fiona.

"For what?"

"For ye to die."

Hugh was not the only one surprised by the abrupt change in Fiona's voice. Ewan did not think he had ever heard a woman sound so hard, so cold and threatening. He tensed as she began to ever so slightly back up toward him. Out of the corner of his eye he caught a glimpse of red hair and nearly smiled. All he had to worry about now was that his brave little wife did not get injured in the battle that was about to begin.

"Ye are mad. Surely ye cannae think that one wee lass like ye could do me any harm."

"Weel, aye, I could, but I believe I will let someone else do it."

"Who?"

"Me," said Sigimor, and he grinned when Hugh whirled around to face him.

Fiona moved to stand close to Ewan as the battle began. She put her basket down and armed herself, a dagger in each hand. She wished she could reach his bonds and get him down, but not only were they up too high, she could not afford to take her attention from the Grays.

"I will beat ye when I am free and healed from these injuries," Ewan said.

"Ye may try," Fiona said. "It will be a quick battle."

"Verra quick." Then he saw Helena turn to glare at Fiona, as if she had only just realized the trick that had been played upon them. "Ware, lass."

Fiona tensed as Helena approached. The woman had obviously been in the midst of the battle. Fiona now recalled hearing that whip crack a few times. Since Helena no longer carried it, she had to assume that one of Ewan's men had taken it away. She was sorry they had not killed the woman when they had done so. Helena did, however, now hold a large, sharp knife.

"Ye are the one he married, arenae ye," hissed Helena.

"Aye, I have that honor," Fiona replied.

"Honor? To marry him? I suppose ye couldnae get anyone else since ye are marred."

"And ye are an idiot."

"I am going to kill ye," Helena said, "and then I am going to cut this pig up into small ugly pieces. Ye had best run, ye wee fool, as I am the one who gave him many of those scars."

"I ken it, but I will be merciful and nay make ye suffer when I kill ye."

Ewan cursed his bonds when Helena attacked Fiona. An instant later he calmed and watched his wife with admiration. Her skill was easy to see, her grace in battle a wonder to watch. It took several moments for Helena to realize she was just being toyed with, that the smaller woman could have killed her already if she had chosen to. For a brief moment, fear flickered in her expression, but then she glared at Fiona.

"I will take ye with me," Helena snapped, silently acknowledging that she would be losing this battle.

"Nay, ye will go alone."

A moment later it was done, Fiona calmly cleaning her blade upon the dead woman's skirts. She was just standing up to look at Ewan when the last of the Grays fell. He knew a brief pang of disappointment when he realized he had not seen Hugh die.

"Sigimor made him sweat," Fiona said.

"Ye can read my thoughts, can ye?"

"Nay, after what he did to ye, it took no great gift to ken what ye would think."

Gregor and Sigimor untied him. He collapsed to his knees, his legs too weak to hold him. It did not take any urging for him to rest his head in Fiona's lap. He closed his eyes and breathed deeply of her scent as she began to gently clean his wounds. All around him, he could hear the sounds of his men removing the bodies of the Grays.

"Oh, Ewan," whispered Fiona as she gently bathed the blood from his ravaged back, "I wish we could kill them all again. Your poor fine back."

"Twill heal," he said. "Helena didnae have the strength in her arm to do me as badly as a mon would have."

"I am nay sorry I killed her."

"Good. Ye shouldnae be. Ah, lass, ye took too great a risk just to save my battered hide."

"I had no choice."

He wanted to ask her what she meant, but his brother Gregor arrived with a blanket and his breeches. Fiona helped him sit up, and Gregor carefully tugged his breeches onto his rapidly weakening body. Trying to understand the meaning behind the tone of Fiona's voice when she had spoken would have to wait until he had his senses back. The wealth of emotion he had heard could be no more than was natural for a woman after such an ordeal. Or it could mean she felt a great deal for him, he thought happily. Later, when he was clearheaded, he would think it out all very carefully.

"Can ye sit a horse?" Gregor asked him.

"Nay without being tied there or held very securely," Ewan answered. "How did ye ken what was happening?"

"I had realized ye had left without me and followed. Found Sigimor already here. He had followed ye, too, although he ne'er said why," Gregor said and frowned at Sigimor as that man stood next to Fiona. "Why were ye there?"

"Thought he was acting odd," replied Sigimor. "Thought he might have himself a leman and decided to find out if I was going to have to pound some sense into him."

Fiona giggled, both at Sigimor's calmly spoken threat and in relief that she was not the only one who had wondered if Ewan was sneaking away to visit a woman. "Ewan is going to need to be held firmly if he is to stay on a horse all the way back to Scarglas, and care must be taken with his back."

"I will do it. He can sit up behind me, put his arms round my waist and we will tie his wrists together to hold him like that if he swoons."

"I ne'er swoon," muttered Ewan, but Sigimor just smiled.

Sigimor winced as he helped Ewan to his feet and caught a glimpse of his back. "That woman loved her whip. Just what did ye do to make her hate ye so much?"

"She blamed me for the death of her mother and sister," replied Ewan, leaning heavily on Sigimor as the man walked him to the horses Simon was just bringing into the clearing. "From the tale she told, I believe her father was mad and killed the women, then killed himself. I could tell that Helena suspected it, but the MacFingals were raiding the Grays that day and so she decided to blame us instead."

"And Hugh wanted Scarglas."

"Aye, but he, too, had gotten everything all tangled up in his mind until I became his demon to slay." Seeing that Fiona was a few steps behind them speaking with Simon, Ewan asked Sigimor, "What about the people in the cottage? By God's mercy, Hugh forgot about them."

"Ye mean the old couple and your son?"

"Oh, curse it, Fiona has seen the boy."

"Aye, he and the old couple are at Scarglas. Ye should have told her."

"It had only been three days since I had learned

about him myself. I was trying to think of the best way to tell Fiona."

"Weel, while ye are recovering, ye will have time to think of the best way to soothe her temper."

"She was angry, was she?" Fiona grimaced at the look Sigimor gave him, a look that clearly told him that was a stupid question. "Aye, of course she was. Tis hard for a lass to accept her husband's bastard."

"Oh, she wasnae angry that ye had bred a bastard. Her brother Diarmot has five. And Fiona has the good sense to understand it was e'er ye met her, that she was still just a wee lass herself, nay a woman yet. Nay, she was angry that ye hadnae told her. Mayhap hurt a wee bit, as weel."

"I dinnae suppose ye ken of a way a mon can grovel without looking as if he is doing so." He sighed when Sigimor just laughed.

By the time they got him settled on the horse, his arms tied around Sigimor, Ewan knew he was soon going to make himself a liar and swoon. He looked down at Fiona when she paused by the horse and stroked his thigh with a trembling hand. Ewan knew he was not imagining the emotion in her expression. There was far more there than the concern of a dutiful wife.

"I will be fine, Fiona," he said. "Get on your horse and let us be on our way. And pull up your gown. I can see your nipples."

He nearly laughed when she blushed, yanked up her gown, and then glared at him before hurrying to her horse. It would have been better to have stayed locked in that emotional moment, used it to pull a few sweet words from her, but Ewan knew it was not the right time for that. He comforted himself with the knowledge that she did feel deeply for him. It had been there to see, clearly, in her tear-filled eyes. Later, when he was healed, he would try to find a way to pull those words from her. That look had given him hope, but he needed the words. It was his last clear thought, for Sigimor started to ride and Ewan lasted barely a minute before his pain sent him tumbling down into blackness.

Chapter 20

"Hello, Father."

Ewan cautiously opened his eyes and looked at the small boy standing by his bed. The next thing he became aware of was that he lay on his stomach and his back was no longer the mass of fiery agony it had been. His memory of how he had gotten into his bed and who had done what to tend his back was very dim. Instinct told him it had been more than a few hours since he had swooned during the ride back to Scarglas.

"Hello, lad," he said, his throat so dry it felt as if he had eaten sand.

"I am nay called just laddie now. I have a name."

There was so much pride and joy in that statement, Ewan had to smile. "And what is your name?"

"Ciaran MacFingal or Ciaran Cameron. Sigimor and Grandsire keep arguing about that."

"A fine name either way. Who gave it to ye?"

"My new mother. She e'en got the priest to christen me all proper. We wanted ye to be there but ye were still sick."

"I have been sick, have I?"

Ciaran nodded. "For days and days. Mama and Mab made ye drink medicines and put muck all over your back."

"Verra kind of them. Um, Ciaran, do ye think ye can get me something to drink?"

"I will do it."

Ewan stared at his wife as she approached the bed with a tankard and sat down on the edge. She looked calm, but perhaps a little too calm. There was a lack of feeling in her touch as she slipped her arm beneath his head to help him hold it up as he drank the cool cider she offered him. There was no doubt about it; she was angry.

"How long was I ill?" he asked after he finished his drink and she rose from the bed.

"Three days," she replied as she stood next to Ciaran. "I thought about waiting for ye to help name our son, and see him properly christened, but I couldnae abide the fact that he had no name for more than a day. And e'en that was a trial. Your father has told him that, when ye are weel, we shall have a proper ceremony and feast where he will be introduced, officially, to all his uncles and cousins and his name will be entered into The Book."

"Ah, The Book." He smiled at Ciaran. "A very important occasion. A very big book," he murmured, thinking of the ledger where his father recorded all of his sons and their sons, their births, christenings, mothers' names, and all other information he could gather. He had recorded his daughters, too, but they were only three amongst the multitude of boys. "I am pleased that ye have settled in, Ciaran. Ye arenae waiting for the ceremony to meet everyone, though, I hope."

"Nay. I need to meet them one at a time, though," the boy said in a very serious voice. "There are a lot of them and I dinnae want to forget their names. Tis verra important to ken a person's name."

"It certainly is." Ewan became aware of a suddenly pressing need to relieve himself. "Ah, do any of my brothers happen to be close at hand? I could use their assistance."

"Aye. I will get one," said Ciaran even as he raced to the door and flung it open. "I need a brother here," he bellowed. "My father has to piss!"

"Oh, my God," muttered Ewan, torn between embarrassment and the urge to laugh as hard as Fiona was, although she was trying to hide it. "I guess he *has* settled in weel."

"Och, aye," she said in a choked voice. "O'er the last three days he has come to think that is what *needing assistance* means. Ah, I hear one of your brothers coming. I will go and get ye some food."

"Nay gruel," he called after her as she grabbed Ciaran by the hand and hurried away, passing a laughing Gregor on her way.

Ewan just glared at him as Gregor helped him tend to his personal needs. He was pleased that he did not feel as weak as he had feared he would. Soon, he would not need such assistance. As he sat on the edge of his bed, he found he was intensely curious about what had happened to make him lose three days.

"Ye were slightly fevered," Gregor told him as he sat in a chair by the bed. "To keep ye from thrash-

ing about and making your back bleed, we tied ye
to the bed for two days. Fiona made ye some verra
soft binding ropes."

Despite his efforts not to, Ewan felt himself
blush slightly, but stoutly ignored the glint of curiosity in Gregor's eyes. "That was kind of her. And
the third day?"

"Ye were sleeping off the rest of the potions she
and Mab kept pouring down ye in an effort to
make ye sleep soundly. And keep still. Ye did wake
up once last night, but ye werenae verra coherent.
Ye werenae seriously ill. Twas mostly the need to
keep ye on your stomach until the wounds upon
your back could begin to close." Gregor peered at
Ewan's back. "They are looking verra good. I suspect ye willnae have to lie upon your stomach for
more than a few days longer. They werenae deep
enough for stitching, ye ken, although Fiona was
upset that the woman had undoubtedly given ye a
few more scars."

"And I have seen that my son has settled in comfortably," he said, then laughed as he thought of
how the boy had bellowed out the door, embarrassment no longer dimming his amusement.

"Aye. Fiona and our father couldnae wait for ye
to help name the lad. For once they werenae arguing, but in full agreement that it was a crime that
had to be set right immediately."

"He seems pleased with their choice."

"He introduces himself to everyone he meets.
And if ye call him lad or laddie, he quickly corrects
ye. I think it will be a while before he allows such
an informality. For that crime alone, that bitch deserved to die."

"Aye, but I wish Fiona hadnae been the one to kill her. She has gotten a fair bit of blood on her hands since coming here."

"Both times it was a matter of kill or be killed. I have seen no sign that she is troubled by having had to kill Helena. In truth, she didnae e'en have to rush off to empty her belly."

"Nay, she didnae, did she."

"She wanted that woman dead from the moment she saw ye hanging there at the cottage. I think she has wished she could kill her again a few times since then, especially as concerns her treatment of your son."

"*Our* son," Ewan whispered, suddenly aware of the meaning of the words Fiona had said. Acceptance. "He calls her his mother."

Gregor nodded. "Aye, ye didnae need to worry about whether or not she would accept him. E'en when she first met him, she quickly hid her shock and was most kind and welcoming. Da is good with the lad, too. Tis odd, but watching him with Ciaran, I started to remember things and, weel, for all his faults, he has been a verra good father."

"Ye didnae think he had been?"

"Ne'er gave it much thought once my mind was taken up with how odd he was. Still is, although much calmer, as if he is, weel, happy."

Ewan nodded and glanced toward the door, his stomach grumbling. "Do ye think she will bring me gruel?"

"Only if she thinks it will soothe her anger at ye in some way. Ye better have some good explanation for nay telling her about the boy. She cannae decide if it was just a *stupid monly thing,* as she calls it, or if ye have insulted her by thinking she would be angry and take that out on the boy."

"A stupid monly thing?" Ewan muttered.

"Aye." Gregor grinned. "Seems Sigimor's sister is fond of saying that and he has decided Fiona has picked up Ilsa's bad habits. Fiona told him her Gilly often mutters about the same thing, that 'tis nay just Ilsa who is an intelligent woman."

"She argues with Sigimor?" Ewan had to grin at the image of the small, delicate Fiona squaring off against the large Sigimor.

"Aye, and our father finds it verra amusing. He and Sigimor nip and bite as weel. The alliance ye wanted is firm, Ewan. Da has accepted these Camerons he cursed for so long."

"That is good, but why are the Camerons still here?"

"Sigimor says that, after so many years of having the gates slammed shut as he approached, he is determined to come to ken all of us. Says we are nay the only ones pleased with gaining an alliance. He isnae at war with all of his neighbors, but they arenae exactly his allies, either. He and Da may argue, but 'tis because they like to. If all of the tales Sigimor tells are true, that clan is nearly as odd as this one." Gregor looked toward the door as it opened and Fiona walked in carrying a tray of food. "Ah, there is hope, brother," he whispered. "Tisnae gruel."

Gregor helped Fiona set the food out on a small table by the bed, then left. She sat down in the chair by the bed, waiting to see if Ewan was going to need any help with his food. It pleased her to see that he was not very weak at all. Despite all of

Mab's assurances that neither the fever nor the wounds were very serious, she had been worried. Now she could just be angry.

As soon as he was done, she helped him lie back down on his stomach. When she started to move away, however, he caught her by the wrist and tugged her close. She sat down on the bed and looked at him, her anger soothed a little by the faintly contrite look he gave her.

"I wasnae worried that ye wouldnae accept the boy," he said. "I was worried about how ye would feel about me having made him."

She stared at him, thinking that he had gotten very good with words if he could so easily banish most of her anger with one sentence. "That was eight years ago, Ewan. I was but eleven or twelve. Wheesht, our Gilly hadnae come to Deilcladach yet and I was still being raised as just another brother."

"I ken that now that I am thinking clearly. I wasnae thinking clearly back then. I havenae seen or heard from the woman since the day she betrayed me to Hugh Gray, and suddenly, I get a message that she gave me a son and he is at Old Robbie's cottage. I am sure Gregor has told ye all about how we thought it was a trap, but I had to go to be sure. One look was all it took to ken that he was my son."

"Tis all I needed."

"Weel, that was a shock. Then, ah, Jesu, Fiona, to hear that she hadnae e'en named him or had him christened. People called him bastard." He tightened his grip on her hand slightly when she lifted their joined hands to her mouth and kissed his knuckles. "He asked if, when he came to Scarglas, he could sleep inside." He nodded when she cursed. "If she had just told me about him, I could have spared him all of that."

"What is done is done. Ciaran is a verra resilient boy. There are wounds to his heart that may ne'er completely heal, but he grew as bold and saucy as any lad of seven should be, and so quickly once he was accepted, that I think he will be fine. But now I ken why he was so thrilled with the wee bed in the nursery. Helena treated her own child as if he were nay more than some stray dog. How can any mother do that?"

"I havenae got an answer to that, sweetling. I dinnae really have an answer to the question of why I didnae tell ye about him immediately. So many thoughts churned about in my head. I even recalled all the bitter arguments my father and his wives had over his bastards."

"If ye bred a child with another woman whilst wed to me, 'twouldnae be an argument ye would need to fret o'er, but a battle, mayhap e'en a painfully slow gelding."

He grinned and tugged her close so that he could lightly kiss her scowling mouth. Even the thought of him being unfaithful had obviously stirred her anger and that delighted him. Jealousy might not be the best of emotions, but it was usually a sign that a woman's heart was engaged. When he was healed enough to make love to her again, they were going to have a very serious talk about how they felt about each other. It was time to stop guessing and fearing the answers. While he healed, he would have time to build up his courage, and some of her actions and reactions over the last few days had given him the hope he needed to do so.

"I was confused, Fiona. Nay more, nay less. I was bringing him home the day I was caught by Hugh and Helena." He frowned slightly. "Does Ciaran ken what happened to his mother?"

"Aye, I told him." She sighed. "I thought about telling him only some, or e'en lying, but in the end, I told him everything. This is a tale that will be told too often for him not to hear it, and I wished it to come from me first. He kens she tried to kill ye, and what else she did to ye. I but mentioned the whip and he kenned exactly what she had done. He also recognized what had put those marks upon your back."

"Och, nay, she didnae—" He cursed when she nodded.

"He isnae badly scarred, so either he was good at hiding or running or there were some people at that keep who stopped her. He also had Mary, whom he loves, and by the sound of it, she loved him as weel. So, I told him that I killed Helena because she was trying to kill me. He didnae doubt that for a minute. He then seemed to simply put it all aside. He doesnae mention her at all."

"'Twas hard for ye, I ken it, but the truth was for the best. And mayhap he doesnae particularly care what happened to her."

"She wasnae really a mother to him, was she?"

"Nay, she wasnae. But ye will be, aye? He already calls ye that."

"His choice. I told him he could call me Fiona if he wished, or Mother, but that he was now our son."

"Thank ye."

"For what? He is just a little boy, a wounded little boy, and ye and I were naught to each other when ye made him. And oh, Ewan, he sees e'en the smallest thing ye do for him as such a gift, it fair to breaks my heart. I was so pleased to hear him yell out that door like a proper little boy, that I didnae even scold him for the words he used. The hardest thing to do will be to keep from spoiling him. That, and hugging him each time he gets that look in his eye, that uncertainty and fear. I think it will be a long time before he can fully accept that he is welcome here." She yawned. "Pardon."

Ewan slid across the bed a little, carefully turned onto his side, and tugged her down beside him. "Rest here." He tucked her up in his arms, pressing her back against his chest.

"Your back," she began to protest.

"I am nay lying on it. We have slept this way before and I havenae turned onto my back until the morning. Without those potions ye and Mab gave me, I suspect I would also feel it the minute I did turn onto my back and move ere I did any damage."

That was true, she thought, even as she closed her eyes. She knew why she was tired and soon she would have to explain it to him. Too many people had begun to notice her very hearty appetite and the way she tended to rest in the afternoons. Talk would begin soon and she did not want him to learn through gossip that he was about to become a father—again.

"Helena was a verra beautiful woman," she murmured.

"Her outside only. Seeing her again, I suffered a brief moment of utter embarrassment that I had ever touched her."

"Ah, but if ye hadnae, Ciaran wouldnae be here."

"True, and that would be a sorrow." He kissed the top of her head. "There was one moment when her ugliness was revealed upon her face. I had wondered why God would wrap such vileness in such fair skin. I think lust had blinded me to that rot, but I excuse myself by telling myself I was a young mon."

"Hmmm. Nay such a heedless one, though. She had to come to you."

"Ah, true. Mayhap there was a small bit of wit left in my stupid monly head."

She giggled sleepily. "Aye, mayhap."

"I still havenae scolded ye for taking such risks," he said, slipping his hand up her side to cup her breast and smiling when she made a soft sound of contentment.

"Weel, ye can scold me in a few minutes."

"Why wait a few minutes?"

"Because I will be asleep by then and nay have to listen to it."

"Such an impertinent lass. Ye put yourself in danger, Fiona."

"As ye would have done for me. And it wasnae a verra great danger. E'en ye ken that they would hesitate to just kill me. E'en if they had guessed who I really was, and the chances of that were verra slim, they wouldnae have killed me right away. All we needed was but a few minutes where all eyes were fixed upon something so that your men and

Sigimor's could get across that open space unseen. Ye may nay like it, but e'en ye have to admit that I was the perfect choice."

He grimaced, reluctantly recognizing the truth of that. "Aye, ye were, and aye, I dinnae like it."

"I fooled them, though, didnae I?"

"Aye, ye did, but if ye ere do anything that dangerous again, I *will* beat ye."

"Ye may try."

And he just might, she mused as she let the need for sleep wash over her. Once she told him about the child she carried, it would not take long for him to realize she had been with child during his rescue. So would Gregor and Sigimor. She was going to be lectured until her ears rang. As she placed her hand over his where it rested upon her breast, she decided it was a small price to pay to have him back at Scarglas, alive and complaining, his worst enemies dead and gone.

Ewan smiled as he felt her body grow lax with sleep. She cared for him. He had no doubt of that. It might take a little while to turn that into the love he needed, but he could see it happening now.

It might be time to have a talk with Gregor, he mused. It galled him to go to his younger brother for advice, but it was no secret that Gregor had a winning way with women while he did not. The time had come to woo his wife, to turn that caring she felt into love. He wanted her bound to him in body, heart, and mind, as he was bound to her. Gregor might be able to help him with his inability to speak the pretty, amorous words women seemed to like.

He would stop keeping her at a distance, pathetic though his efforts had been. Ewan knew she wanted to be part of his life, all of his life. She had tried to be subtle, but he had often sensed her frustration with the way he was hesitant to tell her things, to speak of his thoughts and feelings, to share his plans for the future. Fiona never hesitated to tell him such things, and it was time to start returning that trust and confidence.

The sound of the door opening drew him from his plans for winning his wife, and he watched Ciaran creep up to the side of the bed. The boy looked at Fiona, and Ewan could see the longing in his eyes. Ciaran wanted a mother, and Ewan knew he could not have chosen a better one for the boy. She would be firm yet gentle with Ciaran, and she would know how to heal his wounds. Because of the way she had been raised, she would also have a tolerance for a young boy's ways as many another woman might not.

"Is she ill?" asked Ciaran in a soft, slightly tremulous voice.

"Nay," Ewan whispered back. "She is just having a little rest."

"She did work hard to make ye better."

"I ken it."

"I am sad that my old mother tried to hurt ye and my new mother."

"Ye have naught to be sad about. Ye didnae do it and ye didnae want her to, either, did ye?" Ciaran vigorously shook his head. "So, ye must not think that ye need to apologize for what she did. She may have been your mother, but she was a grown woman and made her own decisions and choices."

"That is what Mama and Grandsire tell me."

"And they are right. A child shouldnae have to bear the weight of his parents' mistakes."

"But I *am* sad that my old mother made my new mother have to kill her."

"So am I, but 'tis done and there is no changing it. Tis in the past, and it should be forgotten."

Ciaran nodded, then yawned, belatedly remembering to put his hand over his mouth. "I think I am feeling a wee bit tired, too."

Ewan had to bite back a smile, although he also felt a pang of tenderness. The boy was looking at Fiona and the bed with a covetous hunger. He doubted the child was really wanting a rest, but he certainly wanted to cuddle up to his new mother for a while. It was a sentiment Ewan could fully understand.

"Weel, if ye are careful nay to wake her, there is room there for ye to curl up next to her."

The boy moved quickly. He also moved with a stealth that made Ewan think too much on where and why he had learned such a skill. The moment Ciaran settled his body next to Fiona's, she murmured his name and curled her arm around his waist, tucking him up close to her. A soft sound escaped the boy, one of pure bliss, as he carefully snuggled up close to Fiona.

Ewan lifted his head just enough to look at Fiona and Ciaran. In three short days, while he had been sleeping, the two had obviously become bound together in some way he doubted he would ever understand. Even in her sleep, Fiona had recognized that small body nestled against hers, just as a true mother would her child.

This was his future, he thought. This woman,

this child, and whatever children Fiona blessed him with. He settled back down and buried his face in her hair, feeling a stinging in his eyes that he was determined to control. All his life, from the moment he had realized that men and women were meant to be mates, he had hungered for a woman he could call his own. Young and foolish, he had briefly thought Helena was that woman. Fiona's arrival in his life had shown him just how foolish that had been. Here was what he had hungered for, and he would do whatever he had to to keep it.

Chapter 21

"I cannae believe it. Married?" Ewan stared at his father and Mab as they stood by his chair in the great hall, then looked to his right at a smiling Fiona. "He is still married to the woman who ran away, isnae he?"

"Nay," Fiona replied. "It seems she died three years ago. I happened to mention the woman to Ciaran and he told me. There was a fever that spread through the clan and it killed her. He remembers her most clearly as she and his mother hated each other and often fought. Seems they both wanted Hugh. Your father talked to the boy and says the woman is the same one. So, he is a free mon."

"And I am going to marry Mab," said Fingal, scowling at Ewan. "I feel foolish coming to ye like some lad, but ye are the laird and 'tis right ye are asked. So, say aye and let us start planning the celebration."

"Ah, Da," Ewan began hesitantly, "I like Mab."

"Aye, and?"

"Weel, ye havenae proven to be a verra good husband."

"Ah, nay, 'tis true. But I didnae care much for those other women. Annie wasnae so bad, but I didnae care enough about her to be faithful, and she may have borne me children but she didnae like the bedding, if ye ken what I mean. Now Mab here likes the bedding just fine—"

"Fingal!" Mab protested, blushing deeply and sending a giggling Fiona a frown.

"And I care for her," Fingal continued as if she had not interrupted him. "I suddenly realized that she and I were, weel, friends. I am nay a young lusty lad, though I am still virile and, weel, I want a wife. I have told Mab I will be faithful and I give ye leave to beat me if I look to be forgetting my vow."

"If ye are giving the vow, Da, I doubt ye will be forgetting it," said Ewan. "No one could e'er doubt your word when ye give it."

"Aye, aye. Tis why I am careful about giving it. Ne'er can tell when ye might find yourself in trouble just because ye gave some fool your word about something."

"That makes sense," Ewan murmured and avoided looking at Fiona, knowing he would see her amusement and not be able to hide his own.

"So? We will plan a wedding feast?"

"Do ye want this rogue, Mab?"

"Och, aye, always have. Ned wouldnae be here if I hadnae. Just had no intention of standing in line. Now there will be but the one." She smiled faintly, but the expression held pure mischief. "I ken a few potions that would cure any mon's wandering ways."

Fingal leaned back and frowned at her. "I made a vow and that be that."

"Of course, my love."

"Then we shall have a wedding feast," said Ewan. "When do ye intend to get married?"

"In two days' time."

"Weel, I suppose we can set out a fine feast in that time."

Fingal nodded and, still holding Mab by the hand, walked out of the great hall. Ewan looked at Fiona. "Did ye ken this was happening?"

"Aye and nay," replied Fiona. "I thought they had gotten a lot closer, but that didnae have to mean anything as far as your father was concerned. She was the one to comfort him when he was reminded of all that pain in the past, and I think that is when he started to realize that she wasnae just Mab, but a friend, mayhap e'en more."

"Weel, I suspect this will cause a bit of an uproar. Nay a bad one, just shock, mayhap amazement, and certainly some hilarity. I hope Mab willnae be hurt by it."

"Nay. She has been here too long. She will ken exactly what is meant. The lads, as she calls them, all like her. Somehow, if there is any concern about this marriage, I believe it will be for her."

Ewan nodded. "Aye, they will fret o'er the chance that he will treat her poorly and hurt her feelings."

Fiona laughed softly at the stunned look that still rested upon Ewan's face. A moment later, he laughed as well. She hoped she was right in thinking Fingal had changed enough to be a good husband to Mab, but it was Mab's risk to take. That worry for her friend did not lessen her amusement over the situation, however.

As they finished their meal, she kept a close watch on her husband. It was his first time out of bed, and although he had certainly appeared to regain his strength, this was the first time he had tested the wounds on his back for any length of time. She did not think they could be easily reopened after ten days of healing, but they were still tender. Pain could tire a person as easily as anything else, and she was keeping a close eye out for any sign of that weariness.

Within moments, Ewan's brothers and nephews began to come in and out of the great hall to express their feelings about their father marrying Mab. As Fiona had expected, most of them were concerned about Mab's feelings. After an hour of such confrontations, Ewan was looking a little pale, and Fiona did not hesitate to use his recent illness and wounds to get him to their bedchamber. Some of his brothers would undoubtedly seek him out here, but not many.

Ewan slowly lowered himself down onto the bed and smiled at Fiona. "Ye have gained a true skill in routing my family when the need arises."

"They have two days to make their opinions known," she said as she poured him a tankard of cider. "Tis a shame they cannae trust your father to be a good husband, e'en though they all believe he will hold to a promise, but that is your father's fault."

"True," agreed Ewan as he accepted the drink. "Tis the first time he has been so blunt about nay caring much for his wives. One wonders why he kept marrying them."

"The first wife was for Scarglas. The rest for legitimate sons."

"Of course. Sad in a way." He yawned. "Curse it, I shouldnae be so weary."

"Ye are nay as weary as ye were yesterday or the day before that. Tis my belief such weariness is all part of the healing. It takes a lot of strength to fight a fever or heal a wound. Ye had both." She took his empty tankard away and set it on the table next to the bed. "Rest, I have a feeling the next few days will leave ye needing your strength."

"Are ye going to have a rest, too?" He smiled and patted the bed beside him. "Plenty of room."

"Nay, I had best start giving orders and making plans for this feast."

He laughed softly as she left, then yawned. It felt wrong to rest in the middle of the day, but he would do it, and he would continue to rest whenever he felt a need. He wanted to make love to his wife again, and that was something that required his full strength. If he had to sleep away the next two days to be at his full strength by his father's wedding, he would do so.

Weddings seemed to make women ripe for wooing, and he intended to woo his wife. He was going to give her sweet words before, during, and after he made love to her. And he was going to speak about the feelings he had for her, and then, hopefully, she would tell him she loved him. Ewan had used his time of healing to slowly teach himself how to share his thoughts with his wife. Fiona had been so obviously pleased, he was a little ashamed he had not made the attempt before. Now he would attempt to speak of how he felt about her. Even thinking about such a conversation made him uneasy, but the prize he craved was nearly within his reach. If it required that he expose himself in such a way, then he would gird his loins and do it. He could only pray that his own hopes and desires had not made him see what was not there, that Fiona truly did hold some affection for him.

"Are ye certain about this, Mab?" Fiona asked her friend as she helped the woman dress for her wedding.

"Aye," replied Mab. "The mon has changed. Mayhap 'tis his age, mayhap 'tis ridding his heart and mind of the hurt and anger of the past, but he *has* changed. Tis time for me to take the risk that he can hold to his vows and cease acting like a rutting swine who cannae look at a skirt without wanting to lift it."

Fiona laughed. "Aye, although he hasnae been acting like that since shortly after I came here."

"I noticed that." She smiled at Fiona. "I have also noticed that ye seem more at ease, at peace, if ye will."

"I am. Ewan has changed some as weel. More so in the two days since ye and his father said ye were getting wed. Mayhap I have finally worn him down. Patience was difficult to cling to at times, but it appears to have worked. Oh, Mab, he has talked to me more since we snatched him from Hugh's grasp than in all the weeks before that."

"I am happy for ye, lass. That sharing, especially in a mon like Ewan, is a verra good sign."

"Now, if he would only share his feelings."

"Patience, lass," Mab said and laughed when Fiona rolled her eyes. "One wee step at a time. Marriage is forever. What are a few months of uncertainty and hard work compared to that, especially if that work brings ye such a wondrous gift as a mon's love, as a love returned in full?"

Fiona nodded as she realized Mab had been patient for years. "I am amazed that ye ne'er gave up on the old fool."

"I might have if some fine mon had come along to offer me love and marriage. He didnae. Since no temptation was dangled before my eyes, it was easy to wait. I just tucked my love for him into a corner of my heart and slowly became Fingal's friend, a companion who asked naught and didnae let him take what he wanted when he wanted it."

"Ye told him nay."

"From the moment I discovered he was wed. And I will keep saying it until the priest finishes muttering o'er us. I did it mostly for my own peace of mind, but that day when ye and I discovered that Fingal spoke to us in a different way than he did to the other women, I looked hard at that. Tis a matter of respect. He simply doesnae respect those other women much, if at all. Fingal appreciates the fact that ye and I stand up to him. I ne'er realized it, but all those years I have been doing exactly what was right and necessary to win the mon. If his wife Annie hadnae been cold in the bedchamber, that marriage might have been a good one, as she also stood strong and he had some affection for her because of it."

"How sad."

"Verra sad. Especially since I dinnae believe all those lasses who so freely toss up their petticoats are actually *warm,* ye ken. They just ken how to make the mon think they are."

Fiona stepped back and looked Mab over carefully. "Ye look verra fine. Ye shall have to keep a firm tether on Fingal or he will be rushing ye off to the bedchamber ere the priest finishes the blessing." She grinned when Mab blushed and giggled like a young bride. "Ye wouldnae want to miss the celebration after we have all worked so hard."

"Nay. If aught else, I want the lads to enjoy it and see their father and I as husband and wife for a wee while ere Fingal starts sharing my bed. I want it set weel in their minds."

"Aye, that would be best."

"Ye are looking verra fine as weel. Why do I think 'tis for more reason than my marriage?"

"Because ye have keen eyes. Your insight obviously stretches beyond what might set in a woman's womb. I am dressed for seduction," Fiona confessed as she stroked the soft skirts of her deep red gown. "I am also dressed to make myself feel beautiful and brave, for tonight I plan to tell Ewan what I feel for him."

Mab's eyes widened. "That is a brave thing, and a verra large step to take."

"I but pray that large step doesnae send me plummeting off a cliff." Fiona sighed. "He has been trying so hard to make me a part of his life. I can see that, feel it. Yet there is a hesitancy there. It could be because he is not used to sharing his thoughts and plans so freely. It could also be because he is still uncertain of me in some ways. Weel, tonight I will let him ken just how firmly he holds me in his grasp and see where that leads us. If naught else, I simply cannae keep biting back the words any longer."

"Sad to say, but the woman oftimes has to be the first to bare heart and soul."

As Fiona linked her arm with Mab's and they started out of the room, she agreed, "Most unfair. But someone has to take that first step. Since I must also tell him of the child I carry tonight, I decided I might as weel cough up all my wee secrets and have done with it. See what a romantic fool I am?" She laughed along with Mab as they made their way to the great hall and Fiona prayed she would soon find the serenity and joy Mab had now.

"Why are ye so nervous?" Gregor asked as he sat in a chair by the fire and watched Ewan pace his bedchamber. "Ye arenae the one getting married today."

Ewan stopped before the fire and stared into the flames. "In some ways, I am."

Gregor frowned for a moment, then sighed and shook his head. "Ye havenae told the lass ye love her yet."

"Tis no easy thing for a mon to do."

"Nay? Ye just open your mouth and say the words."

"So speaks a mon who has ne'er loved a lass. Lusted mightily after a few, but ne'er loved a one."

"I suspicion I will one day."

"Aye, ye will, and when that day comes, I promise ye, ye will open your mouth and those words will refuse to come out past this sudden lump in your throat. Mayhap if the lass ye eventually love tells ye how she feels, freely and often, ye will find it easier. If she hasnae, if ye simply cannae be certain she feels the same, that lump will keep blocking the way out for those little words. A lump of pure fear. And why I can tell ye how I feel, but nay her, I dinnae ken," Ewan muttered.

"Mayhap because we are brothers, bound tight by blood and affection, and have known each other all our lives, 'tis easier." Gregor sipped from his goblet of spiced wine. "Nay sure I like this talk of fear. Didnae ken falling in love involved fear."

Ewan crossed his arms over his chest and leaned back against the heavy stone frame of the fireplace. "It involves a great many of the more unpleasant emotions. Fear, uncertainty, doubt about one's worthiness—"

"Enough, please, or ye will have me disavowing love and lasses for all the rest of my days. Weel, love, at least." He grinned when Ewan chuckled, but then grew serious again. "She loves ye, Ewan. I am certain of it."

"I would sorely like to be certain of it, too. Nay sure I will be e'en if she tells me so, at least nay for a while. What I am certain of is that she has some caring for me and wants to be wed to me. When she came to help rescue me that day, the way she acted o'er me and my wounds gave me the hope that I have won a place in her heart. Tis time to take a chance that she holds back the words I need because she, too, is plagued by uncertainty."

"Ye truly do love her, dinnae ye."

"I think I have from the start, although I called

it lust. A much more acceptable feeling for a mon. I tried to keep a distance between us because I kenned she could twist me into tight knots and devastate my verra soul. It didnae work. I am but verra fortunate that she isnae the sort of woman to use what I feel for her against me, even in small ways."

"Nay," agreed Gregor as he finished his drink and stood up. "I believe she loves ye. And e'en if she doesnae quite yet, 'tis there to be wooed out of her. Ye didnae see how she acted when she kenned ye were captured, how she fretted o'er ye each time ye were hurt, and ye didnae see how your attempt to keep her at arm's length troubled, e'en hurt her. I did. Near all your brothers did. And all of us have seen this as a good match from the start, long before we kenned what she could bring to a marriage."

"Weel, I am nay sure I believe all that, but it certainly gives me courage."

"Ah, Ewan, she is just a wee lass."

"She is my heart, my future," Ewan said quietly, then ignoring the slightly stunned look upon Gregor's face, said, "Weel, let us go and see the old fool married. Again."

Fiona sniffed and wiped away a tear as Fingal kissed his blushing bride. She ignored Ewan's grin as he led her to their table. Men never seemed to be moved by a wedding as women were, and she found that a sad flaw in them.

The celebration quickly got under way, and she was pleased to see how well everything had turned out. The food was plentiful and hot. The music was actually pleasant to listen to. Even Peter was clean although that had been a battle she did not care to recall. How such a small man could have left six hulking MacFingals bruised and battered, she did not know. She caught sight of Ciaran laughing with some of the younger boys and felt a sweet joy warm her heart. At the moment, all seemed right with the world and she intended to savor that feeling.

"The old fool looks quite pleased with himself," said Ewan as he took her hand in his and brushed a kiss over her knuckles.

"He does," she replied after a quick glance at Fingal, who was happily arguing with Sigimor. "The change in the mon is quite wondrous, isnae it."

"Wondrous indeed. He is now simply a wee bit odd."

She laughed. "Mab will be good for him. S'truth, she has been good for him for years, a true friend and companion."

"After I thought on it all for a while, I realized that. She has always been there, for him, and for us, since the first day she rode into Scarglas. In truth, she has been more a mother to us than all of his other wives. I think that is why so many of my brothers were concerned about this. The fate of my father's wives has ne'er been, weel, good, and I realized the thing they all feared was that she, too, would soon be gone."

Fiona nodded. "I got that feeling, too. She isnae going anywhere and I think, this time, your father has met his match. Mab isnae the witless, confused fool some think she is."

"Och, nay. E'en at her worst she could cut straight to the heart of a problem. She is, weel, more at ease with herself, I think. A lot of the little things that made people think unkindly about her are gone. I wondered if it was because she finally had found a companion in ye, someone to talk to besides my father. She didnae really have that before."

"That may be some of it, but weel, I found out why she could seem so, er, odd and distracted." Hoping he would not ask how she found out about Mab's special gift, she told Ewan all about it. "The hiding of it made things verra difficult for her."

"Ye dinnae think 'tis sorcery or the like?"

"Nay. One cannae ken the Murrays for verra long without seeing such things as nay more than a wee, special gift from God. That clan has many people so gifted. Mab and I are working on how she may use it yet nay get people all afrightened."

Ewan nodded and smiled at Ciaran when the boy skipped over and wriggled himself into Fiona's seat, nearly sitting on her lap. "Are ye enjoying the feast, Ciaran?"

"Aye," the boy replied even as he stuffed his mouth with a small cake. "Grandsire has given me a grandmama."

"That he has."

Ciaran looked at Fiona. "Do ye have one?"

"Nay, and I fear I willnae be giving ye either a grandsire or a grandmama. I just have brothers. Ye now have a few more uncles. I suspicion ye will meet them soon."

"Will they like me?"

"Immediately." She kissed his forehead and he giggled.

"Will they like my father?"

"Of course."

"Immediately?"

"Mayhap, but I suspect they willnae let him ken it for a wee while. He wed me without their permission and all. They will have to scowl at him a wee bit ere all is settled. Tis a monly thing to do." She laughed when Ciaran scowled. "Verra weel done."

"A verra monly scowl, son," Ewan said, but he gave Fiona a mock look of severity. "I think I must keep a close watch upon what ye are teaching the boy."

"I am being taught a lot of things," Ciaran said.

"That is what I am afraid of," murmured Ewan and grinned when Fiona frowned at him even as her eyes glittered with laughter. When Ciaran skipped back to the other boys, he grew serious, however. "Do ye think there will be trouble with your brothers?"

"Ah, weel, nothing verra bad. I was allowed the choice of a husband. I chose. Tis just that, e'en though Connor may understand why it was done, he will be irritated that ye didnae tell him where I was for so long."

"Irritated, eh?"

"Aye, irritated. Nothing to worry about." She frowned as she realized that everyone in the great hall had grown very quiet. "What is it?"

"I suspect they are all thinking what I am thinking."

"And what is that?"

"That irritation shouldnae look quite that alarming."

Fiona realized everyone, including Ewan, was looking toward the doorway to the hall, and she tensed. She glanced at Sigimor first, and his wide grin only made her feel even more uneasy. Slowly, she turned to look in the direction everyone else was. Three of her brothers stood in the doorway, several tense MacFingals around them. *Irritated* was definitely the wrong word to describe the look upon Connor's face as he fixed his stare upon her and Ewan. She wondered which one of them Connor was imagining cutting into tiny, bloodied pieces.

"Would ye say that was an irritated look?" Ewan asked quietly.

"I would say murderous, bloodthirsty e'en. I just wish I kenned which one of us he is thinking of slaughtering."

Chapter 22

"Fiona!"

"Me first, I guess," Fiona said as she sank down in her chair a little as Connor, Diarmot, and Antony strode toward the table, Gillyanne and Ilsa hurrying along behind them.

Ewan stood up as Fiona's family approached. Despite the dark look of fury upon her brother Connor's face, Ewan felt something ease inside of him, a doubt abruptly fading away. Connor MacEnroy was big, blond, and scarred. This was a hard man, a man who had known a fight to survive and many battles. This was a man he could understand, one he easily recognized, for in many ways, they were alike.

He had to fight the urge to tell the glowering man to wait a minute because he needed to talk to Fiona now. All his concerns about his scars, about his serious humors, were gone. Ewan knew, without any further doubt, that such things truly did not matter to Fiona. In truth, she probably was more at ease with such things than any other woman he could name. She had been raised amongst such men.

As calmly as possible, considering he faced a man who reeked of the urge to beat him senseless, Ewan performed the introductions then offered seats to Fiona's family. "We are celebrating my father's marriage," he said as he retook his seat and stared across the table at Connor.

"Speaking of marriage . . ." Connor began.

"Tis so nice to see ye," Fiona said, and met Connor's glare with a sweet smile. "I was afeared it would be months yet ere ye could come here."

"Lass, that game willnae work. I mean to speak with your husband. Then I mean to have a wee talk with ye about witless lasses who ride away on a contrary horse whilst a madmon is hunting them round every corner."

"Ye cannae lecture me now, Connor. I am a married woman. Only Ewan can lecture me."

"Ye arenae a married woman until I say so."

Fiona blinked at that remark, which she considered rather foolish. She then looked at Gilly, who was staring at Ewan. Even as she considered asking Gilly what she saw, the woman turned and grinned at her. The wink her brother's wife gave her made Fiona's heart soar.

"Now, ye sit there and hush," Connor ordered, ignoring the severe frowns his wife and Ilsa gave him, "whilst this fool and I have a talk."

Fiona was tempted to argue with him, but Ewan caught her hand in his and gave it a light squeeze. For now, she would leave it all in his hands. She had caused her brother a lot of worry with her rash actions and had not let him know she was safe for far too long. He had a right to his anger, but she would not let him pummel Ewan with it for too long.

"I read your letter and may concede that ye are a good choice for my sister," Connor said, keeping his gaze fixed steadily on Ewan.

"I thank ye," Ewan murmured. "It was impossible to get word to ye any sooner than I did."

"So ye explained, yet we had no trouble as we rode here."

"Matters have changed somewhat since I wrote to ye. The worst of our enemies is now dead, and his clan has already made a small gesture of peace. The new laird of the Grays is as wearied of the feud as we are. They were the ones who would have made any journey from here to Deilcladach or back verra treacherous."

"Since my sister was your hostage, was here without any kinsmen to approve your marriage or protect her from being forced into one, I could end this."

Ice flowed through Ewan's veins, but before he could speak out, a small voice from his side said, "Ye willnae take my mother away."

Ewan looked down to see Ciaran giving Connor a very manly scowl and almost smiled despite the fear Connor's words had bred in his heart. "Nay, Ciaran, he willnae."

"That is yet to be decided." Connor looked at Ciaran. "Since I ken this child cannae be Fiona's, may I ask just why he claims her as his mother?"

"Because he is my son and she is my wife."

"Aye," said Ciaran, "and she is going to stay here or I will have to get verra mean."

"Hush, Ciaran," said Fiona as she tugged the boy to her side. "Twill be all right. Just let the men speak, and if they say any stupid monly things, we can set them aright, later."

"How kind of ye, Fiona," murmured Connor.

"I am but being patient," she said, but did not hide her irritation in the look she gave Connor. "I am a married woman and a mother and 'tis important to learn patience. I find 'tis oftimes verra useful when dealing with men, as weel." A glint of laughter flickered through her brother's eyes, but she was not ready to relax yet.

"Patience? I didnae ken ye e'en had that word in your vocabulary." Connor looked back at Ewan. "All of this has not pleased me at all. I dinnae ken ye and your clan, but what little I was able to find out doesnae make me feel any better about this marriage. Tales of murder and sorcery, the fact that ye have been at war with near every clan within two days' ride, and that ye are irritating Camerons for all ye call yourself MacFingals."

"I resent that slur," Sigimor said amiably.

Connor ignored Sigimor, although his lips twitched slightly. "She was a rich prize and I but wonder if it was stolen or given."

"A bit of both," Ewan said bluntly.

"A bit of force added to all the other problems with this marriage is enough for me to get it set aside."

"I wouldnae suggest ye trying."

"Enough," snapped Fiona. "This is a wedding feast. Sir Fingal has just married Mab."

"From what I have heard, Sir Fingal getting married is a fairly common occurence," murmured Connor.

Fiona ignored that. "I willnae have all this monly posturing ruining the celebration." She was pleased to see both Ilsa and Gillyanne nod. "My marriage to Ewan wasnae forced." When Ewan started to say something, she clapped her hand over his mouth. "It wasnae. There will be no more talk of setting it aside. Ye may be able to do such a thing, but I willnae stand for it."

"Nay?"

"Nay. He is my husband, I love him, and we are going to have a child." She felt Ewan's body jerk beneath her hand. "I believe that settles that. So let us have a nice visit, get to ken each other, and—" She screeched when Ewan suddenly rose up out of his seat, picked her up in his arms, and started for the doors. "Ewan," she began to protest, blushing beneath the grins and shouts directed their way.

"Hush," he ordered in a hoarse voice. "Just hush for a moment."

Since her brothers were not chasing him down, swords drawn, Fiona decided to hush. A quick glance over her shoulder as they left the hall revealed her brothers all grinning, and Fiona grew suspicious. She wondered if Connor had been trying to press Ewan into declaring himself. If so, he had failed, for she was the one who had spoken out, telling Connor things he already knew. She had made her feelings for Ewan very clear in the letter she had written him. Then she looked at her husband's taut expression and wondered if Connor had really failed. He had certainly seen a reaction from Ewan. Fiona remained silent, wondering if she would soon discover why this particular reaction had so obviously delighted Connor.

"Verra weel done," said Sigimor, grinning at Connor.

"Thank ye," Connor said as he began to help himself to some of the food. "I had hoped for some words from the fool, but this was good."

"My son is besotted with the lass," said Sir Fingal.

"It would appear so," agreed Connor, "but ye must forgive a brother, who has been more a father to her than a sibling, for wishing to see that she is happy. From what she said in her letter to me, he wasnae completely successful at that." He winked at Gillyanne. "Sometimes a mon has to have his back against the wall ere he begins to see sense."

"Does that mean ye willnae try to take my mother away?" asked Ciaran as he climbed up into Fiona's seat.

"Nay," replied Connor. "I believe your father would fight that verra fiercely."

"Aye. Me, too. So, ye are my uncles?"

"Aye, although it appears that ye already have a lot."

"One cannae e'er have enough family."

"Truer words were ne'er spoken, Ciaran," Fingal said, but then he scowled at the MacEnroys. "I suspicion ye will be wanting to stay here for a wee while too."

"At least until I have a chance to see my sister," said Connor, then he grinned as he lifted his tankard of ale in a small toast. "I believe it may be a while ere that happens. The way that fool looked as he carried her out of here tells me they will be sorting themselves out for a while."

"Tis about time," said Mab, and blushed when everyone laughed.

Fiona found herself naked and sprawled on Ewan's bed before she could think of one word to say. She was quickly diverted from any attempt at conversation when he swiftly removed his clothes and joined her on the bed. His lovemaking was almost frantic, and she was soon lost to the passion he roused within her. He drove her into incoherency with his hands and his mouth, leaving no part of her untouched or unkissed. She felt cherished despite the ferocity that seemed to tremble through his long frame. They reached the heights as one, their cries blending in a harmony she found incredibly sweet.

Ewan nuzzled Fiona's breast as he sought to recover from the madness that had seized him. The moment she had said she loved him, announced it to everyone gathered in the great hall, his whole body had screamed out with the need to make love to her. She was his, all his, and she carried his child. He placed a trembling hand over her womb.

"Ye are certain?" he asked.

"Aye," she replied, combing her fingers through his hair and praying that the news of the child was not the only reason he had acted as he had. "I have kenned it for a while, but I wished to be certain it was set firmly in my womb. Mab feels it is. Ye are pleased?"

"Jesu, of course I am, but I am also afraid." He lightly ran his hand over her hips. "Ye are so small."

"Connor says I look exactly like my mother and she bore six healthy bairns with nay trouble at all. Mab feels I will have no trouble, either."

"I want the bairn, but I want ye more."

"Do ye, Ewan?"

He looked at her, raising himself up on one elbow and shifting slightly so that he rested more to her side. "Aye, lass." He kissed her, and whispered, "Say it again."

"I love ye."

Ewan pressed his forehead against hers and closed his eyes against the strength of the emotion tearing through him. "I have long hoped that ye might. Someday. If I tried hard to woo ye and make ye happy."

"Ye make me happy."

"Nay completely, Fiona." He turned entirely on his side and pulled her into his arms. "I could see that. My brothers could see it. I tried verra hard to keep ye at a distance. I was a coward, afraid of feeling more than passion for ye. I had tried that once, and I didnae want to feel that pain of failing again."

"I am nay like Helena," she snapped.

He grinned as he kissed the top of her head. "Nay, ye arenae, but forgive a foolish mon for his fears. Nay, I kenned ye were naught like her almost from the beginning. But then, that was some of the trouble."

"How could that be?"

"Because I am an idiot." He chuckled when she laughed softly, her warm breath caressing his chest.

"I kenned that I wanted ye more than I e'er wanted her. I also, verra quickly, realized that ye could hurt me far more than she e'er could or did," he added in a soft voice.

"I wouldnae hurt ye, Ewan. Nay apurpose." She hugged him and kissed his chest.

"I ken it. That, too, came to me weeks ago. Ah, and then I began to plan ways to woo ye, to win your heart."

"Ye have held that in your hands almost from the beginning."

"But I couldnae be sure. I am a dark, scarred mon."

"I think ye are beautiful."

"Aye, weel, we can discuss your poor eyesight later." He loved the sound of her laughter, he decided. "Ye are beautiful, m'love. In face and heart. I just didnae see how ye could want me. I am always a wee bit astonished when ye turn to such sweet heat in my arms. Then, slowly, I began to believe that ye did care for me a wee bit, that, if God was merciful, I might be able to win your love. I needed it, ye see, for ye had won mine." He felt a dampness on his chest, took her chin in his hand, and turned her face up to his. "That makes ye weep."

Fiona kissed him, wrapped her arms around his neck, and pressed her face against his throat. "From happiness. From relief. From utter, blind joy. When did ye ken that ye loved me?"

"When Menzies took ye. I might nay have called it love, I cannae recall, but I did ken that I would have naught, would be without a future, if I lost ye. Then I plotted ways to woo ye. Then Ciaran arrived, and I feared I would lose ye. Then, when ye came to my rescue, I saw that ye might care for me more than I had realized and I began the struggle to rouse my courage and tell ye how I felt. I was going to tell ye tonight, after the feast." He stroked her cheek when she lifted her head to stare at him.

"I was planning to tell ye that I love ye tonight, as weel. And then, tell ye about the bairn."

"Why didnae ye tell me when ye first kenned ye were carrying the bairn? Was it truly just to be certain?"

"Aye, and nay. I wanted to be sure, but I also wanted time to try and make ye love me ere ye kenned there was a child. If ye kenned about the child ere I kenned how ye felt, weel, I feared I would drive myself mad trying to judge your every word and deed as to whether it meant ye cared for just me or for the woman who carried your bairn." She kissed his chin and whispered, "Ye havenae actually said the words, Ewan."

"I love ye," he said against her mouth, then kissed her with all the passionate emotion he was feeling. "Ye are my heart, my future. I ken I am nay good with sweet words . . ." He stuttered to a halt when she brushed her lips over his to silence him.

"I dinnae need sweet words. I dinnae need flatteries, poetry, song, or gifts. I just need ye to tell me every now and again that ye love me."

"That willnae be so verra hard to do, nay if ye do the same. Tis odd, but I thought of my feelings as a weakness, and I cannae believe that anymore. Kenning that ye love me makes me feel strong, whole in some odd way."

"As if a part of ye is finally where it belongs," she

said. "The moment I saw ye, I kenned something special about ye. It wasnae long ere I realized ye were the one I had been waiting for. After ye kissed me in the herb hut, I kenned ye were my mate and I was determined to make ye see it, too." She sighed rather dramatically. "I hadnae realized it would take ye so long to understand."

He smiled at her teasing, but was deeply moved by her words. It was going to take a while for him to fully accept that this beautiful, passionate woman loved him, saw him as beautiful, as her mate. Such great gifts needed getting used to.

Gently turning her onto her back, he began to make love to her, whispering his love against every inch of her soft skin. She returned his every caress, telling him of her love for him in words and touch. When he eased their bodies together, he looked into her eyes, and felt humbled by what he saw there.

"I love ye," he said, finding it easier to say every time he did so.

"And I love ye." She suddenly grinned and grasped him by the hips, pushing him deep inside her. "I will love ye e'en more if ye move."

Ewan laughed and began to move. Soon, despite all his efforts to make it last, they reached the blinding heights together. As he rolled onto his back, their bodies still joined, he held her close as he tried to regain his breath.

"That is what should have told me that I loved ye, that ye loved me," he said. "I should have seen that such pleasure could not be possible without true, deep emotion. I have ne'er felt such passion before." He touched a kiss to her mouth when she started to speak. "Nay, not e'en with her. She was lust and mayhap a touch of vanity and pride. I havenae been with many women, have always feared becoming like my father. One reason I found ye such a trial was that ye roused the beast in me, that passion and fire I had thought weel controlled."

Fiona sat up on him, wriggling a little as she felt him begin to grow hard inside her. "I like that beast."

"I begin to like him as weel." He ran his hands up her ribs and over her breasts. "I saw him as a dark part of me, something to be caged, yet I think he helped me reach out for ye. He wouldnae be still, wouldnae be pushed back into the fetters I had put upon him. He reared up each time ye walked into sight."

"I can feel a wee bit feral myself from time to time when I look at ye."

"Sounds intriguing." He moved a hand down to stroke her still-flat stomach. "I did fear that part of me, Fiona. Feared it would turn me into a mon as careless as my father. Yet, as he changed, I began to see that it wasnae his lusty nature that was really the problem nor was madness. I began to see that my lusty nature was only roused by ye, that it was-nae really some mindless beast within me, but all part of what I felt for you."

"And it had best continue to be roused by only me," she warned, lightly touching his chin with her fist.

"No one but ye, my wee Fiona-of-the-ten-knives."

"And I shall ne'er want anyone but ye, my dark warrior."

"If ye keep wriggling like that, this dark warrior's beast is going to rear up again."

"That was my plan."

He laughed and pulled her down into his arms. "Love me, my sweet Fiona."

"Always."

ABOUT THE AUTHOR

Hannah Howell is an award-winning author who lives with her family in Massachusetts. She is the author of sixteen Zebra historical romances and is currently working on RECKLESS, which will be published in September 2004. Hannah loves hearing from readers and you may write to her c/o Zebra Books. Please include a self-addressed stamped envelope if you wish a response.